THE RETIRED DETECTIVES' CLUB

See No Evil

D1603905

Shawn Scuefield

NEWMAN SPRINGS PUBLISHING
320 Broad Street
Red Bank, NJ 07701

First originally published by Newman Springs Publishing 2019

ISBN 978-1-64531-070-9 (Paperback)
ISBN 978-1-64531-071-6 (Digital)

Printed in the United States of America

For my girls, Leila and Maliea

Prologue

I WANT TO BE THE NIGHT STALKER

Summer, 1998
Chicago, Illinois

*H*IS *CONFIDENCE HIGH,* he stalked the streets like a prowling animal. He always imagined himself as a lion, or tiger, maybe, patrolling the night—surreptitious, stealthy, clandestine. And his prey—well, they never saw him coming.

It had taken him some time to decide what he wanted to be called—when he was in this mode, that is. He had always liked *the night stalker*; he thought it was fitting—appropriate. But he wouldn't call himself that, not since the name had been bestowed upon the 1980s serial killer Richard Ramirez. Even though that was before *his* time, it didn't make sense to have *two* night stalkers. That just wouldn't do, not when you wanted to stand out on your own merits, anyway.

He hated the name the local papers had given him. It lacked creativity.

In the interest of originality, on nights like these, when he was in this mode, he called himself Azrael—the angel of death.

Dressed head to toe in black, his hoodie pulled tight around his head and face, his military-style boots made a soft thudding sound as he strolled. He made his way onto Lower Wacker Drive. The dimly lit, just over two-mile stretch of near subterranean concrete tunnel was built in 1909 to ease traffic flow in downtown Chicago. Azrael often wondered if the architects who designed the double-decker street ever foresaw what it would become or if they were rolling over in their graves right about now.

Lower Wacker Drive served as a "home" to many of the city's homeless—his prime targets, his prey.

Here, the homeless congregated like Cape buffalo at a watering hole. This made the lower drive Azrael's favorite hunting ground. Chicago's a big city, with a large populace. He could find a homeless victim just about anywhere. There was just something about this area, though—something intoxicating. Maybe it was just the soothing sounds the water churning in the Chicago River produced that, well, relaxed him.

Unlike those prowling big cats Azrael often envisioned, he didn't have three-inch canines and retractable claws. He had something else, something more suitable for an angel of death—a *night stalker*. With his Kevlar-gloved hand, he drew the four-inch karambit from the Kydex sheath he wore on his belt. He glanced down at the serrated, curved blade, admiring it, as he slid his index digit into the finger guard and gripped the handle.

He held the blade closely against his right side, away from the view of any passing cars on his left. On this night, however, there would be very few cars cruising the drive. Just about everyone in the city was too busy celebrating—celebrating another NBA championship won by the hometown Bulls. Azrael wasn't into the Bulls, or basketball for that matter. Though, hold his feet to the fire, he would admit that Michael Jordan was something special. He didn't follow any of the other major sporting teams in Chicago either.

Hunting—that was his thing. Now that was a real sport.

Let the city celebrate tonight all along Madison Street; let people go out and make fools of themselves as they march out into the streets, overturning cars and looting; let them occupy CPD's time—that was perfect.

Azrael knew it was always better when he was alone with his work.

*****

The angel of death casually took in the scene on Lower Wacker.

He had many potential victims to choose from. He'd seen stories on the news about how some of the homeless were dead set against sleeping in a shelter. They'd rather take their chances on the streets. He thought about how that decision was going to come back to haunt someone tonight.

Some of the city's less fortunate were congregated in groups of three or more in the corners and alleyways that ran along the drive. Oblivious to the few vehicles that roared by, others had staked out their own private bit of real estate among the filth and grime that had accumulated throughout the years. Many had all of their worldly possessions crammed into (what Azrael assumed to be stolen) shopping carts or large garbage bags. Some were bedding down for the night with thin layers of cardboard between them and the concrete sidewalk. A few managed to own ragged and torn sleeping bags.

It was a dismal existence, living among what was easily a ton of pigeon shit, sharing space with rats, and breathing in auto exhaust and diesel fumes all day and all night—a dismal existence that someone would be freed from tonight, Azrael thought.

Crossing Garvey Court, at once, he saw him, tonight's prey.

The man had a noticeable limp as he pushed his (stolen) grocery cart further east along Lower Wacker Drive. One of the front wheels on the cart spun furiously, counterclockwise first and then whipping back around. Each time it caused the man to struggle keeping the cart straight.

He appeared to want nothing to do with the other huddled masses along the drive. He was a loner. He wanted his own space, his own piece of the shitty Lower Wacker Driver pie. The man's cart was filled to the brim with a variety of knickknacks: crushed cans; an old worn, torn, and dirty sleeping bag; a traffic cone; and what looked to be several pairs of raggedy, mix-matched shoes.

Azrael moved in swiftly once he believed the man was out of view of the others. He strolled by at a brisk pace, bringing the curved, serrated edge of the karambit down in a powerful slicing motion across the back of the man's neck and around to the front of his throat, much like how one of the big cats would use their claws.

The homeless victim fell to the ground, gurgling blood, unable to scream. The angel of death grabbed one of the man's legs and dragged him further out of sight, further into the dark. He could hear the sounds of the Chicago River over the few vehicles that roared past at speeds higher than the posted speed limit—more Bulls revelers no doubt. Just the same, it was…relaxing. He took the karambit and, in one swift, powerful motion, sliced along the inside of his victim's right thigh. Crimson gushed like water overflowing a dam.

His homeless victim was dead in minutes.

Azrael felt no pity. He felt no sorrow. He had only relieved the man of a life that little had been done with, after all. *And you can't ruin a future a person doesn't have, now can you?* Judging by looks alone, he placed the man's age over forty, and to Azrael it was clear: If this was as far as the man had come in life by that age, his death tonight was more of a mercy killing than anything else. He was doing him a favor, saving the poor soul from this harsh, cruel world that had chewed the man up and spat him out like a flavorless piece of chewing gum, down on Lower Wacker Drive.

What you don't use, you lose, right?

After staring at his latest conquest for a moment, Azrael then took the dead man's left hand in his. He separated the pinky finger from its counterparts and, with a swift stroke of the karambit, removed the digit. He pocketed it—a lasting memory of their encounter.

The next morning, Azrael couldn't help but chuckle when the *Times* reported the murder in a blurb. The paper proclaimed that the latest man was the fourth such victim. This statement was just one of the reasons the homeless had come to be his favorite targets, because if the mainstream media, the police, and society itself actually gave a fuck about these people at all, they'd know that this latest victim was the twentieth.

Part One

RELAX. WE'RE JUST GETTIN' STARTED

CHAPTER 1

Pollock, Louisiana

IGNORING THE SCARED, shivering, young blonde strapped to the gurney before him, Orrin Robicheaux turned away from her and headed over to the cellar steps. He craned his neck and strained to listen. He could hear a feeble voice—a male voice—call out again, "I can't see."

"Don't worry," Orrin called back. "You'll be able to see just fine. I promise."

Orrin returned his attention to the shivering blonde. She was shaking uncontrollably, like a leaf in the wind. Her blue eyes were stretched wide and dilated with horror. Tears streamed out of those baby blues and down her face, dragging her mascara in thin, black, veinlike streaks along with them.

Orrin checked her bonds once again. He was meticulous that way. Certain that they were tight, he wheeled the gurney over about three feet to the right of where it had previously rested.

"There," he called out. "You should be able to see just fine now."

The frightened blonde turned her head side to side as best she could, in an apparent attempt to look for whomever the large man before her might have been talking to. "Be still," Orrin said to her. His gruff voice, along with his gruff appearance—the thick mustache and beard, his lumberjack build, and harsh countenance—was horrifying.

Orrin rubbed her bare thighs with one of his large, meaty hands. He then slid his hand under her skirt and grabbed a handful of her privates. He worked his fingers against her vagina. The blonde tried to jerk away, clench up even. Tied down spread eagle on the gurney as she was, she could not do either. Orrin Robicheaux let out a chuckle. "Relax, darlin'. We're just gettin' started," he said.

He removed his hand from between her legs and placed his fingers under his nose. He inhaled deep. Orrin enjoyed her scent. He smiled. Satisfied, he put those fingers in his mouth and sucked on them for a moment. "This one is sweet," Orrin called out, again. He stepped away from the gurney and over to a workbench that lined the far wall of the cellar.

The tools on the workbench were laid out in a neat and seemingly particular order. Craftsman socket and pipe wrenches, hammers, and screwdrivers were on one side. On the other were knives. There were *plenty* of knives. Each item had its own place. His fingers quickly found what he was looking for. Orrin picked up a blade with a serrated edge, his favorite Buck knife. He ran his thumb down it.

"Oh yeah," he muttered.

Orrin Robicheaux turned toward the frightened blonde and held the knife high for her to see. Within moments, the sound of liquid running onto the floor filled the room. Her physical reaction, but more so the terror in her eyes, excited him. Yes, oh yes, it excited him. He felt a bulge growing in the front of his pants. His breathing increased from its normal, shallow rhythm to an audibly heavy, whooshing sound like leaves rustling in an autumn breeze.

"Guess what, Pa!" Orrin yelled. "We got a pisser."

CHAPTER 2

CHRISTA MILLER FELT her bladder loosen and its warm contents empty down her legs and onto the gurney and then the floor.

She wanted to scream; and oh would she scream, if the large man standing before her, holding that knife, had not already stuffed a ball gag in her mouth. And he certainly wasn't gentle when he did it. She could taste blood on her tongue. She coughed, gagged, and choked as it pooled at the back of her throat. The metallic taste upset her stomach.

Christa watched him play with the edge of blade, running his index finger back and forth along it, almost as if he were in a trance. As uncomfortable as it had been, both physically and mentally, when he had thrust his hand deep between her legs, when she felt the cold, sharp steel slash against her thigh and a second warm liquid, blood this time, run down her leg, it was downright excruciating—both physically and mentally.

She struggled mightily against her bonds, which, from what she could tell, only seemed to delight the lunatic standing before her even more. He jumped around and howled with glee. "Let's do that again," he said to her. Then Christa felt him slash her other leg. The warm blood began to flow quickly. She let out another muffled scream.

Christa's mind raced. She couldn't believe she'd come to be in a situation that she'd seen played out on the evening news or repeatedly on some television show like *Criminal Minds*. But here she was, exactly where she never expected to be. Christa thought back to the ad she saw on You Trade It—the latest trading app, the new *Craigslist* or *letgo*, or so she had heard. She was in the market for a pet, a baby kitten. The ad promised just that. The owner's cat just had a litter. Kittens were going for twenty-five bucks, *a steal!*

When the waiflike woman with the dirty blond hair pulled the white cargo van into the parking spot next to hers at the laundromat, it did not raise any red flags. The woman introduced herself as Emily, just as Christa was expecting; so when Emily asked Christa to follow her to the back of the van, again, there were no red flags.

After Emily opened the rear doors of the van and the large mitts of the man tormenting her now suddenly appeared, clasped her in a vicelike grip, and easily hoisted Christa and her 120-pound frame into the van in one motion, it was too late for red flags. The large, brutish man placed a wet towel over her mouth and nose. She didn't know the nature of the fumes she was breathing in—but within moments, consciousness left Christa, and she knew nothing but darkness.

Then she woke up—tied down to the gurney, the ball gag stuffed so deep in her mouth she felt like she was drowning in her own saliva—just in time for the man to ram his large paw in between her thighs.

The big man turned his attention away from her momentarily, retrieving a small suitcase from beneath his workbench. He set it down gingerly, then turned, and gave her a wink before undoing the latches. Christa couldn't believe her eyes at first—she half-expected him to pull a chainsaw out of the case, but it was…a record player. Within moments, the rhythmic voices of The Chordettes blared out:

> *Bom, bom, bom, bom, bom*
> *Mr. Sandman, bring me a dream*
> *(bom, bom, bom, bom)*
> *Make him the cutest that I've ever seen*

Writhing in pain, with blood seeping from the light cuts he made into her legs, Christa could see that he reached down between his own legs and began to stroke himself as he bobbed to the music. The words he had spoken chilled her to the bone. *Relax, darlin'. We're just getting started.* The big man had said that as if things were going to be just fine—fun even.

But Christa Miller had no idea if she would be alive when they finished.

Part Two

THE CLUB

CHAPTER 3

Chicago, Illinois

THE ROAD TO insanity begins with obsession. An FBI agent—explaining criminal behavior—dropped that little nugget on me when I spent some time at the FBI facility in Quantico back in 1996. I was there for profiler training that the feds were providing to police officers. I was working as a cop in Chicago at the time. Now that I had reached the ripe old age of sixty-three, having just recently retired, I realized that those words could just as well apply to my current situation.

I retired because I had decided that I wanted nothing more than to step away from the muck and mire that I had to wade through day after day as a homicide detective. I saw my retirement as a chance to smooth over the rough edges that had inevitably formed like a crust on my marriage, due to all of the time I spent chasing down murderers—suffering from the detective's curse the whole way. I was always able to find clues that led to a suspect's capture, but missed all the clues at home that my marriage was falling apart—that my wife, Elena, was lonely and that she resented the job and me. So I was going to use my retirement to fix the years of damage that I had unwittingly done.

Or so I had thought.

I had promised my wife, and myself for that matter, that I wouldn't be one of those old lawmen who spent their golden years consumed with their old cases; but it didn't take long for me to realize that while I didn't miss the day-to-day grind, I did miss the thrill, the thrill of solving a puzzle—breaking down a suspect's alibi—figuring out the whos and the whys during an investigation. I missed the thrill of getting the confession.

In that realization, I found that I suffered from a need—an *obsession* actually—the need (my mind won't let me keep referring to it as an obsession because then I'd always think back to what that profiler told me) to resolve unfinished business.

There were five cold cases left unsolved on my watch. That's five cases where I did not find justice for the victims or their families. Those families did not get the closure it was my job to provide. And while morning walks with my loving wife, hours of binge-watching her favorite shows (including reruns of *NYPD Blue*—Elena always said I reminded her of Sipowicz, in both looks and temperament), and nights out with various activities sufficed at first, my mind began to wander.

Elena noticed it too. The number of times she had to repeat herself because I had mentally checked out of a conversation we were having continued to rise. My mind could no longer stay in our living room with my wife, Andy Sipowicz, and the boys from *NYPD Blue*. It was off and away, pouring over clues from those five unsolved homicides, wondering what had I missed. Was there someone who needed further looking into? Was there an alibi that I didn't try hard enough to break?

Soon after those questions began swirling in my head, I went on fewer walks with my wife in the mornings. I opted instead to head back down to the precinct. As I was close with my former sergeant, he didn't mind me perusing old case files. "Rob, just don't let me catch you poking around any new cases," he had said to me.

More and more, that was how I spent my mornings, down in the basement at the precinct, rummaging through old case files. Soon, it was how I was spending my evenings as well. As had been the case when I was on the job, I was putting together clues, just not the ones at home, the ones that should've really mattered to me, until it was too late.

"Robert Randolph Raines," my wife had said, as she stood in the doorway upon my return home one evening. It had been another long day of research. The hours had simply gotten away from me. It didn't escape my notice that she had used my full name. That's never good. "I can't do this anymore," she continued. There was a hitch in her voice, as if she had something caught in her throat. It made her sound strange to me. Later, I would realize just what that was.

"I wanted to give this a chance to work," she said. "I really wanted to see if we could try to fix our marriage. Lord knows why, given all I put up with over the years."

"But…" was all I could muster in response as I looked into her eyes. Those eyes, for the first time in our marriage, carried a look of defeat. She looked older than her fifty-nine years, much, much older. She was tired—tired of me and tired of being a cop's wife, tired of sharing the man she loved with a selfish mistress, a selfish mistress that, more times than not, kept her husband out all day and sometimes all night. The packed bags at her feet said so.

In that moment, I knew that her leaving was going to hurt me. Yet, all I could offer was a three-letter word, "But." I knew I should've said more. I knew I should've listed the myriad of reasons I believed she should stay, but the pain in her face and in her voice that night told me the message would've fallen on deaf ears, and quite possibly rightfully so. How much could I expect her to take? Didn't I owe her the peace of mind of being away from me, if that was what she wanted? So I said nothing more.

And just like that, she walked out of my life after forty-two years of marriage.

CHAPTER 4

FOR THE NEXT few weeks, I drowned my sorrows in bourbon, plenty of it. I'd always been particular to Blanton's, but either Bulleit or Maker's Mark would do in a pinch. Commiserating with me during this time was my best friend, another former copper, Dale Gamble.

Dale had retired from the force just about six months before I did. We had worked a few cases together during our time on the force, and I wouldn't mind saying that as good as I thought I was in the interrogation room, Dale was a master in there. I wouldn't be exaggerating when I'd say he'd have a read on a suspect, yay or nay, in five or ten minutes. Everyone whom he sat across from was like an open book that he could read at will. That was the main reason I never played poker with him.

Aside from our shared love of bourbon, he, like me, was a worker. Dale spent countless hours—days and nights just as I did—nose deep in case files, drinking bad coffee and eating takeout. His wife, Millie, I could only assume, felt the same way Elena did. But Dale and Millie were still together, toughing it out. But, make no mistake, they had their issues too—big time.

What we discovered while drinking, talking about the good old days, and me using Dale as a sounding board about Elena was that he too had an obsessive mind. There were cold cases that haunted the recesses of his conscience in between his trips down to Florida with the wife and that cruise they took to Jamaica.

His face lit up when I explained what I had been doing. "Are you going into the station tomorrow morning?" Dale asked.

My answer was "yes"; and sure enough, he was at my door the next morning, bright and early. We began reviewing those old cases together, and I didn't know if it was the extra hours of sleep I'd been able to get since retirement or the better coffee, but we began to make headway. Two old lifers who couldn't seem to give up policing even after retiring scratched up enough clues to get three of those cold cases kicked back upstairs to the active pile. Arrests were made. Closure was provided.

And that's when Dale got what he called "a great idea."

CHAPTER 5

"*WE SHOULD BE* licensed PIs," Dale said to me with a straight face.

"And just why in the hell should we do that?" I had asked, hoping the expression on *my* face really sold the fact that I wanted nothing to do with this "great idea" of his.

I enjoyed chasing down *our* old cold cases. That had been therapeutic—especially after Elena had left me. I worked the cases when I wanted to and at my own pace. I didn't want the pressure of "working" for someone.

"Word will get around, Raines, word about the work we're doing. You think we won't get offers? And it's not like we'd be doing it for free, you know, like we are now. Besides," Dale stared at me hard, "you got anything else better to do?"

Admittedly, he had me there.

And with just a few more days of smooth talking, Dale had me convinced. So we both got ourselves licensed. Then something funny happened. As it turned out, Dale was right.

Word did get around.

Job offers poured in. Some were from private citizens—looking for us to get the goods on cheating wives and husbands—and quite a few offers were from defense lawyers wanting to hire us to handle investigations for their clients. A few weeks in and I had to admit it. Dale *did* have a great idea. Surprisingly, I was enjoying myself to boot. The work—or, put in another way, my obsession—kept my mind off my personal life. If I ever did go crazy, at least I'd know the path that led me to that point.

That entire sequence of events led Dale and me into another discussion, a conversation about doing something else that, at this moment anyway, didn't seem like such a "great idea" to me.

"Will you listen to me for once?" Dale said. The look on his face was serious. Then again, he always looked serious. "This will be great for us. We should do a commercial. Now, I'm not knocking your little ad in the *Times* by the way, but you do know circulation of the printed page is down."

"So what? You want to do a commercial like some ambulance chasing injury lawyer? No, thanks."

"What does Ashe think?"

Cendalius Ashe was our new partner. He joined up with Dale and me this past winter, right before the start of the New Year. An interesting tidbit about the man was he, for what I could only call obvious reasons, preferred simply to go by Ashe. He insisted upon it actually, just the one name—like Prince or Madonna. Ashe was another retired copper, but he found his way to our little club under a different set of circumstances. He retired from the force on a psyche pension. The scuttlebutt had it as something about PTSD or some other kind of stress disorder.

Ashe was a former Marine. He did several tours over in Iraq and Afghanistan before coming back home to the states and joining CPD. So the PTSD story tracked. There had been rumors that he was a little...*off*, to put it mildly. He retired from the job at the ripe old age of forty-four.

"Retired," was the official term applied, but word around the campfire was that he was asked to leave. After reports of excessive force on several of his arrests surfaced, given today's climate where coppers were less and less popular and cellphone cameras were increasingly ubiquitous, none of the brass wanted to risk a major lawsuit. With rumors swirling about his mental state, the superintendent and the mayor feared he could snap and unload his service weapon into a perp out on the street. That was the last thing they would need. As much cash as the city had already forked over in wrongful death lawsuits, they weren't willing to take a chance on that happening. In what I could only see as a raw deal, they managed to find a way to square his dismissal with the police union, and Ashe was gone.

The psyche pension was their "gift," a going-away present for a combat veteran who was being shown the door. I had worked with Ashe a time or two before the end of my run, and in spite of the rumors about him, I came away impressed. He was as solid as any cop I had worked with. He had good instincts and great investigative skills and didn't take any shit from anyone on the streets. It didn't get more solid than that in my book.

When I had heard that he had recently "quit," seeing that Dale and I needed the help, it was only natural to reach out to him. He was onboard with the idea right away. Like Dale and me, it gave him something to do other than sit at home and stare at the boob tube all day.

"You know Ashe," I said. "He's not going to care one way or the other."

"Fine," Dale said. "We'll put this off for now. But this discussion isn't over, Bobby."

"And don't call me Bobby—"

Our office phone rang, interrupting my objection.

Dale answered, "Office of RDC Private Investigations, you got Gamble speaking."

We called ourselves RDC—Dale's idea, using each of our first initials in the order that we came into this line of work. Dale was just full of ideas. We actually didn't have an office as yet. We worked out of the living room in my house. Once Elena left, I certainly had the space. It's a simple setup really. Aside from the sofa that'd been along the right side wall of the living room since the late 1990s, we had two desks, three phone lines, and a couple of computers, both Dell's—the office.

"Sure, sure, he's right here." Dale motioned for me to pick up the other line.

"Raines."

"Bobby?"

The voice on the other end of the phone stopped me cold and not just because the man speaking had called me Bobby. While I never liked being called that, it was the voice itself which gave me pause.

"David? I'm surprised to hear from you."

"I'm actually surprised to be calling you. I heard about you and Elena."

"And just how is your sister doing?" I asked.

"She's holding up well, considering," David said.

"Look. If you're calling to—"

"No, I'm actually not calling about you guys at all."

Relieved, I said, "Well, just what can I do for you then, David?"

"Elena told me about the whole PI thing you're doing. And I heard about those cold cases you guys cracked. It's been on the news."

"Yeah, old habits dying hard and all that."

"Well, some good friends of mine, the McAllisters... I don't know if you remember Michael and his wife, Claire?"

I said that I did not, but David told me that we both went to high school with Michael back in that former life of ours, when we were kids. The only classmates I had kept up with after graduation were David and his sister, who later became my wife, so the name McAllister was of no consequence to me.

"Their granddaughter, Cecilia..." David's voice trailed off, and I felt a knot forming in the pit of my stomach. Hearing the tone in his voice, it didn't take a detective to know something terrible had happened to her. I could guess a million different things, but I kept my imagination at bay and waited for David to compose himself and continue. "She's missing. She's been kidnapped."

"Kidnapped? When? Was there an AMBER alert issued? I haven't heard anything."

"Not here, Bobby. The family lives in Alexandria. Alexandria, Louisiana."

"Louisiana?" I asked. "Well, I would imagine the police down there are all over this. I'm not sure what we could—"

"That's just it, Bobby. They're not all over it. According to Michael, their granddaughter has been missing for three weeks, and the police don't have a clue, not one single, goddamned clue. And here's the kicker, Bobby."

Oh, great. There's a kicker.

David continued, "There was a string of disappearances down in Alexandria that started just about eight years ago—all women. Then suddenly, the abductions just stopped like late last year. None of those women were ever found."

"And the police are thinking there's a connection? The McAllister girl and the past cases? That the abductions are starting up again?" I asked.

"The police haven't divulged that information. As you can imagine, the family has no clue. They're at their wits' end."

"I'll just bet. Look. In my opinion—"

"They're not looking for an opinion, Bobby. They're looking for answers. And they want to hire you to get those answers."

CHAPTER 6

GOING INTO SOMEONE else's backyard and taking over the sandbox had never been anything I ever wanted to be a part of in any way, shape, form, or fashion. Conducting an investigation in someone else's jurisdiction was tantamount to showing up at the officer's home and asking if the lady of the house was available because you had a few hours to kill.

It doesn't play well.

Regardless of whether or not you had the noblest of intentions, there's going to be tons of resentment, and rightfully so—even more so as a PI. At least here at home, I knew most of the players, so it's not as if I was stepping on anybody's toes. And generally speaking, we didn't get involved in any active police investigations.

"Look, David. I don't know that it's such a wise idea."

"The McAllisters are offering to retain your services with ten grand up front, another ten if you resolve the case, no matter the uh…final outcome. But they want answers."

Twenty-grand? I didn't remember Michael McAllister at all, but it sounded like he'd done well for himself over the years. Then again for all I knew, he's up to his eyeballs in debt and was possibly mortgaging his home to find out what happened to his granddaughter. What wouldn't someone do for a loved one? I could only imagine the chaos her disappearance had caused the entire family, especially given the recent history down there that David had mentioned. And I knew the pain and devastation that losing a loved one could cause a family. I knew it all too well. So on that note…

"We'll talk with them. I make no guarantees," I said, grabbing my pad and pen. "Give me Michael's information. I'll give him a call and get all the particulars."

I took down Michael McAllister's number and jotted down a few other details that came to David's mind before he hung up the phone. I was just glad that what I thought was going to be some long, drawn-out lecture about how I'd mistreated his sister all these years turned out not to be. He was still her big brother, after all, and he still acted like it when he felt he needed to—we butted heads more than once in the past. I simply didn't need that headache.

To my surprise, what he provided instead was exactly what I needed, more work to keep my mind off my troubles. As it so happened, I kept my mind off my troubles, by getting knee-deep into someone else's.

"So what was that? A case?" Dale asked. His face seemed to light up at the notion.

"Yes," I said. "We have a case."

Part Three

THE HUNTING GROUND

CHAPTER 7

Pollock, Louisiana

*J*OLIE EVERSON CHECKED her watch. It was already half past three in the afternoon. *Oh no! Girl, you're gonna be late!* Getting settled into her new apartment had taken the twenty-four-year old much longer than she had expected, thanks in no small part to the cable guy.

He was affable enough, but had arrived outside of the two-hour appointment window—*big surprise*. After several trips back and forth to his van and a few false starts, he finally completed her installation. Though flustered, Jolie managed to keep a smile on her face. That was her gift, after all. She didn't wear her emotions on her sleeve. She just kept smiling as she signed the cableman's paperwork and ushered him out the door. Within minutes, she hit the road, driving as fast as she dared in the hopes of keeping her other appointment.

There was still more work to do in the apartment—more boxes for her to unpack. There were more memories—family photos, knickknacks, and such—to hang and put in their new spaces. More work to do to make the new apartment feel like *home*. Before completing those tasks, however, Jolie's plan was to pick up her new guard dog—guard dog-to-be, actually. A pit bull pup that she found for sale on the You Trade It app was going to be a nice and welcome addition in her new home. Her new four-legged friend would be the only company she intended to have for the immediate future.

Jolie Everson had arrived in Pollock with only two days of freedom before starting the first leg of her new career—working as the head nurse at USP Pollock, the federal lockup. Initially she had felt a lot of trepidation about working in a men's federal prison. Actually, she still felt apprehensive; however, she had made her peace with it. Besides, being head nurse at the facility would look impressive on her resume.

The move to Pollock marked the first time that she'd ever been on her own in life; and right now, it was all coming together, just as she had planned. Moving to the small town of Pollock, miles and miles away from her family in New Mexico, was daunting to say the least. But she found the nerve to step out on her own. She liked what little she'd seen of her new city thus far. It would take some getting used to, though. Pollock was much smaller than Albuquerque. But she would get used to it. It was part of her plan, and she was in it for the duration. Her next feat, which she fully expected to accomplish within a few years, was to be the head nurse of a trauma ward at a hospital back in her home state. Albuquerque was her hope, although she wouldn't mind Las Cruces.

She had been the first in her family to have gone to college—gone and graduated, that is. In spite of all those who thought she wouldn't make it, here she was. Of course, given her history and that wild—albeit brief—period in high school, they had reason to cast those doubts. This was her chance to show them all, and that was just what she intended to do. She took pride in that.

The woman selling the pit bull pup, Emily Robicheaux she had called herself, suggested they meet near the laundromat on Fifth Street, which was great for Jolie. The place was only minutes from where she was now making her home. Jolie held out hope that she wouldn't be so late that the woman would leave.

Had she an inkling, however, of the horrific fate that was to befall her, she'd do one better than simply being late. She would never arrive at all.

CHAPTER 8

Chicago, Illinois

MY CONVERSATION WITH Michael McAllister
lasted about twenty minutes. He filled me in on all of the
details of his kin down in Alexandria, Louisiana.

He told me how his son, Timothy, and daughter-
in-law, Alicia, had moved to the Bayou State, for his
job, just as their daughter was graduating high school.
Cecilia, Michael's granddaughter, was in the midst of her
first year at Tulane University and was home visiting her
parents in Alexandria when she went missing.

He recounted most of the details that David had
already given me, that it seemed the police did not have
any clues, at least none that were going to lead to them
solving his granddaughter's disappearance. Michael
McAllister went on about that string of similar kidnappings—women who had gone missing down in the

42

Alexandria area—some time ago. Also like David, he mentioned that none of those women had ever been found.

After getting his son's information, I confirmed we would take the case and ended the call. Dale, who had been sitting on the sofa the whole time I was on the phone and seemed to be chomping at the bit, said, "Well? So when do we leave?"

"You do know we're probably not going to be received warmly when we get down there, don't you?"

"Yeah. And?"

My observation did nothing to curb his enthusiasm. I said, "Never mind. Go ahead and get packed. We can roll out in about an hour, hour and a half. It's a four-teen-hour drive, but I'm betting we make it in twelve."

"Will Ashe be joining us?"

"He has something personal going on. I gave him a heads-up, though, that if we need him, we'll call him in."

"That works for me," Dale said. "And by the way, I'll be ready in thirty minutes."

I quickly packed a bag (I traveled light, so that didn't take me long), and while waiting for Dale, I made a quick call to Timothy McAllister. I thought it import-ant that he heard from me prior to our arrival. His voice was shaky when he answered, as I had expected it would be given the circumstances. I didn't want to keep him long, figuring he and his wife were going to have a hard enough time answering questions and recounting details when Dale and I got to town.

I asked some of the obvious questions, questions that I was certain he'd already answered for the Alexandria

Police Department (PD): *Did your daughter mention problems with anyone? Do you know of anyone who would want to hurt her? Was she seeing someone? Did she do drugs or hang out with people who did drugs?*

He answered each question with a painfully terse "no."

Keeping the call brief as I had said I would, I wrapped it up by assuring Timothy that we'd be arriving soon and would get to work immediately. As I hung up the phone, in my mind I compiled a quick list of what we'd need to do right away if we were going to have any chance at all of finding out what happened to Cecilia McAllister. We needed to determine what she did in the twenty-four hours prior to her disappearance and whom she was with, if anyone. And hopefully within those details, we would find the devil who took Cecilia McAllister.

True to his word, Dale returned to my place in thirty minutes. Across one shoulder was a garment bag with what I was willing to bet was three or four of those nice suits Dale liked to wear. Me, I still bought my suits off the rack at Sears. Slung across Dale's other shoulder was a large duffle bag, which seemed stuffed to the gills. That bag looked like it weighed a hundred pounds easy.

"Alright, old-timer. Let's hit the road," he said.

Only half-kidding, I said, "Jesus, Dale. You got Millie stuffed in that bag?"

"What? This?" Dale unslung the duffle from his shoulder, took it by the handle straps, and easily raised it up and down a few times. "This is me traveling light." He always liked to show off how great of shape he was in for his age. He managed to stay relatively thin, as he got older. He certainly didn't put on weight around the middle like I did. Nor did he start going bald up top like me, though he did have more gray. He's all salt, no pepper. The sad thing was he's three years older than me, but to look at us, anyone would guess me to be the oldest. He's definitely in better shape than I am. I'd give him that. Unlike Dale, I was never the workout type. My version of arm curls consisted of lifting a bottle of beer and shots of bourbon up to my mouth.

Dale stepped inside the doorway and said, "So you ready?"

"One moment," I said, as I took my SIG Sauer P250 from my desk drawer and holstered it. I also grabbed my backup gun, a Glock G43, and a few extra magazines and tossed them into my travel bag, which, compared to Dale's oversized duffle, looked like little more than a gym bag.

"This…is traveling light, by the way." I grabbed my bag by the handles and did the same up-down-up motion with it as Dale had done moments ago.

He chuckled and then said, "You drive the first leg. I'm going to grab some shut-eye. Wake me when you need me to take over."

"Works for me." I grabbed my keys off the desk and hit the lights as we made our way outside. Dale sleeping gave me time to mentally prepare to get into this case. Going in, we had no idea of what we'd find; but in my experience, when someone was missing for this long, there's usually only one outcome, only one way they're found, if they're even found at all.

They're found dead.

And right now, it's just a gut feeling, but I was pretty sure we'd be making that exact statement to the McAllisters at the end of all of this—that young Cecilia was dead.

I hated making notifications when I was on the job. After retiring, while I might have missed the puzzle solving, I didn't miss that aspect. Seeing the pain, raw emotion, and agony that's released when a parent or family member heard that they had lost a loved one was always heartbreaking for me, not because I was a sensitive guy—my wife (*was she my ex already?*) would tell you that I was not.

Death notifications always broke me down and tore me up inside—because it made me remember my own pain. It always made me relive the agony that I suffered with the loss of my son.

CHAPTER 9

MY SON, ROBERT Junior, died just two months shy of his twenty-fifth birthday. Or, to be more accurate, he was *murdered* just before his birthday.

My son grew up admiring his dad. He also admired what I did for a living. At the age of twenty, he followed me into police work. His mom, Elena, didn't like the idea of her only son working the streets as a beat cop, no matter how much I assured her that he would be just fine. She was always a nervous wreck whenever he was on his shift.

One major difference between my son and me, though, was that he had higher ambitions. For me, from the first day I hit the streets out of the academy, I fell in love with the profession. I'd found my dream job, my calling. My son, on the other hand, had designs beyond working the beat or making detective grade. As a matter of fact, he was eyeing a different path in law enforcement altogether.

He had enrolled in college (something else I never did) and was majoring in criminal justice. After that, he was headed to law school. He hadn't made up his mind as to whether he'd work in the state attorney's office or private practice, but felt the experience of being a cop, of seeing this side, would give him a greater perspective. He also felt that he had plenty of time to decide.

We all thought he had plenty of time to decide, until *that* day.

I'll never forget it. It was the worst Friday of my life, April 18, 2003. I'd just gotten home, poured myself a glass of bourbon, and settled in to watch the Cubs. They were taking on the Pirates that day. About twenty minutes in, there was a knock at my front door.

I was aware of what had happened the moment I'd opened the door. I'd stood on the other side so many times before. As much as I wanted to hold out some hope, the looks the officers carried on their faces gave away the grim news before they'd even opened their mouths to say a word.

In that moment, all of my years on the job, my experience with death and crime, didn't matter. It couldn't help me. My heart dropped into my stomach, and I crumpled in my doorway when one of the officers began to speak similar words to ones that I had recited without much thought or emotion on several occasions.

"Detective Raines," the officer, whom I would later come to know as Officer Carl Hoyne, said, "I'm so sorry to tell you your son, Officer Robert Raines Jr., was killed in the line of duty, today."

Before I had even realized it, Elena was down in a heap right next to me in our front hallway. Tears and screams of pain rolled uncontrollably out of us. The offi-cers said something else in the way of offering condo-lences, but we weren't listening. In that moment, we were alone in the world.

After sometime, I managed to get myself back under control. I got Elena to our bedroom and left her there, sobbing on our bed, while I went to speak with the offi-cers. I needed answers. I needed to know what happened to my son.

The story recounted to me by Officer Hoyne, who along with his partner was first on scene after everything went down, was that my son and his partner were respond-ing to a 10-1—a call of officer needing assistance—that came across the radio. What should've been a routine traf-fic stop had turned into a total cluster fuck. A Mercedes SLR that apparently was full of cocaine and cash—and two heavily armed, desperate men who didn't want to be taken in—opened fire on the squad car that put out the call.

My son and his partner arrived on scene and began taking fire as well. Details are somewhat sketchy from there, but a foot chase ensued. What witnesses did report was that one of the fleeing suspects, later identi-fied as Arthur "Art Dog" Murray, a midlevel drug dealer who had made his way onto the DEA's radar, turned during that foot chase and fired the fatal bullet that killed my son.

Murray died in the ensuing shootout. His passenger, and partner, James "Big Time" Griggs, took several rounds during the carnage also. He, however, survived. Griggs went on trial for the death of my son and the attempted murder of several other officers. Of course, he pleaded not guilty. He swore that it wasn't them who opened fire first. The cops did. He and "Art Dog" only fired in self-defense. The cops on scene, including my son's partner, Elliot James (who luckily survived without a scratch), testified to the opposite effect. Griggs, for his part, stuck with his story all the way to death row. Of course, the governor of Illinois, in his infinite wisdom, had suspended enforcement of the death penalty just three years before this happened.

For now, James Griggs gets three hots and a cot. If the death penalty comes back however, Griggs gets the needle. And God willing, I'll be there to see it.

My son would be forty years old were he alive today—a lawyer of some sort, no doubt, and successful. I often thought of the conversations we would've had through the years—him asking me for advice, maybe? I'd thought about the fishing trips we'd have went on. Maybe he'd be married now, and I'd even have some grandchildren running around. All of those possibilities were stolen from me that day. My life would never be the same. And I couldn't get over the feeling, though such words were never spoken, that Elena felt I'd broken my promise—my promise that our son would be okay doing this line of work, protecting our city. I could just feel it. It seemed as if she wished I'd talked him out of joining CPD.

Although, sometimes, I understood that was how *I* felt, it was just easier to project that as coming from her. That way, I could live with myself and not want to eat a bullet. I would've gladly traded my own life to keep my son alive. Life doesn't work that way, though. You don't just get to swap.

We have to live with our losses, like it or not.

Chapter 10

Pollock, Louisiana

JOLIE EVERSON PULLED into the parking lot of the World of Bubbles laundromat that sat on the corner of Fifth and Dennemore Streets. The offer of "Dry for Free" that was prominently displayed in the laundromat window caught her eye. That was good to know. There was one other car parked in the lot, but it was not the white van Emily had said she'd be driving.

"No, no, no…don't tell me I'm too late," Jolie muttered as she parked her Hyundai Sonata. She looked at her watch again. It was three forty-five. She was fifteen minutes late. She slapped a hand against the steering wheel. "Damn." She'd really wanted that dog.

She checked her phone, but it showed no missed calls and no follow-up texts. Just as she had resigned herself to the fact she'd missed her chance, a white Chevy cargo van pulled into the lot and slowly rolled toward her car.

The van had seen better days. It was more than just a little beat up. The white paint had faded to a dull dirty gray, and dents ran along the length of the driver side. In the driver's seat was a tiny, waif of a woman with dirty blond hair. She smiled sheepishly as she put the van in park.

Jolie didn't sense that anything was wrong—that there was something sinister or nefarious about to take place. She wasn't supposed to. That was the whole idea, after all.

Jolie Everson rolled down her passenger side window. She called out, "Emily?"

"Yeah, hon, sorry I was runnin' a bit late," Emily said and flashed a smile. It was an awkward smile—Jolie Everson thought so, at least. It seemed as though Emily was determined not to show any teeth with that smile, and her lips didn't quite seem to understand how they were supposed to form one.

"Oh, no worries. No worries at all. I was running late myself."

"No kiddin'? Well, how about that? You still interested?" Emily flicked her hair from side to side.

"Of course!" Jolie said.

The little blond woman got out of the car. She was dressed in jogging sweats and a tank top that almost seemed too big for her. She was also visibly dirty. Jolie couldn't help but notice the grease smears on her white tank as well as the smears that ran along her arms and down the side of her face. Emily looked as if she'd been working underneath that van she came pulling up in. *That could be why she was running late*, Jolie thought and held back a giggle. Then it occurred to her. She didn't know anything about cars at all herself. If her Hyundai broke down, it's AAA to the rescue. Maybe getting a little dirty wasn't so bad.

She got out of her car and headed to the back of the van after Emily. Sitting in the air conditioning (AC) on the ride over had made her forget just that quickly how hot it was out. The humidity was stifling. Jolie felt overdressed in the sundress she wore. Just looking at the sweats Emily wore was making her feel hot. *What an odd choice on a day like this.*

"Okay, this little fella is 'bout three months old but eats and shits like a big ol' sum'bitch, so make sure you got plenty of kibble on hand. Oh, and be ready to scoop up plenty of poop." Emily flashed that odd, crooked smile of hers again. This time it made Jolie Everson slightly uncomfortable. She didn't know why, but she immediately felt that the sooner she got the pup into her backseat and paid the gaunt woman with the waiflike appearance and got on her way, the better off she'd be.

"Alright then," Jolie said. "I'll be ready for that." She cleared her throat as Emily put her hand on the rear door handle. "Thirty-five dollars, correct?"

"That's right, dear," Emily Robicheaux said. That same crooked smile still etched across her angular face.

Jolie looked down into the small purse she had slung crossways on her body. As she grabbed three ten-dol-lar bills and a five, she heard the van door open. When she looked up, her eyes grew wide with terror. A large, bearded man, looking just as grimy as Emily—in a pair of grease-stained overalls—lunged forward and pulled her into the back of the cargo van. She tried to scream. She kicked her feet and flailed wildly, but the big man pinned her down with ease and put a large, meaty hand over her mouth and nose. Jolie Everson was no pushover. She was a star athlete in college—track and field. There were so many trophies that she still had to put up in her new place. She lifted weights regularly, but couldn't match the large man's strength in the slightest. She didn't think he could even feel her resisting.

The van doors slammed shut. The big man yelled, "Shut up, whore! You just shut it, now!"

The big brute quickly had a wet towel over her mouth and nose, in one fluid motion. It was as if he'd done this before. He was prepared. It was like color by numbers. Jolie felt her head begin to swirl as she inhaled what she knew to be chloroform. The scent was very distinct. She remembered it from one of her science courses back when she was in school. *School*—it was that memory, growing ever distant now, that escorted Jolie Everson into darkness.

Emily Robicheaux looked around nervously. No one was in sight, no one peering out of the neighboring storefronts at the van, wondering just what in the hell was going on. She quickly picked up Jolie's keys and purse and got into the Hyundai. Emily cranked the ignition, dropped the car in gear, and slowly pulled out of the lot. Moments later, after having secured his latest catch, Orrin Robicheaux cranked the beat-up van.

He calmly shifted into gear and followed Emily out of the lot.

CHAPTER 11

Pollock, Louisiana

"*YOU DID GOOD,* girl," Orrin Robicheaux called out to his wife, Emily. She had just finished parking the Hyundai Sonata over by his toolshed. It was a rickety structure of sun-splintered wood that had seen better days, but still served it's purpose.

She always parked the new girls' cars there. Orrin would either sell them for cheap or drive them deeper out into the marsh and abandon them there, except for any of the newer, fancier cars, like the Mercedes that one girl, Cecilia, had. No, those cars would have GPS tracking systems and other fancy whatnots—making it easier for law enforcement to find them. Orrin was too smart for that. Those cars were ditched, somewhere far, far from the family land. And all cellphones were destroyed, period.

She walked over to the rear of their van. The cargo doors were open, and she could see her husband crouched over the prone, unconscious figure of their latest capture, Jolie Everson.

"I thought we was gon' miss her, on count of our bein' late."

"Yeah, well, girl, if that had happened... I'd a beat you somethin' fierce." The congratulatory tone Orrin spoke with just moments ago had vanished. His stone-faced expression caused Emily's eyes to drop down some-where over her feet.

"I'm sorry, baby. I just couldn't find the keys at first is all," Emily quickly stammered out the apology she had been issuing since they had left their property earlier. "But didn't I handle her well for you, baby? Didn't I get her to the back of the van quickly?" She went on, seeking to abate his fury.

"Yeah, girl. Yeah, you did."

"And nobody saw us, baby, nobody. I was sure of it."

"Okay, girl. You handled her well. An' we got what we went out fo'." Orrin's tone softened to the point that Emily meekly looked up at him again. Seeing that his facial expression had softened along with his voice, she managed a weak smile. He turned his attention away from her and back to the unconscious Jolie Everson.

Emily continued to watch. Her eyes flickered back and forth between her husband and the ground below. In between, she saw Orrin stick his hands down the girl's pants, working his fingers around in there. After a moment, she then saw him stick those fingers in his mouth.

Orrin finally turned his attention back to Emily and said, "Help me get this one set up inside."

"Yes, baby."

"And hurry up an' get supper on. I'm starving."

Chapter 12

I HAD OUR CHEVY Tahoe rolling steady at seventy-five miles an hour on the highway the past ten hours. It was plenty of time for me to get thoughts of my son off of my mind, but also plenty of time to think of other dark thoughts. Such were the trappings of an obsessive mind. It's hard to turn it off. We were off I-57 and through Arkansas and onto US-167 heading south before Dale woke up from his slumber.

"Need me to take over, partner?" Dale asked, wiping the sleep from his eyes with the backs of his hands. He yawned and stretched, nearly clipping me across the chin in the process.

"Nah, I'm good," I said. "But since you're awake now, sleeping beauty, let me ask you something. I've been thinking about it ever since we hit I-57."

"Shoot."

"You remember the first case we worked together? It was in '02 I think."

"Yes, I do. The three little black girls who went missing in Englewood."

"Now those girls went missing over what? A period of six, eight months before we realized the cases were connected?"

"That's right," Dale said. "We put in a lot of hours, a lot of hard work solving that case. And that was in spite of the negative publicity the department got on handling that one."

"That's true. I remember feeling like a member of the walking dead during that case. And in the end—"

Dale cut me off mid-sentence. He knew exactly where I was going.

"We didn't find any of them alive. I know." Dale's voice was pained. That case still affected him too.

"And I had a feeling the entire time that we worked that case that we wouldn't."

"We found their killer though, Bobby. We did do that."

Fighting back the anguish being alone with my thoughts had stirred up, I said, "It didn't bring those girls back. And I'll tell you something else. I've got that same feeling right now."

"We weren't hired because we guaranteed that we'd find the McAllister girl alive. We were hired to find answers. And I'd bet green money that we're going to do just that." Dale didn't take his eyes off of me the entire time he spoke. He wanted me to know he meant those words. Then, in his most encouraging voice, he said, "Now, come on. We don't want to show up and be the voice of doom and gloom, regardless of what we think. Let's do our investigation and get this family some answers."

"You're right," I said, finally getting my emotions in check. I needed that little pep talk. "Go back to sleep. We're just a few hours out. I can take us all the way in. And don't call me Bobby."

Interlude 1

HOW TO MAKE A MONSTER

CHAPTER 13

Summer 2010
Pollock, Louisiana

THE YOUNG MONSTER-IN-TRAINING, now four-teen and had already stretched past his father in height, never once thought of looking away as he observed the techniques that his father not just simply recommended, but prescribed.

Over the course of the entire summer, the elder monster, William "Willie" Robicheaux, inducted his son, Orrin, into his world—his world of kidnapping, tortur-ing, and raping women. The practice became a bonding exercise for them. Doing something sane (or in their mind trite) like going fishing, hunting big game, or taking in a sporting event just wasn't their way. But this—this shared exercise in depravity—drew them closer together.

As far back as he could remember, Orrin Robicheaux had always wanted to have a close relationship with his dad. After his mom died when he was twelve—cancer, his dad had said—the two of them rarely interacted, not in any significant sort of way. Their lives followed the same routine day in and day out. Orrin got up in the mornings to a soggy bowl of cereal on the kitchen table, and after finishing it off and getting dressed, he was off to school. The elder Robicheaux worked all day, then returned home, and spent the majority of the evenings down in the cellar. The relationship was by no means abusive. It was simply…nonexistent.

Orrin would spend his evenings, alone, sitting in front of the television, switching between mindless reality TV programs and music videos. That was his life, until the day, young Orrin, a freshly minted teenager at thirteen years old, found himself playing "explorer" in the crawl space above the cellar. He was there for no other reason than he had never been in there before—that and simply because he had nothing else better to do. It was a way to pass the time, those sluggish summer hours that for him passed by in a sort of slow motion.

Orrin found a sizeable hole in the floor of the crawl space. With his eye against it, he could see a vast portion of the cellar. And the things he saw, the things he witnessed through that unintended glory hole, *excited* him.

He watched—without flinching, captivated even— as his father would beat, rape, and torture multiple women. He was most excited and awestruck by the violent beatings, even more so than the rapes. Every time he would watch, Orrin's breathing would get heavy.

His pulse raced. And one day, there was something else, something new, something that he had not experienced before up to this point in his young life. In between his legs, his penis went all stiff one evening as he observed his father and his playthings. Orrin had never experienced that sensation before.

He liked it!

From then on, it was a sense of euphoria he felt, a hint of nirvana even, every time he watched. Discussing these feelings with his dad was out of the question. They barely talked at all, and he was spying on the old man, right? *What would Daddy do*, he wondered, if he was found *essentially trespassing on the old man's cellar time?* He didn't know and wasn't sure he wanted to. Orrin's voyeurism from the crawl space was his little secret, his twisted little secret that he would lie awake at night in bed with and fondle himself to, his little secret that he enjoyed thinking about all day long over the course of the following year, especially when he was at school, staring at all of the girls in his class.

He often got lost in thought when he should've been listening to the day's lesson. Instead, he found himself wondering just what would it be like to punch Brenda Martin in the face until blood flowed freely from her nose and mouth. How about choking Marie Baptiste until her eyes rolled into the back of her head? Or the new girl—Sylvia *what's-her-name*—she was built more heftily up top than most of the girls. What would it be like making her scream and beg for mercy while he carved his initials on her big ass tits? The song his father listened to all the time, the one about the sandman and dreams, or whatever those old cunts were singing about, swirled around in his head on repeat as his fantasies played out.

He continued his clandestine trips into the crawl space until just by chance, one day during the perverted peepshow, he got a little too excited. He squealed in joy, and slightly out of fear, at his first seminal release. His father had heard. Instead of being ashamed or worse (for Orrin's sake) angry that his son found out about his hobby, when he noticed the boy's delight, the elder Robicheaux was *overjoyed!* They'd just had a moment. They had just shared something.

They had a bond.

Not long after that day, the elder monster decided that his young son would gain an appreciation and *learn* while getting a close-up look. No longer did Orrin have to stare in secret and take in the view from the glory hole. He had a ringside seat.

Young Orrin was delighted. After watching from the cheap seats, he now had an all-access pass. Not just front row, he was part of the show, *a player*. Now he was going to learn just how this whole thing, this wonderful new thing he was sharing with his dad, worked.

And in the throes of the year's hot summer, he was getting that chance firsthand.

When Orrin entered the cellar for the first time, his heart pumped in his chest like a jackhammer, and his breathing quickened. Unlike before, when he was merely peering through the hole in the floor, now he could take in the entire scene.

He took in huge gulps of air, one after the other, when he saw that there were multiple women locked up in cages. His father had actually built cages, just like the kind dogs would be housed in at a kennel, down in the cellar.

There were eight of them—eight cages, eight women. The look of fear in their eyes excited Orrin. The confusion on each woman's face seemed to indicate that they did not know what to make of his presence. He stared long and hard at them. The women stared too, sheer disbelief drawn across their faces.

The boy's presence only served to make the horrors suffered that much worse. Their plight became that much more denigrating, if that were possible, with this child watching—watching and getting off on their humiliation and pain. His giddy chuckles could be heard over the music and their screams as they filled the cellar and blood dripped to the floor.

The young monster-in-training soaked up all the tips his father gave like a sponge. He consumed his father's methods and adopted his brutality.

"If the slave behaves, son," his father had said, "you can choose to be merciful. Ya' hear that, boy?"

"Yes, sir."

"But that is always yo' choice, son, not theirs. And remember this: You *always* want to hear the screams. If she tries to be tough, tries to deny you the pleasure of the moment, you beat that bitch harder. You hear me, son?"

"Yes, sir," the monster-to-be said eagerly.

"This is for our enjoyment, our enjoyment only. That's all that matters."

His education continued right on through the dog days of August, when the heat and humidity intensified and the sour scent of women's hygiene gone unattended—times eight—along with traces of vomit and fecal matter, assailed the nostrils upon entry into the cellar. The air inside was thick and heavy. The elder monster, when the scent got too strong for even him, would simply hose the women down, right in their cells.

It was all they deserved. And time marched on.

Chapter 14

WILLIE ROBICHEAUX ALWAYS moved with purpose. But then again, everything about Willie Robicheaux was steeped in purpose. One prime example was the house he had bought. The house sat on three acres of land out in the middle of nowhere in Pollock. Its location served a purpose. It was secluded—and quiet. For a man with Willie's predilections, quiet—and solitude—was exactly what was needed.

The changes he had painstakingly made in his cellar all took time and care. His location gave him the privacy to complete those changes unnoticed. Though the eight-run six-by-ten roof-paneled galvanized steel dog cages he installed, with cots for each, took up most of the room in the cellar, they too would serve a purpose.

A workbench, two gurneys, a slender medical cabinet that housed medical supplies, and a queen-sized mattress casually laid out on the floor in a corner made up the rest of his torture room—his chamber of horrors.

Willie was living the dream, *his* dream, a twisted, evil dream that with him traced all the way back to his childhood, if that thresher of an existence could simply be summed up as such.

His father had been long gone by the time he was born; and his mother, Ruby, was pure hell on wheels. His earliest memories were of being slapped in the face for one thing or another—quite possibly for pissing his diaper or maybe simply for being hungry and crying about it. By the time he could walk, the beatings were becoming severe. Just his luck, he was born to Ruby Robicheaux, who, as it turned out, was a full-blown, class A drunk. She had been since she was sixteen—and a violent drunk, at that.

Her ire for her only son wasn't saved just for the times she was loaded up on whatever cheap hooch she could afford, either. If she couldn't find the remote, obviously, that shit-for-brains son of hers had hid it, so that earned him a beating. Anytime she got fired from one of the many waitressing jobs she worked during the course of her adult life, well, it was only on account of her being late all the time fussing over that no-good William. That would earn him a beating too.

The fact that she couldn't get any of the men who made their way in and out of her life faster than her bedroom door could swing open to stay—well, that was only on account of the fact they didn't want to have to deal with that weirdo kid of hers.

Even she thought he was weird.

One night, Ruby caught little William, who was about ten years old at the time, standing in her bedroom doorway. She turned and saw him staring at her, her legs pointing at high noon, a man on top of her, grunting and groaning. The boy just stood there with a stupid, bewildered look on his face. While Ruby seemed fine with ignoring his presence, the man she was with wanted out once he'd seen young Willie. The man moved like comic book speedster *the Flash* as he dismounted Ruby, scooped his pants up from the bedroom floor, and was out the door all seemingly in the same motion.

Willie got a good whipping that night too. He had to stay home from school a few days after that one. The beating was just that bad. It was during that severe thrashing, though, that for the very first time, Willie realized that he really, really wanted to hurt his mother. The thoughts occurred to him in violent flashes as she punched and kicked at his small frame. She slung his frail body across the living room and into one of the rickety end tables that was part of her hillbilly chic décor.

After the first five minutes, he didn't even feel pain anymore. He concentrated on those thoughts—those wonderfully vivid, violent thoughts of doing the same thing to her. She was much stronger than he was, at this point, though. He couldn't even defend himself, let alone inflict any pain on her. He would just have to draw his comfort from the idea. And he did.

CHAPTER 15

TWO YEARS HAD gone by since the night of that fateful, yet enlightening, beating that William had suffered. There were no more strange men darkening his mother's doorway during that time, which didn't make her any nicer. There was one night in particular, however, that stuck out in Willie's mind more than any he had endured up to that point.

He'd come home from school, and his mom was in her usual place when she wasn't working. Ruby lay stretched out on the couch, in front of the TV with a bottle of Seagram's Gin and a pack of cigarettes at her side, dressed only in her lime-green nightgown with the flowers embroidered along the hemline. Looking at the number of butts in the ashtray, Willie could only assume she'd been there since he'd left for school that morning. It was where she would spend the remainder of that evening, well into the night. What happened next, though, was quite possibly the moment Willie Robicheaux—*the monster*—was truly born.

After finishing the last of the gin, Ruby ambled to her bedroom, calling after young Willie. Ruby gave him a coy smile as he entered her room. She went to the record player she kept on the nightstand and turned it on. It wasn't long before The Chordettes were doing their thing, and Ruby began singing right along.

"My mom and dad used to listen to this all the time. They were really in love," she said before launching into the next verse. "I felt my dream had arrived when I met your no-good son-of-a-bitch (SOB) of a father," she railed once the song completed. After a moment, it cranked up again. Ruby then did something that she had never done before—as far as he could remember, anyway—as she crawled onto bed and had him come sit beside her. She complimented him and told him just how fine of a young man he was growing into. Closest she had been to paying him a compliment prior to that was during report card pickup the previous semester. After looking over his grades and noting that he had gotten all Cs, she looked at her son and said, "Well, I guess you could've screwed up worse."

As he sat on the edge of her bed that evening, she began to stroke his hair. Her voice was soft as she said, "You look just like him, y'know, your father." When she reached around with her free hand and began rubbing between his legs, he shuddered. It was unexpected. It was different from the beatings, but yet, his young mind still could not grasp what was happening. Willie moved to get up. "Uh-uh," she said, pulling her top over her head. "Get undressed. You're gonna sleep with your momma, tonight. It'll be just like old times, like when you were little, my little baby."

It was *not* just like old times, not like any old times that young Willie could remember. She made him strip bare. "To your naked ass," she had said. Within moments of him sliding under the covers, she was on top of him. He'd experience his first erection on this night. While he had heard the boys at school talk about them, talk about having sex with girls even, he had no idea of what they were talking about, or if any of what they had been saying was true.

He felt himself slide inside of her; and as she leaned in and kissed him, forcing her tongue inside his mouth, her breath was heavy with the taste of gin and cigarettes. He wanted to vomit. As she reared and bucked back and forth atop him and The Chordettes carried on, *Give him two lips, like roses and clover…* he knew he hated Ruby Robicheaux and would like nothing more than to see her dead. *What would be great, even better than that*, he thought, *was if I had a knife right now, a knife to cut her tits with, and to then take that knife and jam it deep between her legs, over and over again.* The idea had passed moments later when she rolled from on top him. She kissed him on his cheek and said, "Goodnight, my handsome young man."

But the thought had its moment of conception. And it began to grow. He found, on that night and on future nights that his mom invited him into her room, that thinking of inflicting pain on her while she got her rocks off on him made him excited. One day, one day he was going to surprise her. He'd sneak a knife into the bedroom and then have fun his way. *Just wait and see, Ruby. It's gonna happen, one day.*

The desire continued to grow.

CHAPTER 16

WILLIE ENDURED SEVERAL more years of Ruby's sordid parenting.

To Willie, those years went by slow. The physical beatings had stopped, but the sexual abuse to the one-song soundtrack continued. By the time he reached seventeen, he finally had begun to grow, taller at first and then finally adding size and weight to his frame. His shoulders had grown broad, and he developed increased musculature.

Though he had thought many times of slicing and dicing his mother with a knife on their "special nights" together, he truly did fear her. The beatings she had doled out through the years ensured that. But he was finally reaching a point where he realized he was bigger and much stronger than her now. He didn't have to fear her anymore.

He vowed that the next time she called him into that bedroom, he was going to make her pay and make her hurt. *Then we'll see, Ruby. We'll see just who fucks who!* The thought excited him. He couldn't help but stroke the erection that had grown in his pants as he relished the thought. How fitting it was going to be that she would feel the knife penetrate her skin while riding the erection she caused him to have. It was all he could think about.

But the moment never came.

Willie began to sense that his mother was different. At first, he thought the fact that he had grown so was why she had looked small to him, small and frail. But that wasn't it. That wasn't it at all. He knew something was wrong when she could no longer drink gin.

It made her sick. Gin had been her favorite thing in the world to drink, and now she couldn't keep it down. As a matter of fact, she seemed to be sick all of the time. She barely ate anymore. She was always tired. And she never did call him back into her room. One night, he even knocked on her door, knife behind his back, hoping to coax her into it; but she asked that he "go away." She didn't feel well.

By the time they both noticed that her skin and eyes had yellowed, her health was really beginning to fail, and she ended up in the hospital. Two weeks later, Ruby Robicheaux was dead. The doctor had explained to her young son that his mother had passed of complications from advanced-stage cirrhosis of the liver. Young William stared at the hollowed-out husk that used to be his mother as she lay motionless, lifeless, on her hospital bed. Her eyes, though closed, had sunken in. Her yellow-ish skin had flaked and peeled all over. Willie collapsed in the doctor's arms and cried.

The doctor did the best he could to be consoling. Only the man with the white coat who had just delivered the devastating news could not know that those tears streaming down the face of the young man in his arms were not due to the loss of a mother. No. That wasn't the reason for the water works and the histrionics displayed in the hospital room. Willie Robicheaux cried because in that moment, he knew. He knew that he'd never get the opportunity to inflict as much pain on that woman as she had on him. He hated her for cheating him and taking the easy way out.

Now she'd never pay for what she had done.

CHAPTER 17

INITIALLY AFTER RUBY'S passing, Willie found that he couldn't shake the feelings she had stirred up inside of him—that want, that *need*, to inflict pain on a woman. He couldn't shake the arousal that came along at the very idea.

Since the introduction initiated by his mother, sex and violence had fused as one act in his mind. He couldn't think about one without the other. He didn't want one without the other. Now with Ruby gone, any woman would do. Any woman would be perfect.

Or so he thought.

Meeting Francine Armaio was, at once, just plain old dumb luck and at the same time the best thing that had ever happened to him (aside from the fifty grand the life insurance policy paid off when the woman shuffled off this mortal coil).

Francine worked as a clerk in the Pollock insurance office of the carrier that held Ruby Robicheaux's policy. Stopping in to sign some paperwork, Willie Robicheaux came face to face with Francine, who happened to be in the office because a co-worker called in sick; otherwise, she'd have been out that day.

Looking Francine in the eyes as they spoke, Willie noticed right away something was different, something in him. Unlike other times when he looked at women, or talked to them, this time he was not immediately consumed with the thought—the desire—to inflict pain. He didn't feel those violent, sexual desires that had become part of his life wash over him and drown out all reason.

He liked that.

He steeled his nerves, and before he knew it, he had asked her out. She accepted.

Francine, unknowingly, tamed the anger and rage that had grown during the traumatic teen years of Willie's life. She was a calming influence. The first night they made love, he didn't want a knife in his hand. He didn't want to *cut her tits*. She made him feel good. She made him forget all about the horrors he endured with Ruby. Willie forgot about revenge.

Using some of the insurance money to start his own business, he garnered several local contracts working for both Grant and Rapides Parishes. Willie would go on to marry his sweetheart years later. She eventually bore him a son. Life it seemed had taken a positive turn, at least for a while.

They had enjoyed a solid fifteen years—a good run. But then, Francine took ill, gravely so. She was diagnosed with ovarian cancer. Unfortunately for the Robicheauxs, she had been relatively symptom-free until the disease had progressed well beyond her nethers. Treatments were aggressive and debilitating. The chemo seemed to be just as bad, if not worse, as the cancer. Francine fought hard; but like an untended plant, Willie could only watch her wilt, wither, and die.

Her passing left him cold and angry, about as angry as he had been that day when Ruby passed. *Women— either they're abusing you or abandoning you*, he thought. Like weeds returning in the spring, his rage, his hatred, grew back. And along with it was the sexual fantasy he'd created while on his mother's bed. It was back in spades. There was no denying it or getting around it this time. Someone was going to pay.

Monster number one was finally born—unleashed. The keeper who held the demons at bay was absent—gone.

Willie didn't rush, however. He took the time and honed his craft. He was finally going to let the beast out of the cage and enjoy the damage it would do, no way was he going to leave anything to chance. He enjoyed preparing for the hunt. Riding around in his van all day gave him the opportunity to observe. In secret, he planned his work and worked his plan. Over the next few weeks, he was able to find and stalk his victims. He chose to operate in Alexandria. It was only about a twenty-minute ride from his home. It made sense, not operating in his own backyard. What was that expression? *Don't shit where you eat?* Yeah, that was it.

His reign of terror began. After kidnapping the first of what was to become many victims, he realized something else, no doubt a direct and proximate result from the death of his mother. The fun wouldn't be in simply raping and killing women. It couldn't be. He remembered how empty Ruby's death had left him, how it left him feeling that she had escaped something.

The real fun was in inflicting pain—over and over again. Keeping them alive became paramount. And for that, he needed a place for them to stay. The property in the woods was purchased soon thereafter.

Hell on earth began for his victims.

CHAPTER 18

Summer 2010
Pollock, Louisiana

WILLIE SET HIS tools on his workbench. Items—wrenches, pliers, knives, all going into a predetermined position—were laid out in neat rows of five. Shackles and chains took up the remaining space on the bench. Satisfied that everything was where it should be and as it should be, Willie looked over at his young son, Orrin. "What-d-ya think, Orrin?"

A smile crept across the fourteen-year-old's acne-riddle face. "Looks good to me, Pa," he said. Orrin's eyes had been studying his father carefully the whole time his old man had been making preparations. Observing his dad's every move, he continued to take mental notes just as he had all summer long—learning.

"I got a surprise for you, son. You ready?" Willie said. A sly smile spread across his face.

"Yes, Pa. I'm ready." Orrin Robicheaux's giddiness matched that of his father's.

"I know my boy is ready," the elder Robicheaux said.

"Yes, Pa. I been watchin' you. I know what to do." The fourteen-year-old's voice was still somewhat soft, despite his size. He was already big for his age, standing at six three. He was over two hundred pounds already also. Puberty simply hadn't yet added the manly bass that his voice would come to possess in the future.

"Well, then," Willie said, "I guess we shouldn't keep the guest of honor waitin' any longer!"

The elder Robicheaux walked up the cellar steps past his son. Orrin sat still, at attention, as he heard the door of his father's stark-white work van slide open. A moment later he heard it slam back shut and could hear muffled whimpering and a dragging sound. Orrin watched, nearly in a trance as his father dragged the young, bound, terrified girl down the cellar steps past him.

The girl's eyes were glazed over in fear. Tears had caused dirt-smeared streaks to run down both sides of her face. The bandana tied in her mouth kept her screams muffled, not that it mattered given the isolation of *casa de Robicheaux*. The terrified girl looked to be no older than somewhere between ten to twelve years old.

"Leave her alone, you evil bastard!"

Chapter 19

THE FRENZIED, HARROWED cry had come from a woman in her early thirties, caged in the cellar. She was in the cage second from the cellar entrance, which would've made her Willie Robicheaux's second kidnap victim. She had been around long enough to not only experience but also witness the horror that the psychotic madman visited upon women—all while his son watched.

Like the seven other women caged with her for what now had to be well over two years, she wasn't sure— she too had endured the brutal rapes, the incessant torture. Watching that sadistic madman violate the other women imprisoned along with her had been bad enough. Hearing their blood-curdling screams all hours of the day and night—screams and pleas for help and mercy that went unanswered—made the nightmare worse; but to see this young girl, this child being brought into this sanctum of horror, realizing the brutal fate that awaited her, made Irene Mallineu's blood boil over.

"Don't you touch her, you freak!" Irene yelled again.

Willie paused, looked over at Irene and the other women cowering in their cages, and let out a deep, sinister laugh. He looked over at Orrin, whose facial expression bordered on shock and fear at Irene's outburst, and laughed even harder. Orrin then relaxed, and he began to laugh as well.

Willie walked over to Irene's cage. He unzipped his pants, pulled himself out, and proceeded to urinate all over her.

"Shut it, tramp!" he yelled.

He leered at the urine-soaked Irene, who by now had tried to make herself as small as possible inside the confines of her space. The other terrified women too were huddled tightly in the corners of their cages, having done so to avoid getting splashed by the impromptu golden shower or otherwise courting Willie Robicheaux's ire.

Even in the aftermath, Irene didn't regret her outburst, the intent of it anyway—hoping to somehow spare that young girl—possibly even offering herself up in sacrifice. Willie's next words however let her know that plan had been for naught.

"That lil' treat over there's for Orrin. But don't you worry ya'self none, sugah. When he get done with her, me an' you's gon' have us some fun, since ya volunteered."

Irene knew before she spoke out that she would pay a horrible price. Willie Robicheaux was already a mean SOB when he wasn't angry. Spun up as he seemed, she expected he'd be downright vicious with her when her *turn* came around. The revelation that drawing his wrath would do absolutely nothing to save that poor young girl from this horror show melted her will and crushed her spirit. She slumped against the cage and cried.

"Orrin," Willie called out as he finally turned his steely stare away from Irene, "go on. Get that girl up on the gurney. Get her strapped in."

Orrin guided the crying teen over to the gurney; her fear seemed to make her very compliant. Orrin was turned on by that fear. He quickly strapped her in.

"Go on, boy. Go on," his father exhorted. "Do just like I taught ya."

"Listen to me!" Irene yelled out. Already in for an unbelievable amount of torture later, she was getting her money's worth. "Little girl, keep your eyes closed, honey. Don't watch him, whatever you do. Just keep your eyes closed, honey!"

Willie kicked the cage door hard. That outburst of anger caused all of the women to jump back in fear. "Shut it, slut! It's really gon' be hell for ya. Ya hear?"

Orrin made his way over to the workbench. He clicked on the record player, just as he'd seen his father do many times, and The Chordettes again haunted the cellar. His eyes perused the assortment of knives and the various tools laid out neatly on it. He settled on the Buck knife. Orrin picked it up and, after gazing at it in some joyous wonder, turned and walked back over to the frightened girl. He gently moved a few strands of her hair, matted to her face by her tears, back behind her ear.

"Don't worry," Orrin Robicheaux said to her. "We're gonna have us some fun."

The fledgling monster had spread his wings. It was time to fly.

End of interlude 1

Part Four

THE MISSING

Chapter 20

Alexandria, Louisiana

I*T WASN'T MUCH* longer, after Dale nodded off to sleep again, before I saw a sign welcoming us to Alexandria, Louisiana. Just as I had predicted, we made it in twelve hours, having only stopped for gas and a few bathroom breaks.

I had never been to Alexandria before, or anywhere else in the state of Louisiana for that matter. I took in a few of the sights, the ones that were visible in the dawn's early light, as we rolled into town while my partner and passenger, who was doing his best Rip Van Winkle impression, snoozed away. I was surprised that I wasn't tired myself, even more surprised, stubborn old ox I am, that after refusing to hand over the wheel to Dale, I did not fall asleep and drive us off the road.

Dale finally stirred. He yawned and stretched like a cat after one of those naps that they were famous for, turned to me, and said, "Where are we?"

"Welcome back to the land of the living, Dale. As of five minutes ago, we are officially in Alexandria, Louisiana."

He stared at his watch. "It's early."

I nodded in agreement.

As it was only just after six in the morning, we decided we'd stop and stretch our legs before visiting the McAllisters.

"Let's see if we can't find us a good breakfast spot," Dale said.

"I could eat." I had to stifle a yawn as those words came out of my mouth. "And I definitely could use a cup of coffee."

We stopped at the first diner we came across. We're not picky. After forty-plus years of eating at various dives and greasy spoons, one finds that bacon and eggs are pretty much bacon and eggs everywhere you go. Their coffee, while unremarkable, was more than enough to get the job done. I was feeling awake, more like myself. The demons that prattled around in my mind on the ride down—the fear of finding the girl dead and having to report that back to her parents, which in turn would take me back down the path of thinking about my loss—were gone.

Then Dale promptly decided he would single-handedly ruin my morning.

"So have you reached out to Elena lately?" Dale asked.

"Seriously? Right now?" I nearly choked on a forkful of eggs.

Dale tried his best to look innocent. "What?"

"No. No, I haven't reached out to Elena."

"Are you going to?"

I frowned at him and said, "When I do, Dale, I'll be sure to let you know."

Dale put his hands up like a perp and leaned back away from the table. "Just a question, old-timer. Just a question."

Ordinarily it would've been. I'd been purposely avoiding thinking about her. All of the misgivings I'd had about coming here, working this case—thinking about my boy—it allowed me to escape thinking about her. Despite those misgivings, I believed exactly what Dale had said earlier on the ride in, that we were going to get answers for the McAllisters. But I had no answer as to what I was going to do about my wife leaving me.

And that scared me shitless.

CHAPTER 21

Pollock, Louisiana

AT SEVEN THAT same morning, Pollock Police Officer Dakota Quinn, after hanging up her phone, called out, "Got another one, sheriff." She got up from her desk and carried her notepad into the sheriff's office.

"Another what?" Sheriff Abraham "Abe" Noblise grunted. He was always grunting, at least as far as Officer Quinn was concerned. She couldn't tell if he didn't like having a female officer under his command—one who had a brain and who, unlike her male counterparts, produced thoughts that were not in line with his own—or if there was something else about her personally that he didn't like. Maybe being sheriff for so long (and getting up in years) had finally taken its toll on him.

"Missing girl," Dakota Quinn continued.

"Christ almighty, Quinn. Do you ever have any good news?" Sheriff Noblise rubbed his fat stubby fingers across his balding head. He was a short, portly man, running about sixty years of age. He looked a lot like Boss Hogg from *The Dukes of Hazzard*. The only thing he needed to complete the look was the white suit.

"We have a Christa Miller, aged twenty-three. Family has her missing approximately forty-eight hours. She makes three, sir. That we know of. At this point, it'd be too much of a coincidence to consider these abductions unrelated."

"Now hold on, Quinn. What we have this morning is *a* missing person. Singular. And while I'll grant you it's conspicuous, nothing we have right now says abductions, related or otherwise."

"That's for true," Officer Wayne Ellington leaned into the sheriff's office and chimed in. He was the senior officer under Sheriff Noblise. He pretty much parroted any idea the sheriff had. Ellington was young—much younger than the sheriff anyway—and a good-looking man with an athletic build. Dakota would have been able to appreciate that more if he wasn't such a dick.

Ignoring his input, Dakota Quinn went on, "Sheriff, I'd like the opportunity to work these disappearances as a serial. I think it's all one case."

"No," The sheriff's reply came quick and terse. "What we don't wan' go an' do is get the good people of Pollock worked up thinking there's some serial kidnapper out there. Understand me? Bring me proof that these cases are connected, proof that these girls ain't just done run off, and we'll talk about it. Unless you find me an abandoned vehicle, signs of a struggle, or a witness, these are individual cases, missing persons cases. Til' we have proof otherwise, you keep the Miller girl. Guilliame and Faraday are working the other two."

"But, sir—"

"Quinn," Noblise's voice grew stern, "unless you have plans for the rest of this week that don't involve you being here, I suggest you drop it and carry on."

Both men stared at Quinn for a few moments. *Got that?* She expected at least one of them to say. Then finally, Sheriff Noblise said, "Anything else?"

"Oh, one other bit of good news for you, sir. Rupee is back. Says she has information on the other two abduct—umm, missing women."

"For Christ's sake! Goddamn psychics!" Sheriff Noblise bellowed. He furrowed his brow and then looked to the heavens. *Lord, why hath thou forsaken me?* He looked to say.

"Want me to throw her out, sheriff?" Ellington asked, the fervor in his voice indicating he wanted nothing more than to do that very thing. It would seem that just like the sheriff—and most likely *because* of the sheriff—he hated psychics too.

"No. No, just have her wait is all. That Rupee is crafty. And you better believe she'd like nothing better than to run to local media and say how we jus' kicked her outta here, without listening. Down here, boy, psychics still get some respect among the hoodoo crowd, folks believin' in that bullshit. Rupee is probably gon' tell me it's the damned Rougarou behind it all. I'll speak to her. Let's just have her wait an hour or two."

Quinn returned to her desk. She was glad to leave the sheriff and his pet alone to discuss how they would handle the resident psychic. Nevertheless, she was not happy. *Proof*—the sheriff wanted proof that these cases were connected. *Whatever happened to gut instinct?* These disappearances just felt wrong. She could feel that they were wrong and had only been on the job a few years. A man in his position should be picking up the same thing.

She didn't want to let her mind assume the sheriff's reticence was tied to the gender of the victims. But her mind was already made up that getting Guilliame and Faraday to play nice and let her see what they had on their cases would be about as easy as prying food out of the mouth of a gator. Those two nitwits definitely had a problem with her gender. And like the sheriff (and his parrot, Ellington, for that matter), they didn't believe the cases were connected.

But that feeling that resided in the pit of her stomach—that gnawing, clenching sensation telling her that something was rotten in Denmark—wouldn't let her agree with them.

No, not at all.

CHAPTER 22

Alexandria, Louisiana

IT WAS JUST about eight thirty in the morning when Dale and I arrived at the McAllisters' place. I had my game face on by the time Timothy McAllister opened his front door. We formally introduced ourselves, and Timothy invited us inside. Their home was very nice, exquisite even. Obviously, Timothy was doing pretty well himself. The interior design of the house suggested *extremely* well-to-do.

There were expensive-looking things each way I turned. I recognized one of the paintings hanging on the far wall—*Schooner on the High Seas.* That bad boy cost them thirty grand easy. There were several others that, while I did not know what they were, I was certain carried a similar price tag. *La-ti-da! To be one of the haves!*

There were also family photos, now stark reminders of happier times, all around the living room.

Tim was snappily dressed already. While I had already gotten the impression that he wasn't the type to lounge around all day in jogging pants and tee-shirts, I wouldn't have expected he'd be wearing what I could only guess to be a custom-made suit this early. It fit him perfectly too. The Mercedes Benz S560 out in the driveway also hinted at his successes. But none of that mattered now, not in this moment. Right now, he was simply a frightened parent whose only child was missing.

"Please, come in. Have a seat," Timothy said, his voice cracking just a little. He motioned us over to the sofa. His wife, Alicia, entered the living room from the kitchen. Her face was pale and ashen. She was not wearing any makeup, unlike the visage in the family photos. I could not help but notice, by the pictures anyway, she was an attractive woman—prior to this incident. It seemed to have aged her by at least ten years or more. She probably hadn't been eating since…

They both looked as if they hadn't been taking good care of themselves.

"Can I get you some coffee or tea?" Alicia asked. She was working hard to put on a brave face.

Dale took some coffee. I declined. Any more for me and chances were my sixty-three-year-old bladder was going to stop cooperating with me. It gets…agitated after too much coffee, and I'd had my fill at the diner.

"I'm so sorry to be meeting you folks under these circumstances," I said. I looked them over as they sat down across from us. They both looked frail, ragged even—

physically and in spirit. But this type of thing could take that type of toll, so it was to be expected. There was a stack of fliers on the table in front of us. The fliers had their daughter's beautiful, smiling face splashed across it. Her eyes seemed to peer through me as I glanced at it. Across the top of the flier it read, HAVE YOU SEEN ME? It went on to give details, her full name—Cecilia Marie McAllister—her height at five six, her weight as 115 pounds, and so forth. Her eyes, and that smile on the picture, certainly seemed to be piercing the hearts of her parents in this moment.

"We're sure you might have been asked some of these questions before," Dale began. "But bear with us, please."

"Ask whatever you need to," Alicia McAllister said in a voice every bit as shaky as her husband's was.

"But to be clear," Timothy McAllister added, "the police have already vetted us, both of us. We didn't have anything to do with our daughter's disappearance, and I would appreciate…not…not being asked."

"I have no doubt that neither of you were involved," Dale said. His response seemed to immediately calm Tim McAllister.

I took out my little notepad and a pen. "Has your daughter ever taken off like this before? Run away from home? Has she ever run off with friends, say back to Chicago—or New Orleans, for that matter—without telling you guys?" I asked. I scanned their faces as the replies tumbled out of their mouths.

"No! Absolutely not!" Timothy said resolutely.

"Cecilia has always been responsible. She is not a wild child, or impulsive in any way," his wife added.

I scribbled a few notes before continuing, "The area her car was found in, was that an area she frequented?"

"No. Not that we're aware of." Alicia's eyes began to water as she spoke.

"And her cell phone is missing, yes?" I asked.

"Yes. Her phone is missing. The police reached out to our service provider to get her records," Tim said.

"Okay. That's good. The last time you saw your daughter, how was she acting? Did she seem nervous about anything? Depressed, maybe?" Dale asked.

The tears that had been welling up in Alicia's eyes since this conversation began streamed down her face. She could hold back no longer. "She...she was fine, just fine." She managed to stammer out. "Cecilia was home visiting from school. We went shopping for God's sake! Everything was fine. It was just another day. Why would anyone want to hurt my baby?" Her voice carried pain— and the love she felt for her daughter—as she spoke.

Her husband put an arm around her to comfort her. "I didn't notice anything odd, either," he added in that dull, shaky voice. Their emotions were quickly becoming my emotions. Their tragedy made flashes of my own race across my mind, escaping the place where I had buried it.

Come on. Keep it together, Raines!

After a moment, I found my voice and said, "Her friends, have you spoken with any of them?"

"Well, we don't know most of her friends, certainly not well, anyway. There's two of her friends who have been by the house before. We did speak with them."

Alicia provided the names, "Curtis Wakefield and Sarah, Sarah Marsh."

"We'll definitely want to speak with them," I said. "Do you have their contact information?"

"Yes, let me get that for you," Alicia said, wiping away the tears that continued to cascade down her face. She got up and left the living room.

"After we talk with her friends, we'll stop over at the Alexandria PD and see what they have so far," Dale said. His voice was as comforting as I had ever heard it.

"Have either of you worked missing persons cases before?" Timothy asked.

It was a fair question, one that, frankly, if the roles were reversed, I would have asked as soon as we sat down on the sofa. He needed to know if his family was getting their money's worth. *Can these two old yahoos whom the family is plunking down a nice chunk of change to actually do something more than has already been done—actually provide answers?*

"While we were on the job, back in Chicago. Yeah. We both did. Six cases between the two of us," I answered. While the statement itself was simply true, I did my best to sound just as reassuring as Dale had.

Timothy took a step toward the next room, no doubt checking to see if his wife was returning just yet. As she was not, he stepped closer to Dale and me. Keeping his voice low, he said, "Look. When Cecilia first went missing, the police were here every day. Her story was on the news each night that first week. Now, not so much, if she's mentioned at all." Timothy paused, drawing in a deep breath. His lips trembled. He looked like a condemned man, not one condemned to prison or death row, mind you, but one condemned to bear an impossibly heavy burden for the rest of his life. What's more, that just might be his plight—and it seemed he'd already accepted it.

"You two were highly recommended by David," he continued. "And right now, I have no faith in the Alexandria Police Department. But give it to me straight… In cases like these…after this kind of time has gone by…" Timothy had to choke back tears, "what are the odds that my baby girl is still alive?"

"Mr. McAllister," Dale jumped in before I could open my mouth, probably saving the day, as he knew that question had the potential to take me down a dark path; and he was right. "Each case is different. Until we gather more facts, we don't want to jump to any conclusions about any outcome. And more importantly, you don't want to give up any hope at this point, not just for your sake, but your wife's as well." *Smooth talker, that Dale. Smooth.* He had a knack for having the right words to say at exactly the right moment. Shit, I was certainly impressed.

Timothy swallowed hard after hearing those words. There was not much by way of a promise in them, but just enough of a thread for him to continue to hold on, even if only for just a bit longer. Timothy McAllister managed to get his emotions back in check, just as his wife reentered the room. She gave us a piece of paper with the phone numbers and addresses of both Curtis and Sarah, the two friends of her daughter whom she knew.

"Thanks," I said. "We'll keep you informed of everything we find out."

"Thank you. Thank you both." Timothy extended his hand to show us the way out.

Out on the porch, after the door had been closed behind us, Dale asked, "You okay, Bobby?" He obviously had been watching me closely in there.

I was far from okay, but said, "I'm fine. Let's see about tracking down these friends of hers. And don't—"

"Yeah, yeah. I know. Don't call you Bobby."

CHAPTER 23

CURTIS WAKEFIELD, A big black kid who went six eight and about 250 pounds and at nineteen years of age was a red-shirt freshman power forward for Tulane University, agreed to meet with us to talk about his missing acquaintance.

Our conversation with him, unfortunately, did not reveal much. While he was gracious enough to meet up with us, it turned out he actually had not spoken to Cecilia for over two weeks prior to her disappearance. Much like her parents though, he described her as level headed—unimpulsive—certainly not the type to up and run off, definitely not without letting her parents know where she'd be.

Curtis Wakefield's description of Cecilia McAllister continued with her being a good student, a smart, intelligent young woman. While she might have imbibed in alcohol on occasion, she did not do any illicit drugs. Nor did she hang out with anyone who did. The only tidbit he was able to impart was that while scanning his Facebook page, an update from Cecilia came across on the day of her disappearance. She apparently, in his words, "posted that she had to make a stopover in Pollock."

While it seemed less and less likely that this case would turn out to be about a young woman who could not take the pressure of college life and decided to run away—in my mind, that theory was DOA, before we ever left Chicago—we still needed to be thorough. Also, we needed to make sure there wasn't some boyfriend in the picture whom Mom and Dad didn't know about, some boyfriend who, say, had an issue, if Cecilia decided to end things. We had to dig a little further on that score. We couldn't take anything for granted.

We were going to have to wait until the next morning before we were going to be able to speak with Sarah Marsh. My phone call to her had caught her in the middle of something or another, and she wouldn't be free to speak with us until noon the next day. Dale and I decided then that we'd make our presence known to the Alexandria Police Department. But first, as I'd found myself hungry again by the time we finished up with Curtis, we headed back to the diner we had stopped in earlier for breakfast. The bad news in that, however, was I mistakenly opted for another cup of coffee (my eyes were starting to get heavy again after driving all night and into the morning); and now the ol' bladder had me running to the john every fifteen minutes.

After my third trip, Dale cracked wise about the shape I was in. After a hearty "Fuck you," I mentioned I was going to take a special delight in watching him slip into decrepitude. "If you live long enough to see it," Dale retorted. We enjoyed the laugh. Little did we know at the time, there wouldn't be much we'd laugh about during the rest of our stay.

CHAPTER 24

As THE CLOCK edged closer to noon, the heat and humidity outside increased. I was used to hot and humid summers having lived in Chicago my entire life, but this was next level. It was the kind of hot that seemed to creep up under your skin.

The sun was fully awake and beat down from a cloudless sky. The air was thick and heavy. It literally weighed on you. We were sweating buckets anytime we were out from under the AC. Despite that heat, as we made our way to the police station, we saw the McAllisters and a group of what I assumed to be neighbors, friends, or just concerned citizens outside passing out those fliers that were sitting on the McAllisters' table—those fliers with Cecilia's face staring out from them.

Just how long have they been out doing that? I wondered. *Since day one of her disappearance? How long will friends and neighbors engage in the exercise? They couldn't possibly have the same stamina for it as the McAllisters, could they?* More questions surged through my mind as we drove past the group. *How long before the disappearance of this one young woman gets old in their minds? The story is no longer on the local news, so how much longer before it fades from the public consciousness altogether and it would just be Timothy and Alicia left to carry their burden alone?*

I had no answers for any of those questions so I put them out of my mind and continued on our way. Both Dale and I had ditched our sport coats by the time we arrived at the Alexandria police station. There's no point pretending anymore. It was hotter than hell out today.

A rather thick-necked desk sergeant, Emil Acossi, gave Dale and me a good once-over—looking us up and down in what I could only describe as bewilderment after we introduced ourselves as private investigators from Chicago. He looked to be close to Dale and me in age, probably preparing to ride off into the sunset and call it a career.

"You're joking, right?" he said.

"If I was joking, I'd be wearing a fez and blowing into a kazoo," Dale responded in a snarky tone.

It was all I could do not to laugh.

Acossi frowned. He didn't appear to find Dale all that funny. "And to what, may I ask, do we owe the pleasure of you two big city boys being in the great state of Louisiana?" Acossi then asked, the expression on his face mimicking the sarcasm in his voice.

"We were hired by the McAllister family. They'd like us to look into the disappearance of their daughter,

Cecilia Marie McAllister. I believe you have an ongoing investigation into the matter?"

"Cap!" he called out over his shoulder, not once taking his eyes off us.

"What is it, sergeant?" A younger man than the desk sergeant made his way from an office just about twenty feet away from the front desk. I could see stenciled in gold flake paint on the door the words "Capt. J. W. Freere."

He looked to be in his late thirties, still slim and fit. I took him for a college grad—unlike the desk sergeant, who'd probably been in the force since before it became popular that a lawman had a degree. He walked over, eyes fixed on us, barely even blinking. *Here we go.* Here comes that harsh reception I had predicted earlier.

"So what's all this, then, sergeant?" The young captain's voice had a down-home southern accent to it that was balanced by the quiet confidence with which he carried himself.

"Two private investigators, cap."

"Is that so?"

Before I could open my mouth to speak, Acossi jumped back in. "Yes, sir. And get this. They come all the way from Chicago, no less."

"That right?" Captain Freere asked. His interest was piqued. "And just what brings you boys out here?"

Again, Acossi got the words out before I did. "Say they're looking to work the McAllister case. Hired by the family, no less."

"Seeing as you boys are from Chicago, I do suppose you are somehow licensed to work as investigators in Louisiana?" Captain Freere asked.

"Hadn't gotten that far with them, cap," Acossi went on before the captain's hand on his shoulder quieted him down.

"As a matter of fact, yes, we are," Dale said. "I'm Dale Gamble. This is my partner, Robert Raines. We're also licensed as investigators in the state of Florida. Florida has reciprocity with *the great state of Louisiana*." Dale said that last bit using the same accent and emphasis as Acossi had earlier.

"Indeed it does," Freere said.

And here was an example of another of Dale's "great" ideas in action. With all of the time he and his wife had been spending in Florida, he felt it made sense that we be licensed as investigators there as well. That paid off big time right now.

"You gentlemen armed?"

"The gentlemen are indeed so armed," Dale continued, "in accordance with LEOSA."

Freere nodded. "I'm familiar with the statute."

The Law Enforcement Officers Safety Act (LEOSA), which became law in 2004, basically provided current and retired LEOs in good standing the ability to carry firearms across state lines. That came in handy because it simply made sense to carry, regardless of the nature of the investigation. Besides, I'd always lived by the motto I'd rather have it and not need it, than need it and not have it.

We displayed our credentials to the captain. Acossi nearly broke his neck straining to get a good look for himself.

"Well, why don't you two boys come on back to my office, then?" Freere said. "See if we can get y'all situated."

CHAPTER 25

"*FORGIVE ME. WHERE* are my manners? I didn't properly introduce myself. I'm Capt. John Freere. If you pronounce it like furry, you're close enough. And don't mind old Acossi out there. He's just a cranky—"

"Cranky old man?" I finished for him as we all took a seat inside his office.

The captain couldn't help but laugh as he settled in behind his desk. "Yeah, sorry about that. No offense."

"None taken."

"Well, welcome to Alexandria. Now, the family has hired you to look into the—"

"McAllister case. Cecilia McAllister," Dale said.

"Yes. She was reported missing by the family three weeks ago. Look. I have no problem with you guys working on the family's behalf. Lord knows if one of my little girls were missing, I have three, mind you, I'd want all the help I could get too. But understand this is an active investigation. Anything you find, you make sure you keep us in the loop. Fair?"

"Fair enough, captain." I was stunned. I had braced myself for an argument, a slight dustup at least. Without question, I was expecting foul language. I'll be damned.

"I'll get the officer assigned to the case to share what we have. What I can tell you up front is this: We have no witnesses to an abduction. Talks with her friends haven't revealed any plans for her to run off and disappear, though. We did find her vehicle parked not too far from downtown Alexandria, but no signs of struggle."

"Cameras?" I asked.

"The car was found parked on a residential street. No cameras, unfortunately," Captain Freere said.

"It's like she just vanished into thin air," Dale noted.

"That's exactly what it's like," the surprisingly friendly captain concurred.

"Have you had a chance to go through her phone records?" I recalled Timothy McAllister mentioning the cops had reached out to the phone company.

"We're expecting them in today, tomorrow, or the day after. Either way, we should have them soon. We'll definitely get you a copy once they're available."

"Question for you, captain." Dale was scribbling in his notepad as he spoke. We both made sure to take lots of notes. Sometimes, without even knowing it, you'd jotted down something that later on would give you that "ah-ha!" moment. A seemingly innocuous detail here, an insignificant statement there could help break the case wide open. "Has any connection been made between the

McAllister case and that string of disappearances from some years back?"

"The news media certainly has. The papers are definitely making hay. Now, from an evidentiary standpoint, no. There's no connection. But does that stop the talking heads and the print jockeys from running with it? No, sir, it has not let me tell you."

"Were there ever any breaks in any of those prior cases?" I asked.

"No. Eight women—that we know of—went poof! Just gone. That's eight cold cases doing nothing but getting colder. I was one of the officers working the task force on that one. We had the FBI send a couple of their big brains down here to help us out with profiles and whatnot. Came up empty. We always figured we were dealing with a local boy. Just the same, the feds ran what we had through ViCAP. That came up empty too. Seemed like every time they gave a profile, or we thought we were close, something changed. Y'know, I swear, you'd have thought the son-of-a-bitch behind it all sat right out there in our bull pen and worked every briefing on every clue with us. Whoever was behind it was either very lucky or very good."

"Sometimes lucky trumps good, captain," Dale said.

"Ain't that the truth. And, mind you, we got sightings called in to the tip line all the time. There were reports of some of the missing women being seen in town as well as sightings from here all the way down to Florida. Hell, some of the calls came from as far away as California. We ran them all down. They all came up empty. But that's in the past. I don't see any connection here, between those cases and this one. As a matter of fact, I wouldn't be surprised if that perp from the original case is locked up—probably for some unrelated crime—or dead, even."

"That would explain why the abductions stopped." That certainly made sense to me. "Either that or he moved on, changed his hunting ground."

"Yeah, there's that." Captain Freere rubbed at the stubble growing on his chin, a reflective look planted on his face. "Either way, those poor women who had gone missing back then, I hate to say it, but I'd lay heavy odds on them being dead."

"Given the time that's gone by, any happier outcome is certainly unlikely," Dale agreed.

"Listen. I'm not one for that jurisdictional bullshit. I don't care about glory. I just want this young lady found—God willing, alive. In the unfortunate event not, then, any clues you two dig up that can help us catch the bastard or bastards behind it will be greatly appreciated. Of course, any arrests need to be made, we'll make them."

"Understood," I said. "We're here to do our best, captain."

"Good then." Captain Freere picked up his phone and pressed a button and, after a moment, said, "Williams, my office, please. There's a couple fellas here I'd like you to meet."

CHAPTER 26

WE SPENT ABOUT another hour down at the Alexandria police station chatting with Officer Paul Williams, the lead investigator on the Cecilia McAllister case. He wasn't able to shed any new information from what the captain had already provided, but it was still good to get his take on the evidence, as it were, thus far. He was an amicable enough fella, pretty much like the captain. That's two. It appeared my fears of an entire department disgruntled with our arrival were unfounded. It's nice to be wrong every once in a while.

During our discussion with Officer Williams, Dale had a few thought-provoking questions which led to some plausible, though obviously unsubstantiated, theories. By the time we wrapped up our little chat, I was dead tired. I had been making steady trips to the restroom. My bladder seemed to demand I take the trip. Only when I got there, it's just a few drips that made their way out. More coffee was definitely out of the question. It was time I got some good old-fashioned sleep. I was maybe ten minutes from falling flat on my face, literally. At my age, it's near impossible to recover from such an event.

After checking into the local Motel 6, I made my way to my room, leaving Dale to his thoughts. I downed a quick shot of Blanton's bourbon (smartly packed in my duffle bag). After a shower, I flopped onto the bed. Sleep was coming for me quickly. I normally slept with the television on. That was a habit I developed coming home from work late nights to find that Elena had left the television in the bedroom going. I never bothered turning it off. Now that she's gone, leaving the TV on was the only way I could get to sleep—except today. I was just so tired. I picked up the remote but didn't go through with clicking the power button.

Sleep was on me quickly. But even as I drifted off to the land of nod, where I would be visited in my dreams by my wife and long dead son, there were questions that swirled in my dwindling consciousness. What were the odds that the McAllister girl's disappearance was just a coincidence and *not* related to the previous cases? What were the chances, though, that it was the same guy? However, predators rarely ever change their MO, or their hunting ground for that matter, at least, not in my experience. What were the chances this girl was even still alive for that matter? I wasn't supposed to even think that last one. Dale had already warned me about that. I'd bounce the other questions off him in the morning.

CHAPTER 27

Pollock, Louisiana

AROUND EIGHT THAT evening, Patrol Officer Dakota Quinn arrived home. Tired and exasperated from another long day, she sighed and wiped her brow as she pulled into her driveway. Her hand was wet and dripping with sweat.

Though the sun had gone down, it was still quite humid out. Her car had AC, but Quinn always liked riding home with the windows down in the evening. She liked the scent of the night air. She liked to feel the breeze, albeit warm, generated by the speed of her car. For that indulgence, she ended up sweating more than just a bit. Quinn exited her vehicle carrying a large, thick manila folder. She quickly took the three steps on her porch and entered her home. She turned on the living room light, illuminating the far wall.

The light revealed newspaper clippings pinned and taped to the wall. The clippings detailed the stories of two missing women—Dahlia Movane and Erica Graham—cases that, per Sheriff Noblise, were currently being handled by Officers Faraday and Guilliame. That nearly made Quinn chuckle—"handled" by Faraday and Guilliame. The way she saw it, those two couldn't find their own asses with a map and a two-day head start.

She sat the manila folder on the desk that sat facing her "crime wall" and opened it. Among the contents in the folder was another newspaper clipping. This one was from the day's paper, the evening edition. The headline read, THIRD AREA WOMAN MISSING. A PATTERN? Christa Miller's family had already gone to the press. *Soon enough, the media and probably every other citizen in Pollock are going to piece together that these cases are related—everybody except the good ol' boys in the office, that is.*

There was a map of Grant Parish also pinned to Quinn's wall. Different colored stickpins marked various points in Pollock. White pins indicated where the women's cars were found (if a car was found). Quinn used blue and green pins to identify the location of the cell towers the women's phones pinged last.

Index cards containing detailed information that Quinn had obtained about Movane and Graham, their height, weight, race, DOB, and date last seen, among other things, had been taped to the wall as well. She pulled out a stack of blank cards and a pen from a desk drawer. It was time to get a card on the wall with Christa Miller's details. Sheriff Noblise's orders be damned—she was determined to investigate all three cases. Faraday and Guilliame were decent cops—but less than average investigators at best. And that was if she felt like being generous in her assessment. The biggest problem with those two, however, was that they were prone to follow the sheriff's lead.

She'd seen it far too many times during her five years on the job. If the sheriff didn't see something as a big deal, the rest of them didn't either. Noblise was in charge, and the "boys" in the office weren't going to rock that boat. They all got along too well. Whether they were telling inappropriate jokes like *What's the difference between jelly and jam? Well, you can't very well jelly your dick up your girlfriend's ass!* or making sexual innuendos about her own sexuality or staring at her breasts and mumbling under their breath about what they'd like to do with them, those fellas were all on the same page.

Dakota Quinn was thick skinned; she grew up with four brothers and a mean son-of-a-bitch for a father, so she had the necessary training. In fact, she had become a cop because her father, a hard-drinking iron worker, had told her that she couldn't. "No way you'd make it, Dak. No way, no how. Besides, women shouldn't be cops," he had said. "That's men's work and best left to men. Go on and do something like be a teacher, or settle down and make a man some babies," he'd told her. "You'd be good at that." That was his mentality. And it was what her mother had done.

While Everett Quinn doted on his four boys, he didn't pay much attention to his daughter. She had to work extremely hard to get his attention—and for his affection. Had he known anything about her at all, though, he'd have understood what his words had done. Those words lit a fire under sixteen-year-old Dakota. She knew in that moment, as those acidic words rolled off his tongue, what she'd do with her life. Her older brothers, who didn't mind rough housing with her since she could walk, toughened her right up too. She was able to throw a solid punch long before she got serious about self-defense training after high school.

By the time she hit the academy, she was more than ready, mentally, emotionally, and physically.

Her father had passed, *God rest his soul*, just before she graduated the academy. Though he disapproved of her choice up until the day he died, she did feel some satisfaction in knowing that he was aware that there would be more to his only daughter than cleaning house and making babies.

Dakota's mother, on the other hand, couldn't be more proud of what her daughter had become. Dakota herself always felt it was her determination to succeed that drew the two of them even closer. She always made it a point to visit her mom in Monroe regularly. Only now, in the middle of this current mess, she wasn't able to visit as often as she'd like. Phone calls and text messages were taking the place of face-to-face visits.

Right now, she had to concentrate on the case.

She didn't feel she could leave it up to her fellow officers.

The men's sexist and sometimes racist statements that she'd overheard on occasion aside, they managed to keep some semblance of law and order in Pollock. So while she'd never have a beer with any of them, she was able to let a lot of things slide, but not this, not the way the sheriff and his band of merry men were treating these cases. No way was she going to let this thing slide.

Someone abducted these women. She was 100 percent sure of that. Dakota had already figured in her mind that investigating these disappearances as individual, unrelated cases would be a mistake. If these women weren't dead already, that approach would cost them time that they didn't have. And if they were dead, that approach could possibly cost more women their lives.

She was sticking to her guns on this one, in secret for now. It had to be a secret. There was no telling how Sheriff "Do as the hell I say do" Noblise would react to her disobeying a direct order. He'd probably hand her case over to one of the numb-nut knuckleheads in the office. She couldn't allow that either. She couldn't afford to be taken off the case. Those women couldn't afford for her to be taken off the case. Once she found the connection, once she found the link that proved they're all related, then she'd take it to Noblise. Until then, she's working this on her own.

Quinn removed her gun belt and set it atop the manila folder. She let her hair down out of her ponytail, and after a quick change into a pair of shorts and a tank top, she grabbed a beer out of the fridge and made her way to the desk. On the way, she set her AC to *high*.

It was going to be another long night.

CHAPTER 28

Alexandria, Louisiana

IT HAD BEEN some years—near ten, actually—but the emotions felt the same. The excitement crept up over him as it had back in the late 1990s and those first few years after the new millennium. The experience he'd gained during his years in Chicago, and then Jacksonville, Florida, after that, had steeled his nerves to the point that the forced sabbatical he'd endured as a *guest* of the state of Florida the past seven years didn't cause him to be anxious. He was as calm as a Zen Buddhist monk.

Wayne Elliot Casey, who, when he was in this mode, liked to call himself Azrael, had come to Alexandria, Louisiana, just after his release from Raiford Prison. Alexandria would be just a pit stop, though, just a place to re-embrace all that he had been and all that he could be again, before going *home*.

He'd put the messy affair in Florida in his rearview mirror, realizing that despite the seven-year stretch, he'd gotten lucky. If the Florida Department of Corrections knew whom they actually had in custody, if the prosecutors had even an inkling of what he had done, his body count to this point, he'd have never gotten out of prison. As a matter of fact, he'd probably be in the waiting line to receive a generous blast of the state's electricity—free of charge, so to speak—to send him on to his final destination.

But they didn't know. They didn't do their due diligence. Wayne Casey knew that a cursory review of the contents of his wallet when taken into custody would've revealed he owned a safety deposit box. Not that it pertained to his case, but a curious investigator, a thorough one, might have come up with an excuse to get a court order to open said safety deposit box. They would've discovered his secret then. They would've easily been able to piece together his true identity. They would've found his pride and joy—his trophies!

Those precious, precious trophies were vacuum sealed and as fresh, more or less, as the day they were taken.

No matter, though, the authorities in Florida did not launch the effort required to come across his collection of "pinkie" fingers—the number had to be cruising toward one hundred now. Though he'd lost count, Wayne Casey was certain of one thing. The number wasn't legendary. He'd yet to reach that awe-inspiring figure that would put him over the top and fulfill his ambition. It was all about numbers when the goal was to be the most prolific serial killer in history, and not by some piddling margin either. He wanted to blow the current record away.

Taking an accurate inventory of his trophies was something he knew he needed to get to someday, but he'd just been so busy what with that prison thing and now moving to a new town. The logistics of dealing with it all could drive a person insane!

The count, however, could wait. In this moment, all he needed was the right victim.

Who would be lucky enough to be his first in his new city?

Wayne arrived home from work just after midnight. After scarfing down some leftovers, he then made his way back out into the streets. Dressed in his familiar black outfit and boots, he skulked about underneath the I-49 overpass. Even with his hoodie cinched tight around his head, he found he didn't mind the heat. It helped him focus. While the overpass was not as full of prospects as, say, Lower Wacker Drive had been, there were still plenty to choose from. The guy sleeping on the trashed-out, piss-and cum-stained mattress, for one, slept like he had not a care in the world. Azrael decided he'd call him Jacob.

That was a fun thing he'd started when he moved down to Florida—naming his victims. Sometimes he tried imagining what name they might have been given by their parents when they were born, when they still had promise, before they decided to waste the gift of life. Now, they were being renamed by their *father in death*.

The woman curled up by one of the concrete pillars of the overpass, with her back to him—easy pickings. He named her Ruth. Just a little further down from her, a second man, whom Azrael had watched drink himself to oblivion on whatever cheap booze he'd managed to procure, had passed out some time ago. He named him Raif. It seemed like a name befitting a drunk.

So who would it be? Which one? Jacob? Ruth? Raif?

There were other prospects, spread out along the route of the overpass. They were all spread out, actually, each claiming their own spot of land—spread far enough apart, in fact, that if he moved fast and showed the same skill as he had in the past, he could take…all three. And why not? Now that's a fitting return to action.

Azrael was up for the challenge.

CHAPTER 29

I WOKE UP FEELING refreshed the next morning. My alarm hadn't even gone off yet when I sat up in bed. Right away, my thoughts shifted to the case. Those questions that were hounding me before I fell asleep last night swirled around my head again. I still didn't have any answers, none that I liked anyway.

A few hours later, I was reciting those same questions to Dale as we ate breakfast. We tried a different spot this time, some place called Laney's; Officer Williams recommended it as we left the station yesterday. After my usual bacon, eggs, and toast, I decided I'd try the official state doughnut, a beignet—along with some chicory spiced coffee. I had to admit I thought it was pretty good. I wasn't usually one for sweets, but what the hell. You only live once, right?

Later that day, just about noon, when the sun and humidity were kicking into high gear, we arrived at a local coffee shop—there seemed to be a million of them here—to meet up with Sarah Marsh. I was determined not to make the same mistake as I had made yesterday—drinking a shit ton of coffee. Thank, God, I had gotten some sound sleep the night before. In the very least, that helped remove the temptation given our current surroundings.

Dale and I had been sitting in a booth, maybe five or ten minutes, when a barely twenty-something, petite, young brunette-haired woman walked over to our table and asked, "Are either of you two Mr. Raines?"

"Are we that easy to spot?" Dale asked her.

"Well, on the phone yesterday, Mr. Raines told me to just look for two old white guys who don't look like they belong," Sarah responded.

Dale shot me a look. "That's priceless."

"Thought you'd like that," I said. I slid further into the booth to make room for Sarah. She was dressed for the weather in her loose-fitting t-shirt, shorts, and sandals. I was jealous. I wished I could dress that way—minus the sandals, of course. Just the same, both Dale and I had said "no" to the sport coats today. That lesson had been learned already.

"I'm Robert Raines, and this is my associate, Mr. Gamble. You must be Sarah Marsh?"

"Yes. Is there any news about Cecilia?"

"That's why we're here," Dale said. His voice was doing that reassuring thing again. "To see if we can help find out what happened to her."

"Like I said yesterday on the phone, I talked to the cops already." Sarah slid in next to me and waved off the waitress who was ready to stop over and take her order.

"We know," I said. "We've been brought in by the family to augment the police investigation into her disappearance. If you'd please—"

"Well, hopefully you guys find out more than they have. So what do you want to know?"

"When did you last speak with Cecilia?" Dale asked.

"The day she went missing. At least the day I figured she went missing."

"Around what time was this?" I reached for my notepad and pen, ready to start jotting things down.

"Just after two in the afternoon."

"Did she mention hanging out with anyone that day?"

"She was going into Pollock. She said something about getting a kitten for cheap off some app."

"An app?" I wasn't familiar.

"Short for application, old white man who doesn't belong," Dale said with a smirk. "Do you know which app or possibly whom she was going to meet?" He asked her.

"You Trade It. She found a kitten on You Trade It. Then, after that, we were supposed to go out later that night. She had just broken up with her boyfriend, y'know. We were gonna hang out, have some drinks so she could start getting over it."

"So there *was* a boyfriend in the picture?" I asked. We had come up empty on that thus far. Everybody else had been in the dark on the boyfriend. But girlfriends—girlfriends always would know. "Anyone she saw regularly? Because we talked to her parents, they said she didn't have one. The only other friend we were able to talk to, a…uh…Curtis Wakefield, also said no on a boyfriend."

"You're kidding, right?" Sarah's facial expression matched the incredulity in her voice.

"Am I? What am I kidding about, and why?"

Sarah sighed and dropped her head in her hands. She seemed equal parts exasperated and exhausted. "I can't believe he's still going on with this shit!"

"Who's still going on with what, Sarah?" I asked.

"Curtis!" her voice cracked with raw emotion. "Cecilia was dating Curtis Wakefield!"

CHAPTER 30

CURTIS WAKEFIELD WAS in a hurry. He stuffed as much of his clothing that would fit into his duffle bag with no rhyme or reason and zipped it tight. He grabbed his cellphone off the dresser. He threw the phone to the floor and stomped it hard. He stomped it a second and a third time with all the force he could muster, for good measure. The Galaxy S8 shattered into pieces.

Curtis patted his back pants pockets for his wallet. "Wallet, wallet...wallet!" His head whipped around in a violent semicircle, eyes scanning the room. They finally settled on his wallet resting comfortably on the night-stand near his bed. He grabbed it and shoved it into his right back pocket.

How could he have been so stupid, so absent-minded as not to remember phone records? *Freaking phone records!* And it's not just the call log. That wasn't the problem. He could find a way to work with what the call log would have to say. News flash! Police could also request text messages. He knew that fun fact from watching *The First 48*. It had slipped his mind until the two old geezers came and talked with him. The private detectives from Chicago that the McAllisters had brought in to help find Cecilia mentioned that her parents said police had requested the records. That tidbit meant nothing to him at first, because as her friend, of course his cell number would be on her records.

But the goddamn text messages could be another problem altogether. He didn't know if the Alexandria PD were after the messages, but it only made sense to him that they would be. There was one thing he knew for certain—that he had no doubts about. That was that he didn't want to be around when they got them. How could he ever explain them? *Face it. There is no explaining them. They speak for themselves.*

He had already told the Alexandria PD and the private dicks that he hadn't seen or spoken to Cecilia in over two weeks before she disappeared. The clock was running out on that story, and it was time for him to go. He was going to head back home to Alabama and just lie low, so much for playing basketball for Tulane, let alone any hopes of going pro and playing in the NBA, all because of a few lousy text messages—well those and a missing girl named Cecilia, a missing girl who just happened to have been his girlfriend, another fact he conveniently chose to leave out when talking with law enforcement.

Certain that he had everything he needed, Curtis made his way out the front door of his apartment. As he stepped outside onto the street—

"Freeze! Curtis Wakefield! Get your hands in the air! You are under arrest in connection with the disappearance of Cecilia McAllister!" Three squad cars were parked out in front of his apartment building. Three officers had their guns drawn on him.

His time was up.

CHAPTER 31

WE HAD JUST left Sarah Marsh. Dale was driving us back to Motel 6 where we planned to regroup. We couldn't think of any reason that made sense, to us anyway, as to why Curtis Wakefield would lie about dating Cecilia McAllister. Gut instinct told me that he had nothing to do with her disappearance. That was Dale's read on him as well. But it's not like we hadn't been wrong before. And it was too early for us to dismiss anyone as a suspect.

One thing was clear, though. Both Cecilia McAllister and Curtis Wakefield had secrets. In my experience, secrets and murder went hand in hand. At this point, we had way more questions than answers. We had just pulled into the lot of Motel 6 when my phone rang. It was Officer Paul Williams.

I listened quietly to what he had to say, only interrupting to ask, "Would it be okay if we talked to him?"

After a moment, I replied, "Really? Okay. We'll be there. Thanks." I ended the call.

Dale asked, "Who was that?"

"That was Officer Williams."

"They got the phone records back? Found out about Curtis, didn't they?"

"More to it than that, actually." I adjusted the AC temperature; the day was continuing to get hotter. Or maybe it was just this case.

"So what was that about?" Dale asked.

"Take us over to the police station. Alexandria PD arrested Curtis Wakefield about fifteen minutes ago. He's being charged with Cecilia's disappearance."

"What?"

"Phone records revealed that not only had Curtis talked to Cecilia up until the day she disappeared, but he also sent her some text messages."

"Okay. Given that he lied about talking to her, that appears suspect on its face, but—"

"Apparently, they were threatening messages. The DA is taking his lying about talking to her and the threats as foundation for the charges."

"Circumstantial at best. But then again—"

"Exactly. We're talking about a young black kid dating a white girl, a white girl who's now missing, a girl whom he appears to have threatened. How much of a push do you think a jury would need to convict? Without a rock-solid alibi, he could be in some real trouble."

"Did Williams agree to let us talk to him?"

"As it turns out, Curtis asked if he could speak with us."

A contemplative look rolled across Dale's face, and he said, "That brings two questions to mind, Bobby."

"And they are?"

"One, how do you want to handle the interview? Should we run a West Side Shuffle on him? The Singapore Sling? A California Crack-back?"

I cut my eyes at him and sighed, "Dale, are any of those even a real thing, or are you just making shit up?"

"Well, a Singapore Sling is actually a drink," he said. "The other two are made up. They all sound more exciting than 'good cop, bad cop,' though."

That got me to chuckle just a little. "Well, we'll go 'good cop, bad cop.' And we know who bad cop is going to be."

"Fair enough," Dale said. "Which then brings me to my second question. Why would he *want* to speak with us? You know, instead of a lawyer?"

"I'm thinking he knows what I know. If the DA figures he's responsible for her disappearance, that means the police will no longer be looking for Cecilia. And it also means they're going to try to burn that young man."

CHAPTER 32

WE ARRIVED AT the station and found ourselves greeted by Captain Freere. The captain was actually waiting in the parking lot for us. Standing outside in that muggy, humid air, he didn't seem to be bothered by the elements. Just used to it I'd guess. He was wearing a grin from ear to ear. Right away, I was reminded of the cat that swallowed the canary. As soon as we hopped out of the SUV—

"I know I told you two boys that I don't care about glory and all that, but I have to admit I'm pleased it was the Alexandria PD that pulled this particular rabbit out of the hat." Captain Freere's smile got wider as he spoke. He was starting to look like the Joker from the old *Batman* comics now.

"So he's a solid suspect?" I asked. I felt myself starting to sweat already, but I refused to look as if I couldn't handle the heat.

"Solid? C'mon into my office and have yourself a look-see at these text messages. Soon as ol' Ozzie saw them, he was all in on it, happier than a dog with a long tail." Captain Freere turned and headed into the station. We followed.

"Ozzie?" Dale asked, puzzled.

"Oswaldo Cox. He's the Grant Parish district attorney."

"Well, then," I said, "let's take a look at what ol' Ozzie saw."

Captain Freere led us into his office. Atop the stacks of paperwork strewn across his desk were several documents that looked a bit like invoices. They were from Sprint. He rummaged through the documents for a moment.

"Okay. Here we go." He handed over the page containing the text activity between Cecilia McAllister and Curtis Wakefield. Freere highlighted their last conversation, marking the messages from Wakefield's phone as "Curtis."

I was completely shocked as I read the messages:

> CURTIS. why are you doin this to me cecilia???
> Leave me alone Curtis we're done
> CURTIS. BITCH!!!!!!
> Real classy Curtis
> CURTIS. you gone learn I aint the one you gone pay for this
> you bitch!!! you gone get what you deserve I promise

I'M GOING TO BLOCK YOU CURTIS

CURTIS. block me bitch I guarantee
you getting what's coming to you
You can't treat me like this and get
away with it

In stunned silence, I handed the document over to Dale. The expression that crept across his face no doubt mirrored the one I had on mine. Added to his lies to the police, the messages were definitely damning. I came here under the impression that he was innocent. Taking everything in its totality however, now, I was not so sure. Could I really have been that wrong about him? Dale and I both? Curtis had some explaining to do.

"Looks like you two boys came all this way for nothing," the captain said, finally. "Based on this new information, it's likely we now know what happened to Cecilia, just a matter of sorting through all the details."

I let out a sigh. Captain Freere just might be right. I asked, "Are you still going to allow us to talk to him?"

"He asked for you guys instead of a lawyer. I got no problem with it. Just get what you can out of him. Location of the body would be nice. If he's got any brains in that head of his at all, he's gonna ask for a lawyer at some point—but he's been Mirandized, so he's speaking to you guys of his own free will."

CHAPTER 33

OFFICER PAUL WILLIAMS escorted us into the holding cell that contained Curtis Wakefield.

Even cuffed to the eyebolt in the table, slumped over in despair and abject fear, this kid still looked every bit the giant he was. Seated, he's still over six feet. His face was somber. In the harsh lighting of the interrogation room, that made him look older, older than the happy-go-lucky young man we talked to just the other day anyway. But one look at the *Marvel's The Avengers* t-shirt he was wearing and the gym shoes that looked like he should be able to fly instead of simply run reminded me he's just that—a young man, a nineteen-year-old young man charged with a horrible crime.

"I'll be just outside. Give a rap on the door when you're done," Officer Williams said.

"Thanks."

After the door closed, both Dale and I stared at Curtis for what I was sure he felt was an eternity. Dale walked a complete circle from in front of Curtis to behind and back around in front of him. We both then took a seat directly across from him.

"You wanted to see us," I said, finally. "What for?"

"I didn't do nothing," Curtis began. "I'm innocent."

"Well, that's a relief," I said. "I guess that means we can all go home, including the officers and the DA who happen to think you're guilty of at least kidnapping and, at worst, murder."

"Honest! Look. I know it looks bad, but—"

"Cut the shit, kid!" Dale interrupted. "Help me understand something... You not only threatened a girl who's gone missing but you lied to the police about it. And then they caught you what? Planning to skip town? Care to tell me how, in your mind, this adds up to you being innocent?"

"So what did she deserve, Curtis?" I interjected, purposefully not waiting for him to answer Dale's question.

"What?" Curtis's eyes darted back and forth between the two of us.

I flipped open my notepad. "The text message you sent from your phone, and I quote, 'You gone pay for this bitch, you gonna get what you deserve.' So what did she deserve, Curtis?"

"I know... Look, man, I know them text messages look bad. But it ain't like that."

Dale stood up and leaned into Curtis a little and then said, "Well, then enlighten us, Curtis. What's it like?"

"Look, man. We was dating—"

I cut him off again, saying, "And why did you lie about that?"

"It was what Cecilia wanted."

"How's that?"

"Look at me, man." Curtis wore a look of exasperation on his face. "I'm black. She said her mom and dad wouldn't understand her dating a black dude."

"Wouldn't understand, huh?" Dale asked.

"Man, she said they'd fuckin' flip! So we kept it from them—from everybody."

"Not everybody," I said.

"The only person who knew about us was her friend, Sarah. When Cecilia went missing and everybody asked, I just said I didn't know if she had a boyfriend. I convinced Sarah to go along with it. She didn't want to. But she did it for me."

"Very nice of her," Dale said. "Lying to the police for you."

"She's not in trouble, is she?" Curtis asked. His attention seemed to shift from his plight momentarily.

"I don't know if she will be or not. That's up to the cops. But you know who is in trouble?" Dale let the question linger.

I answered, "Cecilia."

"Now, tell us why you two broke up." Dale leaned in close to Curtis, again, crowding his space. They were almost nose-to-nose. Dale stared into his eyes waiting for an answer. From Curtis's body language, he seemed to be uncomfortable with Dale crowding him, just what Dale wanted.

"Shit, man, that's what I wanted to know. It was just all of sudden. She was like she didn't wanna see me no more. I got angry. I overreacted. I was mad because I thought our breaking up was over me being black. I didn't mean anything I sent in them texts. And now she's gone, man, missing. And they think I did it."

"That's right. They do. They think you did it." I got up from my side of the table, went over, and sat down alongside Curtis. He had to look down at me to see eye to eye. That almost made me chuckle. "Now I'm just gonna ask you straight. Did you do it? Did you have anything to do with the disappearance of Cecilia McAllister?" Dale was watching him closely, waiting for his answer to my question.

"No! No, I had nothing to do with it!"

Dale was immediately in Curtis's face again, in full "bad cop" mode, shouting, "Admit it. Admit it, you little sniveling shit! You did it! You fucking killed her, didn't you?"

"What? No, man…no!"

"Oh, come on. You expect us to believe that shit? She left you, probably started fucking some white stud, and figured she didn't need your black ass anymore. Isn't that right? Made you mad, didn't it? Then you killed her! You got your payback, and you fucking killed her!" Dale was all over him.

"Fuck you, man! No! No, that's not right. I didn't hurt her. I swear to God I didn't hurt her. I didn't have anything to do with her disappearing, man. On my momma's life, I didn't!"

"The DA is ready to nail your ass to the wall on this one," I said. "So tell me. What's your alibi? Where were you on the day Cecilia disappeared?"

"Home. I was home alone, sick in bed." Curtis lowered his head. His voice trailed with it. His alibi was weak. It was weak, and he knew it. But after sitting here, looking him eye to eye (almost), I just might believe him.

"You called anyone?" I asked. "Or did anybody call you?"

"No," Curtis mumbled.

"That's pretty thin, Curtis," Dale said, echoing what I had been thinking.

Tears welled up in the big kid's eyes and began running down his cheeks. "It's the truth," Curtis mumbled. "It's the truth, man."

"This DA is going to crucify you. You hear me? And all you've got to offer is that you were home alone, sick in bed?"

Curtis, near bawling now, said, "Look. It's the goddamned truth, man! I didn't do this! I loved Cecilia. I would never hurt her! And now nobody's lookin' for her anymore, 'cuz they got my black ass up in here! Y'all have to find her, man. Y'all have to find her. It's the only way to prove it wasn't me!"

Curtis was becoming animated. I thought he could possibly yank that eyebolt right out of the table.

"Can't make you any promises, Curtis. But you should've been straight with us from the start." Dale and I looked at each other. We'd heard enough. It was time to go, so we stood up.

"I know…man. I know. But please," he went on.

I rapped on the door. A moment later, Officer Williams reappeared and opened it. "We'll be in touch, Curtis," I said as Dale and I made our way out.

CHAPTER 34

"SO WHAT DO you think?" I asked Dale as we made our way from the interrogation room and back out into the bull pen.

"If he didn't have anything to do with it, he sure did do just about everything he could to look like he did," Dale said. "Having said that, we braced him pretty good, pressed the right buttons in there. I didn't get a read that he's our guy for this." Dale, the human lie detector, had spoken. His mouth speaking aloud what my gut had been telling me.

Reading people was Dale's gift. If Curtis had been sitting there lying through his teeth, Dale would've shot him down. He looked for tics and tells, to get a bead on whether someone was being truthful or not. We all did. If you'd ever been in the box with a suspect, it's what you're trained to do. I just didn't know how Dale did it as fast as he did, but I trusted his instincts. I was glad to see we were on the same page.

"He was stupid, for sure," Dale continued. "The lying and the goddamned text messages don't help his cause none. But he didn't hurt Cecilia. At least I don't think he did. But that's just my opinion."

"Well, fat chance getting everyone else around here to see it that way. At least we agree on—"

"Where is he?" Shouting erupted from the front entrance of the police station. "Where is that black son-of-a-bitch?" It was Timothy McAllister. It's fairly obvious at this point that Captain Freere had already informed the family that an arrest had been made.

"I want him to get the max!" McAllister shouted again.

Officer Williams spoke up. "Calm down now, Mr. McAllister. Calm down. We got him in holding. The DA already said he's going to be charged, so settle down."

"In holding? Why hasn't he been sent down to Angola yet? He belongs in prison!"

"Mr. McAllister, please." I tried to get his attention. A man suddenly invigorated, angry, and bloodthirsty had replaced the frazzled, broken, soft-spoken man Dale and I had met just a day earlier. I found, however, that I couldn't help but sympathize to a large degree.

There was a moment or two that passed before Tim McAllister was able to focus on just whom it was standing in front of him. He finally recognized us, the detectives his family had hired. He asked, "You two, did you talk to him? Did he confess?"

"The only thing he confessed to was dating your daughter and lying to the police," I said.

"Dating my—the hell you say! My daughter would not date a ni—" With Officer Paul Williams staring him down, McAllister cut himself short.

"Date a what?" My voice was stern, angry even. I didn't have tolerance for bigots. I hadn't taken Mr. McAllister for one, but if he could stoop to using that term… As the saying goes, if it walks like a duck and quacks like a duck, it's a fucking duck.

Timothy McAllister composed himself and said, "She…she…my daughter wouldn't have dated him. I don't believe it! I want him to pay for what he did to her."

"Well, that's what trials are for," Dale chimed in. "I don't think a lynch mob has been formed in these parts in some time, certainly not legally. Isn't that right, Officer Williams?"

"That is correct, Mr. Gamble. Mr. McAllister, perhaps you'd like to speak with the captain. He's expecting you in his office. As I stated, Curtis Wakefield is being charged. The law will take it from here."

Officer Williams led Tim McAllister to the captain's office, and Dale and I headed out. Once outside, I said, "The mess has just gotten bigger."

"Meaning?"

"Not only do we have to find out what really happened to Cecilia McAllister, but we might want to do it in time enough to save Curtis Wakefield," I said.

"Oh, you mean that mess."

"From the DA to the police and now the missing girl's parents, I don't think they're willing to accept an alternative theory to the case."

"That alternate theory that Curtis is actually telling the truth?" Dale cracked a wry smile. "Yeah. I don't think they're buying that one. They're ready for sentencing, now."

I walked over to the driver side of our SUV.

Dale tossed me the keys and then said, "Got any bright ideas?"

"I do, actually. It's a long shot, though."

"Lay it on me."

We hopped inside the SUV, out of the heat. I started her up, and though I had the AC blasting, I rolled the windows down in the hopes the black, leather interior would cool off even quicker. On the bright side, it was possible I'd lose a couple of pounds sweating in this heat.

I continued, "We've heard both Sarah and Curtis say that Cecilia had some appointment in Pollock, right?"

"Right. But her car was found here in Alexandria," Dale pointed out as he put on his Oliver Peoples sunglasses. I remembered asking him how much they cost. After he told me, I stopped asking Dale how much things he bought cost.

"That's true," I continued. "But we have no witness who saw her in Alexandria—no witnesses and no cameras where the car was found."

"What are you getting at?" Dale asked.

"What if…and again this is thin…but what if she never left Pollock? What if whatever happened to this poor girl happened right there *in* Pollock?"

"And somebody else—her kidnapper, the *real* kid-napper—brought the car back to Alexandria."

"That's what I'm thinking," I said. A smile spread across my face. Hearing Dale say that aloud sounded even better to me than when it was just rolling around in my head. "Anybody with half a brain knows how easy it is to track newer model cars. Leave it in Pollock, and the police are buzzing around in no time."

"Oh, Bobby. That is razor-thin. But—"

"The McAllisters did pay for a thorough investigation." I arched my eyebrows.

Dale nodded in agreement and said, "Yes. Yes, they did."

We were on the same page. I rolled the windows up and got us on the road. It was a hunch, but a hunch worth playing. What did we have to lose, anyway?

We were taking a trip to Pollock.

CHAPTER 35

Pollock, Louisiana

IT WAS AT about the same time that Sarah Marsh was dropping a bombshell on the two old detectives from Chicago—that Curtis Wakefield was dating Cecilia McAllister—when the monster, Orrin Robicheaux, paid a visit to the women held prisoner in the cages in his cellar.

The women, taking advantage of his absence, had all been sleeping when he entered. He sat watching them, in the dark at first, as they slept. He flicked the light switch on. The lights flickered and danced off and on for a moment until solid light filled the room. The women began to stir. Orrin walked along the cages—only five of them had occupants. That meant three were empty.

Willie always had a full house—eight, always, not seven, not five, but eight. Even if he had to get rid of one, by *properly* disciplining her, Willie Robicheaux went out and found a replacement within days. Orrin knew he was behind in the tally. He wasn't living up to the example set by his dad—not on quantity, anyway. By every other measure, however, they were equals. In other aspects however—brutality, for example—he had his old man beat.

The women shifted and scurried as far back into their cages as they could, knowing at any moment one of them could be selected, selected to be his plaything. The women never knew what to expect from their captor. Was he just in the mood to exert power over them through sex? Or was he in a more violent mood? Would he beat them mercilessly with those large fists of his or break out the knives and make cuts—smearing their blood on his face and laughing the entire time? They never knew. And that was just how he wanted it.

Orrin enjoyed the fear as it crept across their faces. As was the case when he was a teen and watching his dad for the first time, he enjoyed seeing the women react in fear even more than he enjoyed the actual torture—and the rapes. It was their fear that meant the most to him. It always made him grow a big rubbery one. He could have an orgasm from that alone. Their lives were in his hands—and *they* knew it. And he knew that fact scared them to death.

After studying them, he looked at his watch. It was almost time to go, but he didn't want to wait. There was still time enough to choose. He stuck a finger out at the woman closest to the cellar door, Dahlia Movane. He waved that finger back and forth between occupied cages and began, "Eenie, meenie, minie, moe… Catch a pussy by the toe. If she hollers, beat her some mo'. Eenie, mee-nie, minie, moe!"

Orrin's finger landed, with that final *moe*, on Christa Miller. Her once pretty, blond hair was a dirty, matted mess now. She began to scream.

"Shut your mouth!" Orrin yelled. "I got to go to work. We won't have playtime till I get back. But you just get ready."

Orrin walked away from the cages and over to his workbench. He looked over his tools. They were all laid out in the proper order. Just like his dad had taught him. It was time to go to work now—yes, time to do the day job. The day job was so important. It's one of the most critical pieces to the entire operation. He remembered his father explaining it to him in detail. And when it became time, he took over the family business and was ready to hunt on his own.

Just the same, Orrin couldn't take his mind off what was to come later. After reviewing the contents on the workbench, he turned and gave the scared women one last look. He smiled his evil, *I'm-getting-away-with-it* smile and clicked the lights back off.

He exited the cellar and locked the cellar doors using a three-quarter-inch thick chain and Master padlock. He found his wife waiting for him just outside.

"What is it, woman?"

"I got your lunch ready, Orrin."

"Huh? Oh, well, good. I'm getting ready to head off to work. Got a few deliveries and pickups to make. You keep an eye on things. Ya hear?"

"Yes, baby. I will."

"Good. Maybe I'll let you play with the treat I got picked out tonight."

"Orrin, you know I don't like to—"

"I sure as hell don't recall askin' what you like, Emily. I sure as hell don't."

"Yes, Orrin."

He snatched the lunch sack from his wife's hands and made his way over to his van. He cranked it up and headed off to work.

CHAPTER 36

THE TERRIFIED WOMEN residing in the cellar of Orrin Robicheaux relished the return of the darkness after he had left. It was a condition they had become used to. It was the state that they preferred.

The darkness helped to hide the visible scars he had left on each of them: the knife and razor cuts that had healed over as jagged scars and the facial bruising from the beatings. The black, pink, and bluish bruises that lined each woman from chest to toes were hidden in the dark. They didn't have to see the damage done to the other women or to themselves. It also meant they didn't have to hear what to them had become a god-awful song, associated now with acts of brutality instead of the sweet sentiment with which its creators intended.

The women had begun to develop a bond of some sort, if that was truly at all possible in a situation like this. They all had chosen to believe it was. It was as if they were now sisters—their inherited bloodline this unspeakable tragedy, this living, breathing nightmare that they were forced to endure together. *If we ever get out of this alive*, they had often said to one another. But deep down, none of them believed that they would get out alive. It certainly didn't seem that was possible. *How? Just how would it be possible to escape the clutches of this brutish, evil man?*

They were locked away twenty-four seven until he's ready to *play* with them, one at a time, always one at a time. He could easily overpower any one of them. He could easily overpower all of them at the same time, truth be told. Then there's that evil witch he had with him, the one who lured all of the women present with the ads on You Trade It; the one who hopped out of the van all innocent as you please, smiling and making chitchat and shit; the one who helped set all this up.

The blond woman had even helped to strap a few of them down on that gurney, helping him out. Imagine that. There she was, making certain they couldn't fight back—that they couldn't get away. The blond woman was just as much a problem as he was they had all agreed. It was hard for them to believe a woman would be involved in this madness. How could she be? As many times as the captive women had discussed it, none of them had an answer. And as the days wore on, turning into weeks, months, and, in some cases, even a year, they were losing hope, losing hope that they'd ever be found, losing hope that they'd ever get away or even survive. From Dahlia Movane to Christa Miller to Erica Graham and that new girl, Jolie Everson, they were all losing hope.

And though none of the other women would ever say it, certainly not aloud, they were each glad just now when it was the other girl, Christa, and not them who was picked as this evening's entertainment.

You bet your ass they were.

CHAPTER 37

ACCORDING TO GPS, Pollock's just about a half-hour ride from Alexandria going down US-165, so with me driving, Dale and I arrived in no time. I'd had a lead foot ever since I became a cop. For the most part, we all did, definitely in Chicago. We sped, ran red lights, and parked illegally—it's a cop thing. Even though I was retired, I still had that thing about speed. To hear Elena tell it, I would until the day the good Lord ended my run by calling me home.

On the ride down, Dale and I had been discussing all of the possibilities that could lend credence to my theory. As I had said, what I was suggesting was definitely a long shot, but right now, it's the only shot Curtis Wakefield had. We still didn't know if Cecilia's alive. We also didn't know for a fact yet that he didn't have anything to do with her disappearance. But one thing the kid had said resonated. Finding her, dead or alive, was the only way to prove whether or not he was involved.

While the case against him was largely circumstantial, many people had ended up doing life, or getting the needle, on a circumstantial case. Scott Peterson's name came to mind immediately.

The prosecutors had very little, if any, direct evidence of his involvement in the murder of his wife and unborn child. In spite of the fact that the majority of the evidence presented at trial was circumstantial, the prosecution secured a guilty verdict. Now, I'd never say the guy was innocent, not by any means. But I was pretty sure the only thing that he was proven guilty of—in my book, anyway—was of being a world-class douche bag. Just the same, he couldn't get from under the circumstantial evidence, and down he went for the crime.

There were a lot of cases like that.

And I didn't doubt our young basketball player was going to suffer a similar fate if Dale and I couldn't get Cecilia McAllister's disappearance figured out. We're the only ones still actively investigating at this point. Alexandria PD had their man as far as they're concerned. So it had to be us who did it. More importantly, though, I wanted to get this solved for the family's sake, to give them that closure, one way or the other.

As we rode into town, we got to see a full representation of life in Pollock—full as could be anyway, when you're riding by at forty-five miles an hour. Some of it was good; some of it was bad. There were lush forest preserves and well-kept parks that we passed by. We caught views of beautiful creeks and streams (probably good fishing holes), and we saw nice, well-manicured lawns in front of single- and two-story homes, many of which looked fairly new. The homes were tuck-pointed and freshly painted.

We also encountered quite a few homes that weren't so new, nor had they received the same care. Peeling paint, broken steps on the front porches, and gutters hanging along the sides of some of the homes along with overgrowth and weeds in the front yard said that some folks were not as well-to-do as others.

As we passed by, I couldn't help but wonder about the people who lived in those places. What were their lives like? Were they barely getting by as their surroundings would suggest? I knew that as people, they probably were no different than Dale or me or anyone else who lived here in Pollock. Their fortunes however were at least, on the surface, entirely different.

I had another thought too—going on the assumption that it wasn't Curtis Wakefield—could the person who abducted Cecilia McAllister be living in one of these places or maybe even in one of the fancier homes we passed? Either way, if my theory held water, anyone of these people could be our suspect.

Pollock's a prison town. There were three United States Penitentiary facilities here at one time, as a matter of fact. But it still had that down-home country feel and look to it. I liked it.

"Small towns, they ain't so bad you know," I said.

"Small towns have big hearts, Bobby."

"Don't… Ah, forget it."

We arrived at the station. It was an old building, small, and made of brick. It resembled a bunker. There

were three squad cars out front, each parked in its desig-
nated parking spot. The one that caught my eye had the
name Sheriff Abe Noblise. It would appear the head man
was around. That should be good for us, at least saving us
some time. There's no point getting approval from someone who wasn't in position to give it.

"Can I help you, fellas?" A young, cocky officer said
as we entered. The smirk he wore told me immediately
he thought himself more important than he actually
was. Quite frankly, nobody could be as important as he
seemed to think he was. But I didn't care about that.

"My name is Robert Gaines. This is my associate,
Dale Gamble. We're private investigators from Chicago.
We were actually up in Alexandria investigating a miss-
ing persons case, and we believe it may have ties here in
Pollock."

"Is that a fact?" Deputy Ellington, his name tag said
so, chirped at us. "You two's a long way from home, ain't
ya?"

"A ways," Dale said.

"Now how did it come that two Chicago dicks end
up doin' an investigation in Louisiana?" Ellington continued his questioning.

"We were hired by the family. Is the sheriff in?" I
asked. It was passive-aggressive. Giving him an answer
and yet being short, I let him know at the same time that
we're not here to talk to him.

"Yeah, uh, sure," Ellington seemed not to know how
to take that response. He shrugged his shoulders and led
us to the office of Sheriff Abe Noblise.

And I thought I looked bad for my age.

If I had to bet, I'd lay green money down on the sheriff being younger than me, probably by five or more years even; but he looked older. And his gut stuck out further than mine. Making these observations let me know I was getting cranky. I made a conscientious effort not to drink a lot of coffee this morning, and I certainly hadn't had any bourbon yet. I was edgy. I told myself to relax. There's fellow law enforcement present, and right away, that demanded a certain decorum be extended.

"What is it, Ellington?" Noblise asked as we were led in. He didn't seem to be having a carefree day either.

"Sir, these two gentlemen are investigating a missing persons case up in Alexandria. They think there may be some connection down here in Pollock."

"Connection? What in the name of... Who are you two anyway?"

"I'm Dale Gamble. This is Bobby Gaines."

I shot Dale a look. He fought back a smirk. He's having entirely too much fun with that.

"We're investigating a disappearance up in Alexandria. Looks like there may be some foul play involved. Based on some interviews, we believe there could be a connection down here in Pollock. We wanted to ask you and your officers a few questions."

"Look, fellas. I can appreciate y'all been hired to do a job. And given y'all from out of state and already stopped up in Alexandria, I'm sure I don't have to ask if ya properly licensed to operate in Louisiana. Those boys up there pretty good 'bout that type of thing."

"Yes, we are, sheriff." We displayed our credentials.

"That's good. Would'a hated to have to lock you two up for not dotting Is and crossing Ts. Know what I'm saying? Just the same, you can investigate all you want, but right now, I don't have time to deal with your case. That's Alexandria. This is Pollock. We deal with Pollock cases in this office."

"Sheriff, that's kind of our point. There could be a connection. We just want to cross-reference against any recent open missing persons cases you may have."

"Could be a connection? Could be a connection? Oh, so what? Some big city boys come rollin' down here, and we should drop everything we're doin' 'cause you all feel there's a connection to a case elsewhere?"

Guess I had just found the resistance I had been expecting. *Small towns have big hearts, Bobby*, Dale had said. I'd have to find time to mention to him that sometimes they had small minds too, apparently.

"Look. We understand you're busy," I said. "We were on the job back in Chicago ourselves. We're not looking to take up a lot of your time. We were just hoping for some professional courtesy is all." I thought I had put that rather nicely.

"Oh, professional courtesy? Really? And we just owe you that 'cause you all used to be big shot detectives back in Chicago? Stop the world! The PIs from Chicago need some assistance!"

"Okay, fuck the courtesy part then!" My voice rose. I was nearly shouting. "Think maybe you can be professional? We have a missing girl, and by your attitude, I'm guessing that doesn't mean much to you." There it was— that temper my wife always spoke of. I knew I was cranky from the lack of caffeine, and maybe I shouldn't have let him get under my skin, but he was under it. So I had to let him know. He really shouldn't fuck with me right now. There's too much on the line. Curtis Wakefield's life and quite possibly Cecilia McAllister's hung in the balance.

"Now wait just a damned minute! You questioning my integrity, city boy?" The sheriff slowly made his way to his feet from his chair. He moved like a dinosaur, but he was angry. Good, I was angry too.

"City boy?"

Dale stepped in between the two of us and said, "Couldn't help but notice as we were rolling into town, sheriff, that there's an election coming up."

"What? What the hell does that have to do with—"

"Be a real shame if we were to appear with the parents of the missing girl on the local news. Have them spin a story about how the sheriff of Pollock didn't seem interested in helping out with the investigation into their missing girl. Now wouldn't it?"

"You tryin' to blackmail—"

"I get that our arrival seems to have made you a bit apoplectic, sheriff," Dale continued, cutting off Noblise mid-sentence. That seemed to make the stubby little sheriff even more livid. "And maybe now you're even thinking you won't move on our request with any alacrity, but I assure you that's a bad look just before an election."

Flustered, Noblise bellowed, "I lack what? What did you just say?"

That was Dale at his best. When he wasn't being sarcastic, he was injecting ten-dollar words into the conversation while the rest of us were using ten-cent ones. He always knew how to get under someone's skin—without flying off the handle. He was enjoying it too, although he didn't crack a smile.

"I can take them, boss," a female voice came from behind us in the doorway—interrupting our little tiff with the sheriff. I turned to see a pretty, petite redhead, dressed in the same uniform as the other officers standing behind us.

"Huh? Take 'em? And do what?"

"Just answer a few of their questions. Send them on their way, boss."

"Fine, Quinn. You take 'em! Babysit 'em! Whatever the hell. Just get 'em the fuck outta my office, now!"

We followed the pretty, redheaded officer out of the sheriff's office and over to a desk a few feet away. "My name is Dakota Quinn."

"Pleasure to meet you, Officer Quinn," I said.

"Seeing as you pissed my boss off within five minutes of meeting him, it's a pleasure to meet you two as well."

CHAPTER 38

IT DIDN'T TAKE me long to know that I was going to like Dakota Quinn. She had presented herself as having the opposite of what I had seen in my brief interaction with the sheriff: a laissez-faire attitude.

In my years on the job, I'd seen all types of cops: the bully, the authoritarian, the good cop, the bad cop. You name it, I'd seen it. I'd even been each of those at some point or another. And while from a personality stand-point either of those versions could rub you the right or wrong way, they could get the job done.

There's also another type of cop I'd seen—an incompetent one. If there's one thing I couldn't stand, it's incompetence, especially incompetence brought on by indifference. Fair or not, that's how the sheriff struck me. And I knew from experience, when you had someone at the top like that, it could affect morale. As the expression goes, the fish rots from the head.

As we talked, I figured Quinn was quite different from her boss. For one, she was smart. Her timely intervention was also helpful because not only did it prevent that matter from needlessly escalating, it also allowed me to get a look at the dry-erase board that she had over by her desk.

Splashed across it in one of the neatest handwritings I had ever seen from a cop were details of a missing young woman by the name of Christa Miller. Her disappearance, based on the date reported, occurred shortly after our girl Cecilia went missing. We began discussing details she had gathered about Christa Miller; and by the end of the conversation, Dale and I were both satisfied that there were no tangible connections to our case, as bad as we wanted them to be. We were all set to leave when...

"There's still one thing that has my panties in a bunch," Dakota Quinn said. "The mom mentioned to me that Christa was going to meet up with someone who was selling a dog. I don't have any proof that the meeting ever occurred, but it could be the one thing."

"That'll be hard to track down," I said. "Besides, she probably was responding to someone on one of those newfangled apps. What-cha-ma-call-it? We Trade It."

"You Trade It," Quinn corrected me. "How'd you know?"

"Wait. Your MP was supposed to respond to an ad on the You Trade It app?" Dale asked.

"Yes. That's right," Quinn said. She searched through some paperwork on her desk and found her notepad. "When I talked to her mom, she said that was the last thing the two of them discussed."

"So was ours. According to two of her friends, she was meeting someone in Pollock based on an ad on that same app. Everyone had pretty much assumed since her car was found in Alexandria that she made it back."

"That could be it. That could be our connection," Dale said.

Dakota Quinn took out one of those dry-erase markers and went over to her board. She wrote, in that neat handwriting, ANSWERED AD ON YOU TRADE IT APP. She then turned back toward us and leaned in close. She was almost whispering when she said, "Can you two meet me at my place around eight? I've got something you should see."

Interlude 2

PASSING THE TORCH

CHAPTER 39

Pollock, Louisiana, June 2017

IT WAS A normal summer day, normal at least for Willie Robicheaux. He had worked his normal shift and had returned home. Delivering supplies and making equipment repairs could take its toll during the run of a day, especially on days when things got hectic. He contracted with several major businesses and even some of the government offices throughout both Grant and Rapides Parishes. There'd been days where he had to work both. On days like those, he sometimes didn't get home until well after dark.

This day though, that had not been the case.

He had just parked his van and shut off the engine when he felt an odd sensation—a tingling sensation. It ran along the left side of his body and down his left arm. He wasn't sure what it was, and at the moment, he didn't really care. All day at work, setting up new printers and returning repaired phones and the like, he had just one thought on his mind, one thought only—his playthings locked away in his cellar. After a hard day's work, he'd earned it. He hadn't made up his mind which one he was going to choose. There were eight to choose from so sometimes that could be tough. *But, hey, why stop at one? Do one, and then go back for seconds with a different one. Hell, yeah! I pay the cost to be the boss! Going to live it up today.*

He stepped out of the van, and the tingling sensation turned into full-on numbness in all his limbs. His vision went blurry, and his head throbbed—hard. The world spun on him furiously and then suddenly went black. He crumpled facedown in a heap, just outside of his van. He lay there, convulsing for nearly an hour or more before Orrin came home to see his father, lying in a heap, seemingly broken, outside of his van in the Louisiana sun.

"Dad! Daddy!" Orrin called out as he leapt from his pickup.

He received no response. He rolled his father over, and Willie's eyes had rolled back in his head. His tongue appeared swollen, and it hung partly outside of his mouth.

"Daddy!" Orrin called out again. His cry was guttural, animalistic even. He picked his father up from the ground, hoisted him over his shoulder, and made his way around to the back of the van. Willie Robicheaux was not a small man, yet his hulking son had no issue carrying him around. He opened the backdoors and laid his father gingerly inside the bay of the van. The moment was bizarre for Orrin, who had always seen his father as a bear of a man who could handle anything, who could take anything in life that he wanted. Now, his own life seemed to be ebbing away from him.

Orrin jumped into the cab, cranked the van, and began the near-thirty-minute drive to Central Louisiana Surgical Hospital in Alexandria.

"You hang in there, Daddy. You hang in there now. We gonna get you some help."

CHAPTER 40

THE WAIT IN the appropriately named "waiting room" was hard on Orrin Robicheaux. *It's Dad! Dammit, this is Dad! And he's down! How could this happen?* He paced back and forth in the dreaded *waiting room*, doing what everyone in there did—wait impatiently to hear word from the doctors as to the condition of their loved one.

He has to be okay! He just has to be! If he's not okay, what does that mean? What does that mean for everything? His mind raced at a hundred miles an hour. *Keep it together, big O,* he told himself (using the nickname his father had taken to calling him). *Keep it together, big man. We'll get through this. We get through everything. We're Robicheauxs. This world is ours!*

And he truly believed that. He recalled the day this odyssey with his father began, the day his dad bought home a treat for him. As Orrin sat, waiting for word, he thought about the conversation they'd had after they had finished entertaining the ladies in the cellar that evening.

"I want you to understand something, son, something I learned from your grandmother. May she burn in hell," Willie Robicheaux said to him in a moment of calm as the two sat on the porch of their ranch-style home, staring off into the acres of nothingness that surrounded them.

It was still hot and humid out though the sun had gone down some time ago. Beads of sweat formed along their brows and raced down their faces. The shrill cries of the tortured had stopped, and all was quiet, save for the quasi-rhythmic chirping of crickets. The mosquitoes were out in force as usual, but same as with the heat, the pair of them didn't seem to mind.

"What's that, Daddy?" Orrin was readily intrigued. It wasn't often his dad talked of his grandmother. He barely knew anything about her at all.

"Your grandmother knew—and in her own way taught me—*we* take what we want. We are takers. You have people in this world who will wait for what they want to come to them. Ruby wasn't like that. We're not like that. Now, ain't everybody gonna agree that we're in the right. That don't make them no different than us. It don't make them no better than us. They think about what they want to do, but we act. Now on account of that, we have to be careful at all times. Your grandma was careful. She hid the fact that she took things. She did things no one knew about. We have to do the same. You understand that?"

Orrin nodded his head in the affirmative, although he didn't understand, not completely anyway. What he did understand, the thing that didn't take long to take root in his mind, was that he liked it. He didn't care *why* they were doing what they were doing. Reasoning and justification weren't required. He wasn't the self-reflective type, not then and not now. All that mattered was what his father had said. *We take what we want.* The world belonged to nailers not hangers. He and his daddy had decided which side of the cross they were on—they damned sure were nailers.

It was nearly three hours that had gone by when a doctor—he read the man's name tag, and it said Dr. Noel—came out and asked was there family present for William Robicheaux. He stood up and towered over the doctor, pretty much as he towered over everyone. Orrin was a grown man now, and he stood a full six five. He easily weighed about three hundred pounds. Anyone who knew him, however, swore he was just a biscuit shy of three fifty.

"Me," Orrin said in that booming voice of his. "I'm here for Willie Robicheaux. That's my daddy. Is my daddy okay?"

"Sir." Dr. Noel, a petite man with thinning hair who only went about five-foot-eight and weighed a buck sixty, looked like a small child standing next to Orrin. He looked up at the large man standing before him and said, "Your father had an intracerebral hemorrhage, a stroke. Right now it doesn't appear he'll need surgery, but that's still a possibility. Based on the scans we've done thus far, we believe he will survive; however, there's a possibility that he could lose, either temporarily or permanently, the use of the left side of his body. We're talking facial muscles, his left arm, left leg. He may also experience some memory loss or thinking difficulties. We believe he may even have difficulty speaking. At this point, it's too early to tell, but we want you to be prepared for that possibility. Now with therapy, it is possible he can regain some function. I don't want you to feel there's no hope. However, having said that, he's really going to need some help. Will you be able to provide the required care?"

"Did you hear what I said earlier, doc?" Orrin's voice boomed as he leaned in over the diminutive doctor. "That's my daddy! Of course I'll be able to take care of him."

"Uh...okay, that's...fine. That's fine then. We're always pleased when family can step in and provide what we think will be the necessary care, especially in cases like this. He's going to need someone to keep his spirits up." The doctor, more than uncomfortable at their proximity, took a step backward. "That should go a long way."

Two weeks had gone by before Orrin took his father home. The paralysis the doctor had described, despite the two weeks of hospital care, hadn't improved at all. His mind, just as the doctor had said, wasn't what it used to be. Orrin noticed that immediately. His dad had been sharp, razor-sharp, before the stroke, that is. And now... well, he just wasn't the same.

His father needed help doing everything now, everything—eating, bathing, wiping his ass after taking a shit. He needed help with it all. It wore on the old man. Six months after the stroke, Willie realized he would no longer be able to please himself sexually, or in any other manner, with the women he had taken hostage. On that same day, he realized his playthings were no longer *needed*. They were now a liability.

Orrin didn't want them. That was a fact. What that meant then was that they'd outlived their usefulness at this point. That was the simple, God's honest truth.

It was a rainy, Saturday afternoon when Willie Robicheaux, in his now slurred Louisiana drawl, called his only son into his bedroom. He wore a look of defeat on his misshapen face.

"You need something, Daddy?" his son and caretaker responded.

"I sure do. Son, I surely do. I need a favor."

"Anything. Anything, Daddy."

"My girls, son. My girls. They don't have their master anymore. Their lead dog is down."

"You're gonna be okay, Daddy. Just give it more time. You're gonna be okay."

"No, I'm not, son. Your daddy is far from okay. I can't walk on my own, eat on my own. Hell, you been wiping my ass the last six months. And I don't think I got to tell you my pecker don't even work no more. I can't have my fun no more. You know, son, our special kind of fun."

"I know what you mean, Daddy."

"Well, I need you to do something, son. Ain't no need of you keeping my girls around. You understand? You understand what I'm saying to you, big O?"

THE RETIRED DETECTIVES' CLUB

"I know that I do, Daddy. I understand what you mean, but I think you gonna be fine. It's just going to take more time is all."

"Goddammit, O! No, I'm not gonna be fine. *This* is my life now. You hear? This is what's left for Willie Robicheaux. This is it. You roll me around in my chair. I have to masturbate in my head, can't pull on my dipstick or make fun with my girls. I'm played out, son. I'm played out. Send them girls on proper, now. You hear me? Send 'em on proper."

"I'll do it, Daddy. I'll do whatever you need."

"I just wish... I just wish I could watch."

"You can watch, Daddy," Orrin Robicheaux said. "You sure can watch."

CHAPTER 41

ORRIN ROBICHEAUX LOADED the clip of his Beretta nine-millimeter pistol with its maximum sixteen rounds. His thoughts raced. *This is real. Daddy's done! He's done!*

Orrin couldn't wrap his mind around his rapidly changing world. He had relished watching his father work with the other women held prisoner in their cellar. Every time he watched, either in the cellar or through the hole he had discovered in the crawl space long ago as a child, it brought a certain erotic satisfaction. And that was gone now—gone. Orrin racked the slide on the Beretta. The weapon was hot now.

When he first entered the cellar, his mind was racing. His pulse was too. He could hear his heartbeat pounding in his head. It reminded him of the time his dad first brought him into the cellar when he was twelve. *Thump! Tha-thump-tha-thump!* over and over again. All of his fears and anxiety hurtled through his mind at a breakneck pace.

The women locked in the cages stared at him in stunned silence as they caught sight of the semiautomatic pistol he held in his hand.

"I'm so, so sorry, ladies," Orrin began. His gruff voice was a bit shaky. "My daddy can't play with you anymore. He had a stroke you see. He's no longer the man he used to be. He can't please you ladies no more. So now, you're no longer needed."

"Wait... Orrin... It's Orrin, right?" Rebecca Wynn, a recent addition under Willie's rule, began to stammer. "We...we could be...everything...you need. Please. Please...don't..."

"No. No, you can't. I'm sorry."

Orrin raised the Beretta and...

Bang! He opened fire. *Bang! Bang! Bang!* Repeatedly, the Beretta let off its ominous report as round after round ripped into the cages. The women's bodies jerked and convulsed with every impact.

A minute later, they were all dead.

CHAPTER 42

THE CRAWL SPACE is the answer! Willie hadn't thought of it himself. That had been Orrin's idea. Of course it was. That was how he had found his way into Willie's world of rape and torture all those years before, after all.

While Willie didn't think it would work at first, Orrin assured him that it would. The crawl space over the cellar would give him what he wanted. It would give him the ability to see—with minimal effort. Orrin had gone out to the garage and returned with the six-wheeled car creeper. A broad smile crept across the elder Robicheaux's face. They were about to have a complete role reversal. The peephole in the floor of the crawl space—exactly the way little Orrin first watched him—would be how he, now, would watch his son in action.

Orrin lowered his father, gently, facedown onto the creeper. He wheeled him into position through the crawl space to the hole in the floor.

"There, Dad. How's that for a bird's-eye view?"

"This will work just fine, son, just fine," the elder Robicheaux had said. He stared through the hole in the floor, able to get a fishbowl view of his cellar. From his vantage point, he could make out the women in the cages though his view of the gurney he had routinely strapped the women down to was somewhat obscured.

The elder Robicheaux watched with keen anticipation as Orrin entered the cellar. He was mesmerized by the multiple flashes from the barrel of the Beretta. The screams of the women carried for him a certain satisfaction. It was over in moments, but he had thoroughly enjoyed the show his son provided. It was a just and fitting end, given his current state. He could no longer look after those women. And Orrin couldn't be expected to do so. That wouldn't be fair to him.

Later that day and into the evening, after having retrieved his father from the crawl space and getting him back into bed, Orrin Robicheaux dug eight graves on the property. He dug them far out enough that standing in front of the main house, one would barely notice the earth had been disturbed. One by one he carried the bullet-riddled, ravaged bodies out of the cellar and placed them into the earth. He said no prayer for the damned, although if he had, it would've been disingenuous at best.

The sun had long bid the day farewell by the time Orrin finished. He worked the last hour or so by kerosene lamp. His hands were raw and bloody by the time his mission was completed, but he felt satisfied. He carried out his daddy's wish and arranged for him to see it to boot. He felt good about that. Yes, sir, that's a job well done. But there was something else, something else entirely that began as a distant thought, a blip on the imagination radar, earlier in the day as he dug the graves.

There were eight openings, eight empty cages down in the cellar now. What sense would it make, he began to reason as he continued to dig and dig, to leave those cages empty? With all of the techniques he learned from his father and with him now about to take over Daddy's supply and delivery business, wouldn't it make more sense to carry on his legacy, to do what his dad had done, but even better? Yes. That's what he would do.

The torch had been passed.

End of Interlude 2

Part Five

THE STING

CHAPTER 43

Pollock, Louisiana

DALE AND I arrived at Officer Dakota Quinn's place at exactly eight. She was just pulling into her driveway.

"You guys are punctual," Quinn said as she stepped out of her vehicle. "I thought you'd be a little late, out seeing the sights or something."

"Not much for us to get into, although I could use a drink," I said.

"Well, before you go back home, you should ride into New Orleans. It's just over a three-hour drive. There's plenty to drink there, and if you're a fan of jazz at all—" Quinn led us up the stairs of her front porch and fished in her pocket for her keys.

"I was thinking about doing that," I said. "I am a big jazz fan actually, and I've never been to New Orleans. I figure that would be nice."

"You boys play your cards right, and I just might tag along, just to keep you two out of trouble," Quinn said with a wink as she stepped inside her place.

We entered behind her and shut the door. "Trust me, Quinn," I said. "I'm nearly twenty years past being able to successfully get into trouble, and ol' Dale here is still a solidly married man. Not much trouble we'd be getting into."

"Wow, you're not married? You seem like you'd be quite the catch." Quinn seemed genuinely surprised.

"Separated. Not too long ago, my wife finally figured out I wasn't quite the catch," I said with a smirk. I actually didn't know why I said that to her, talking about my personal situation like that. But Quinn was easy to talk to. I really felt comfortable around her.

Quinn flipped a light switch. Dale and I were immediately taken aback. On the far wall, there was a map and index cards. Quinn explained she was investigating *three* active missing persons cases—not just the one we'd seen on her dry-erase board at the station.

There were detailed notes about each missing woman on the index cards. One name I recognized, Christa Miller—the name on the dry-erase board at the station. The other two were news to Dale and me.

"Sheriff Noblise doesn't see a pattern. He doesn't see these cases as connected," she said as we gazed at materials on the wall.

"Obviously you think he's wrong," Dale said.

"Good for you," I added.

She took off her cuffs, retractable baton, and gun belt, laying them down on a small end table. Then Quinn laid out for us what she had in detail. The disappearances began over the prior year. They were spaced out, sufficiently enough to, on the surface, not immediately appear to be connected. But good police work would take you beneath the surface. Two of the three disappearances on Quinn's wall, based on her own investigation, were connected to an ad on the You Trade It app. Each of these missing women was from Pollock. While one of the faces on Quinn's wall, Erica Graham, was black and the other two were white, that alone wasn't enough to dismiss the pattern. Something I learned a long time ago, there never is a straight line to the truth.

Also, given that Cecilia was answering an ad from that same app, in Pollock no less, it made sense to make the connection between Quinn's cases and our own. On the other hand, it explained why Alexandria wasn't on alert and wasn't seeing a connection to the string of disappearances they had several years ago. One missing person a pattern did not make.

"We've got to let Captain Freere in Alexandria know about this," I said.

"What? Why?" Quinn was concerned.

"They've arrested a young man in connection with our missing person, Cecilia. We are already fairly certain he didn't do it, but they do have enough for a circumstantial case. And the DA is ready to put his boot on this kid's throat," Dale said.

"What we have may be tangible, but I doubt it's enough to get the DA to drop the charges, not yet, anyway. And as such, I'd rather you didn't mention this just yet. If Noblise finds out I'm working these cases, he may have my job."

She was right. It was a good start, but it wasn't enough yet. And of course Noblise didn't see a connection and would hang Quinn out to dry for disobeying a direct order, even though it's a stupid ass order. However, what we'd just discussed gave me enough hope to keep pushing because now I felt even stronger that Curtis Wakefield was innocent. After gleaning all we could from what Quinn called her "crime wall," she ushered us over to the sofa in the living room where we all took a seat.

"Fair enough. We need to connect all of the dots here. Make sure we have something solid to present to the powers that be."

"Is there any way we can find out which ads these ladies answered?" I asked. I knew nothing about apps and all of that other techy nonsense. That's the exact reason I still had a flip phone and wouldn't upgrade it. But I figured Quinn was young enough to know.

Dakota Quinn shrugged her shoulders and then said, "We'd probably have to get a subpoena and go directly at the app company. That could take some time."

She paused for a moment, staring at the two of us to the point we both blurted out, "What?" at exactly the same time.

"Well," a coy, sheepish grin spread across her face, "I've got an idea I've been toying with. It might seem a bit far-fetched, but I think it's worth it. And it just might get us where we need to go fast."

"Let's hear it then," I said.

"In the cases I have that involved You Trade It, the victims were looking for a pet, right? I was thinking about setting up an account on You Trade It, female seeking pet. I figured I might as well answer any ads for someone selling a pet. Hopefully that's not a ton, but for any responses, I set up a meet."

"A sting," Dale offered.

"With me as the bait," Dakota continued. I'd swear that smile she had got even bigger. "I was already planning to run this outside of the sheriff's office. I'll have more leeway. Can I count on you two to watch my back?"

I looked Quinn directly in the eyes and said, "Every step of the way."

CHAPTER 44

WE HAD A plan—Quinn's plan. And I had to say it was quite bold. Apparently she was prepared to do this, alone, had she not met Dale and me. Without being too crass, I really had no other way to put it—she had balls.

The plan might be a long shot, but Dale and I came to Pollock on a long shot, so we were all in. We spent another twenty minutes bird-dogging over her shoulders as she set up an account with You Trade It. Per our plan, she placed ads under "Seeking Pets" and responded to ads under "Pets for Sale." Luckily, there were only three advertisements for the sale of pets: two cats and a dog. Given that, we shouldn't spend too much time chasing our tails on this, if we're lucky—especially if it's going to end up leading us straight to *Nowheresville*—which was surely a possibility.

While she typed away on her computer, at a speed that obliterated the pick-and-peck method I used, I couldn't help but take a look around her place. I thought it looked a lot like what my place would've looked like if I was single at her age. From day one, Elena put her personal touches on our home, and she constantly redecorated through the years. Young Officer Quinn here, on the other hand, was a minimalist. She had the sofa that we sat on, a recliner, and a small, flat-screen TV that was perched atop a stand directly across from it. No houseplants or candles nor any of the other little decorative knickknacks that my wife saw fit to inhabit our place were anywhere to be found in Quinn's pad.

There was only one photograph out in the open. It sat next to the TV in the living room. The photo was of Quinn with an older man and woman. Based on the likeness she carried from both, I presumed they were her parents, a lovely-looking couple wrapped in a joyous embrace with their young daughter. I couldn't help but wonder, even if only briefly, were her parents still together. And if so, were they happy? (What was their secret?) Of course, I wouldn't ask her either question.

Something else I noticed. Hanging on her closet door was a B-10 target from the gun range. She was twenty out of twenty by my count—all in the "10" ring. When I asked about it, she replied with a grin, "That was my warm-up target."

Dakota Quinn finished up playing around on the computer, setting our trap, and then said, "Can I offer you boys a beer?"

"What? No whisky? Quinn, just when I was beginning to like you," I chided her.

"Slow down, old-timer," she said. Quinn went into her kitchen. After a moment, she returned with three long necks in one hand and a bottle of Jim Beam in the other. Jim Beam might not be my favorite, but I was due for a drink and *when in Rome*. She handed Dale and me each a long neck and, after retrieving some shot glasses from her kitchen, continued her hostess duties and poured us each a shot. She caught me staring at the ashtray on her coffee table. It was empty, but it was obvious it had been used recently.

"I smoke cigars on occasion, Dominican's mostly," Quinn said. She paused mid-pour, looked at me, and asked, "Think that's unladylike?"

"Quinn, I don't think there's anything that you could do that would be unladylike," I replied with a smile. I used to smoke cigars myself as a much younger man. Elena put an end to that too. No smoking in the house was an ironclad rule she instituted immediately. She didn't even want me coming in the house smelling like cigar smoke. First, I kept a change of clothes out in the garage and would put my smoky clothes in a duffle and smuggle them in to be washed later. It turned into too much of a hassle, so I quit.

Quinn sat down in the large, comfortable-looking recliner adjacent to the sofa and asked, "So how long were you guys cops?"

"Forty-three years for me," I said.

"I put in forty-five. Give or take a day or two," Dale replied.

"Wow, you guys have been cops longer than I've even been alive!" Quinn laughed hard, nearly spitting out some of her beer in the process. She had mentioned she was twenty-eight years old. We'd been cops nearly *twice* as long as she'd been alive. That was worth a laugh.

"Go on. Laugh it up, young lady. How about you? How long you been on the job?" Dale asked.

Quinn took another sip of her beer and said, "Five years come this August."

"Holy shit!" Dale laughed. "Forget I asked."

We enjoyed quite the chuckle at our age disparity. In the midst of that humorous moment, the Jim Beam didn't seem so bad. I downed another shot of it. The beer chaser helped.

"You see yourself here long term, Quinn?" I asked.

"I got bigger plans, Daddy-o." Quinn seemed more relaxed, much more relaxed. But then again, she was downing the Jim Beam and beer at about an even pace with Dale and me. I was sure that was playing a role. As I said, I liked her, and she's easy to talk to; so it was good to see her let her hair down, so to speak. "FBI," she said plainly.

"Really? No kidding?"

"Not at all. Already applied." Quinn hiccupped and offered a sheepish grin. "Excuse me!"

Dale laughed. "Need one of us to burp you?"

We enjoyed a laugh at that as well. Quinn then went into detail about how she had long dreamed of being an FBI agent. Her job with the Pollock PD was just a temporary stop, not that she saw any scenario where she would stay in that office. Given the shenanigans with the dickheads she worked with, they would make it impossible to stay even if she wanted to. But she was determined to stay in law enforcement, regardless—personal reasons, as she put it.

As if I needed another reason to admire her, there was one. She was tough and didn't let things affect her, at least not so far. Five years was a small sample size. I also liked the fact that she didn't view herself as "stuck." She had a plan to move on and was already putting that in motion.

After a little more chitchat, Dakota Quinn's phone chirped and beeped.

"Plans this evening, Officer Quinn?" I winked at her.

"That's not a date. That's a response from the app. I gave it that ring tone."

That was fast. I didn't even dare hope we'd get a hit that soon. She checked her phone, then looked up at us, and said, "They want to set up a time for tomorrow. They've got a pit bull pup for sale."

I slammed down another shot of Jim Beam and said, "Well, hell. Let's meet."

CHAPTER 45

Alexandria, Louisiana

AFTER QUINN CONFIRMED through that *thingam-ajig* that she was available to meet the sellers of the pit bull the next day at three in the afternoon, near some laundromat, Dale and I headed out. Drinking time was over. We needed to make sure we were well rested for tomorrow.

We got in to Motel 6 about quarter of eleven and went our separate ways. I hit the shower and then the bed, running our plan for tomorrow through my mind as I began to drift off. Quinn was still playing this close to the vest, keeping the other officers in her unit out of the loop. On the one hand, given the opposition she'd gotten, that's smart. On the other hand, if this blew up in our face, it could come back to haunt her—her FBI escape plan notwithstanding.

Just the same, given that we didn't know if this was going to be anything more than some young lady turning up to sell a pit bull puppy that's cute as a basket of buttons just to be turned away, it was best we kept this under our hats. Besides, Dale and I were pros. We're more than capable of watching her back. If anything went down, we're on it. And I liked our chances.

I drifted on my way to sleep. The television was still on, so occasionally, it snapped me back to reality. One minute, I heard the guy selling the *Slap Chop* saying "You'll love my nuts!" and the next minute, I was dreaming again. Now it's Officer Quinn in the infomercial. She's selling some new nonstick cookware. *The food slides right out of the pan, no mess!* How did you get here, Quinn?

Next, it's my wife, Elena. She's back in my dreams again. But she didn't wait her turn; no, she's crashing the party. She took that nonstick skillet from Quinn and proceeded to clobber me one. She's asking me the same question over and over again. *Why? Why, Robert? Why?* Just like that day on the porch, I had nothing more to say than "But…"

She turned to walk away from me, but on her way out of the dream, she turned back and asked one final, stinging question: "Why didn't you love me anymore after we lost our son?"

That question startled me awake. It was just me in my motel room now, with the infomercial for the nonstick *Red Copper Pan* still playing on the tube. I looked around the room, stunned, double-checking to be sure that I was alone. After the queasiness the last bit of that dream caused me had melted away, I was able to fall back to sleep. We had got a job to do tomorrow. I didn't have time to worry about apparitions asking questions in dreams, especially when it changed nothing. I fell into a very deep sleep.

There were no more dreams. *Thank God.*

CHAPTER 46

Pollock, Louisiana

IT WAS 6:30 a.m. when Orrin Robicheaux pulled in front of *the* building, the building that played host to his most important clients—just as they had been for his father before him.

Orrin parked and then exited the van. The surrounding streets were still sleepy, empty, save for a pair of squirrels chasing one another back and forth. A thudding stomp from Orrin sent them both scampering up a nearby tree. He went to the rear of the van, opened the doors, pulled out his dolly, and then dropped several heavy boxes onto it.

Inside, the office was mostly empty. That was usual for this time of morning. Orrin generally didn't get a chance to see the majority of its inhabitants unless he had an afternoon drop-off or pickup to make. As he lugged the dolly in through the front door, the lone occupant sitting at a desk looked up and acknowledged him, "Hey, Orrin. How's it going, big guy?"

"It's goin' easy, boss. Same ol' same," Orrin replied, seemingly trying to add some cheer to his normally gruff voice.

The man folded up his copy of *The Chronicle*. He leaned back in his seat, kicked his feet up on the desk, and asked, "Still getting enough work in Pollock to keep supper on the table?"

"It ain't like it used to be, but I'm gettin' by, doin' what I can and doin' what I gotta."

"I hear that, big guy," the man said. He absently went back to *The Chronicle*. "You have a good one, now."

"Thanks," Orrin replied and casually went about his business. He unloaded the boxes from the dolly, dropping them at various desks. As he made his rounds, there was something that caught his eye. It was off toward one of the corners of the office, but he could see it clear as day. His blood ran cold for a moment, but then he remembered why his father had told him a long time ago that this was his most important customer. And that they always would be.

"Oh, wait!" his morning conversationalist called out, interrupting his train of thought. Orrin turned to face him, trying not to look like he'd been caught staring around the office.

The man went on, "That damn fax machine is actin' all hooey again. Think you can haul that outta here and get it fixed?"

"I sure can, boss. I'll get it back to you by this afternoon."

Orrin walked into the break room. Next to the coffee machine and the copier, off in a corner, was the fax machine. He unplugged it and lowered gently down on the dolly. He exited the break room and stared again over in the corner. Satisfied, he wheeled the dolly with the busted fax machine out to the van, waving goodbye to his morning companion.

Orrin walked out with his thoughts racing at a hundred miles an hour. He was nearly in a panic. It was happening just as his dad had said it would. His father had told him repeatedly that, at some point, it would come to this. As much as he'd believed everything his father said, it still seemed surreal. Here he was, in the very moment that had been prophesied about, but he didn't want to believe it. His father's words echoed in his ears, "There will come a time where everything about your plans will have to change." And that time was now.

He pulled out his cellphone and selected a preset number. The phone rang for a moment before Emily answered, "Yes, baby?"

"That appointment today, it's cancelled on our end. You understand? We'll be takin' some pictures instead."

"I understand."

"There's gonna be some changes. Ya hear? We'll talk when I get home."

CHAPTER 47

Alexandria, Louisiana

THE APARTMENT WAS one step above the accommodations of a flophouse, but Wayne Elliot Casey didn't need creature comforts.

The building itself was showing its age as much of the brickwork needed tuck-pointing or out-and-out replacing. The paint around the doorframes had cracked and peeled, revealing a history of the colors that had been painted there in the past. Wayne didn't care. That simply was not the reason he was in town. This stay in Alexandria was like being off Broadway. It's a dress rehearsal before going big time, before *prime time*.

Truth be told, he needed the practice. There's more to do, much more to do, if he were to get the recognition he so desperately sought.

Staying in a rundown place like this on a rundown side of town served his purpose. Poverty, drugs, and a healthy dose of apathy saturated this side of town. Everyone seemed to mind their own business. That allowed him to blend in. Blending in had been step 1 in the plan.

Wayne Casey traveled light. He had moved into the apartment with the simple belongings he brought with him from Florida: a rollout bed, his prized trophies vacuum-sealed in plastic, the vacuum sealer, his karambit and what amounted to little more than a week's worth of clothing, and, of course, Azrael's stalking clothes.

As far as Wayne Casey was concerned, this place was perfect. His neighbors oozed the same apathy that had infected the neighborhood who knew how many years ago. They couldn't care any less that a new guy had moved in. They had their own problems, or their own secrets, to hide. Everyone kept their head down. It was the best thing for them really. He didn't need any nosey Ned's or snooping Sarah's poking about, saying "hi" and shit like that. He needed his space, his privacy. And if the neighbors knew what was good for them, they did not want to get to know Wayne Elliot Casey. *No, sir. No, they do not.*

In his downtime from working the shit job at Walmart (not a serious career move, just something to keep a little bit of cash in his pockets as he enjoyed visiting with the homeless here in Alexandria), he relaxed staring at his plastic-encased trophies. The "pinkies" would always be special.

He'd returned that morning with the day's paper after a brisk stroll before it would be time to head in for work. He thumbed through it, his eyes rolling over each headline, searching, scanning, and…nothing!

That's why I love the homeless!

He broke out in a little makeshift two-step as he made his way over to his coffee pot and poured himself a cup. There was no mention in the paper of the three dead bodies he'd left under the I-49 overpass, no mention of throats having been slit, femoral arteries ravaged, or missing "pinkie" fingers, no mention whatsoever. That had been step 2 in the plan.

The homeless were the forgotten members of society. People would see them every day, and yet didn't see them. He wouldn't be surprised if people who passed by them daily—looking down their nose in disgust or fear or possibly even throwing change at Jacob, Ruth, and Raif at one time or another—wouldn't even notice that they're gone.

What was it about being homeless that automatically made square folks think your plight was all your fault, that the homeless were homeless simply because they chose to be? Where did that scorn and derision come from? These questions popped into Wayne's head on occasion, not that he cared. The irony that those question occurred to him at all was not lost on him, either. After all, that was exactly how Wayne Elliot Casey saw the homeless—as at fault.

What was more important to him was the fact that the homeless were hard to keep track of, rarely discussed, and easily overlooked. That benefitted him.

While there had been times where Wayne Casey was able to keep Azrael—the angel of death—under wraps, times when he could resist the urge to don the black hoodie and military-style boots and resist stroking the edge of the karambit before blending into the darkness of night and falling upon a hapless victim, those times were few and far between.

This latest sabbatical was over. The other night's dalliance heralded that. It's Azrael's time now. He would enjoy Louisiana for a little while longer, but what he really wanted—what he really needed—was some home cooking. There was still his legacy to enhance, still that mountain to climb to achieve greatness. That was step 3 in the plan. A few more days then he'd hit the road, heading back to Chicago.

Now, how's that for a return to the game?

CHAPTER 48

Pollock, Louisiana

THE MEET WAS set for 3:00 p.m., so Dale and I arrived at the corner of Fifth and Dennemore Streets around 2:15 p.m.

I parked our SUV just up the block, a few hundred feet from the laundromat parking lot. At two forty-five, Dale hopped out of the SUV. I stayed inside. We were going to have eyes on Dakota at all times and from all angles. My plan was to keep the motor running, not just for the AC because of the Louisiana heat and humidity, which was still kicking my ass; but if something went down, I would be full throttle into the parking lot in no time.

Dakota made up an excuse, personal business (for which I was sure at least one of the nitwits she worked with made a snappy, witless remark), in order to get the extra time out of the office for our sting. With any luck, she'd be going back in a hero.

Dale carried a sack that he had filled with towels from the hotel. Instead of being dressed in one of his snappy suits, he wore a pair of jeans and a loose-fitting khaki button-down shirt and those expensive sunglasses. My eyes followed him as he took up his position inside the laundromat.

Shortly thereafter, Quinn rolled past me in her personal vehicle and gave a slight wave. It was 2:55 p.m. She then pulled into the World of Bubbles laundromat parking lot and slid into one of the parking spots. We were in position, and now came the hard part—waiting. We were waiting on a young woman named Emily. At least that was what the text Quinn received had said. The respondent also indicated they'd be driving a white van.

Every white van (all four of them) that rode by over the course of the next hour got intense scrutiny from me. However, none of them so much as slowed down as they passed by, let alone entered the World of Bubbles parking lot. So we waited some more.

At 4:15 p.m., we were resigned to the fact that we'd been stood up. I had Quinn call the number she'd been receiving texts from. There was no answer. The calls went straight to voicemail each time. There could've been a legitimate reason this Emily character didn't show up. Sure, there were at least ten that came to mind immediately. But the fact Quinn could no longer reach "her" was too much of a coincidence for me. Then again, how could whomever Quinn had contact with know we'd be here, lying in wait? It just didn't make sense to me.

I pulled the SUV into the parking lot. Dale came out of the laundromat, and we walked over to Quinn's car. She hopped out, her phone in hand. She was dressed in a plain cotton tee, gym shorts, and white tennis shoes. She did not look the part of a cop right now.

"I tried calling that number again. Before, it was going straight to voicemail. Now, I'm not getting anything."

"They probably ditched it," Dale said, "yanked the battery and smashed it with a hammer, by now."

"Let me see that," I said, reaching for her phone. I looked at the number and began plugging it into my own phone.

"What are you thinking? Trying to get phone records?" Quinn asked. "No point in that. If it was a burn phone, which it more than likely was, that'll be harder than hell to track down."

"Actually, I'm going to reach out to a partner of ours. He has connections. He may be able to get a pin-point location on where the phone was last. Anything would be helpful—"

My cellphone rang, interrupting our conversation. I took a half step away from those two and answered the call. Both Quinn and Dale appeared as though the heat didn't bother them at all. I'm guessing it's just me. Maybe I was getting soft in my old age. Oh, well, I was even more determined now not to appear that it's getting to me either.

"Just the same, I guess we can call this thing, huh?" Quinn asked.

"Yeah, this was a bust," Dale admitted. "We gave it a shot. Did you get any other responses to your ad?"

"One."

"Well, in the very least, it's worth running down. Might not lead to more than we got today, but…"

"I guess that is the bright side," Quinn said. "If there is one."

"It certainly could've been worse," Dale replied.

"It is worse," I said, having just ended my call.

"Who was that?" Dale asked.

"That was Officer Paul Williams from Alexandria."

"And?"

"He was calling about Curtis Wakefield. He's in the hospital."

CHAPTER 49

JOLIE EVERSON'S 2015 Hyundai Sonata pulled unnoticed into the lot of the 7-Eleven across the street from the World of Bubbles laundromat.

It had arrived at 3:05 p.m. carrying Orrin and Emily Robicheaux. Emily drove. Orrin sat hunched down, trying as hard as he could to sink his large frame down into the passenger seat. Emily parked, and the two sat in silence and stared across the street at the sapphire-blue Buick LaCrosse, the one the young lady, *Angela* she had said her name was, had described to them via text.

She was supposed to be next. She was to have a chloroform-soaked rag stuffed into her face. She was to be bound and tied up in the back of the white work van. That was what was supposed to happen, like clockwork, easy-peasy, 1, 2, 3! That was the plan until Orrin managed a glimpse of that dry-erase board at the morning's drop-off, the drop-off to his most important clients—the Pollock Police Department.

The writing on the board had been about one of Orrin's *girls*, Christa. An 8 × 10 glossy of her smiling face was on that board under her name. But it was the words written in all caps and black marker on that board that got his attention. Those words had been flashing in his mind over and over all day long: ANSWERED AD ON YOU TRADE IT APP.

That was when he knew all of their plans had to change. The way they went about things in general had to change. But that was the beauty of having a service provider contract with the parish. more specifically the police department—access.

And that access—limited though it was to picking up on clues left out in plain sight or eavesdropping at the right time, picking up something no matter how small— was invaluable.

Orrin had learned that very morning that the police were definitely investigating Christa's disappearance and that they were on to how he baited his trap with You Trade It. But he wasn't sure what else they had, if they had anything else at all. Did they have anything on him?

What about the other girls? What do the piggy-piggies have on them?

The entire time that idiot cop sat at his desk in the morning, reading the paper and making chitchat, Orrin's mind raced. Was it safe to keep the girls tucked away in the cellar? Or was it time to give them a proper send-off like he had to do with his daddy's girls?

It was too soon to answer that question. He needed more information first. All things considered, Orrin figured it would be worth their while to get a look at just who was coming for the promised pit bull pup. Instantly, there was something familiar about the woman behind the wheel of the Buick. He was sure of it.

A cop! She's a goddamned cop!

He'd seen her around the police station during past drop-offs. But who was she here with? Was she alone?

Are they on to me? Is Pollock PD on to me?

He determined they'd wait across from the Buick for as long as it took. His patience was eventually rewarded. At 4:15 p.m. a large black SUV swooped into the lot. An older guy ambled out of the laundromat. The man driving the SUV, another senior citizen, and the one from the laundromat walked over to the cop from the Pollock police station.

He didn't recognize either of them. He definitely hadn't seen either of them at the police station before. Orrin turned his attention away from the scene unfolding across the street from him and over to Emily. "You get that new burn phone, like I asked?"

"Yes. Yes, I did, baby."

"Good. Get their picture, the two old geezers. Get a shot of that fancy truck too."

Emily snapped away using the camera on the phone.

CHAPTER 50

OUR FIRST STING operation was a bust, and on top of that, Curtis Wakefield was still sitting in prison, well, in the prison infirmary now, as according to Officer Williams, he had been attacked in the prison chow hall.

Having left Dakota Quinn, Dale and I headed back to Alexandria to get a full accounting of what happened and hopefully get a chance to talk with Captain Freere and the DA. We were just about to hit the interstate when I realized…

"Awww, shit!"

"What is it?" Dale asked.

I pulled a pink-cased iPhone 8 out of my shirt pocket. "I've still got Quinn's phone."

"Didn't figure you for a klepto, Bobby."

"Whatever. I'm going to swing around. We'll drop it to her at the station, then make our way back to Alexandria."

"I guess I'll take a nap." Dale let the seat back to a comfortable resting position and was sound asleep in seconds. He'd probably gotten more sleep than I had since we left Chicago. Maybe that's why he'd been able to maintain that cool demeanor of his.

I pulled into the lot at the Pollock police station. I didn't pay him much attention; but the rather large man parked a few spaces over, unloading what looked like a fax machine or a printer from the backseat of a red Hyundai, did catch my eye for a moment. Frankly, he was too goddamned big for that car. But then again, you drive what you can afford was the way I saw it.

I went inside the station. I got the eyeball from someone (the nameplate on his desk said B. Guilliame), but I moved past him with barely a glance back. I believed I heard the tail end of Sheriff Noblise giving Quinn grief; but as he turned and saw me, he grunted something (probably uncomplimentary) and lumbered off to his office, slamming the door behind him.

No doubt about it, he hated me. Dale too I was sure. After that threat about bringing the media in on this investigation, along with it being an election year for him, he just wanted to see us gone. There's no point in kicking up any more dust. Little did he know, with Wakefield's arrest, Dale's threat had very little teeth. It did sound real enough though, and that was the point.

"What are you doing here? I thought you guys were headed to Alexandria," Quinn said when she noticed me walking toward her.

I held up her phone. "Appears I managed to walk away with this. You can attribute that to old age. You know, they say the elderly steal at a higher rate than any other age group." I shot her a smile.

"I would've been going crazy looking for that later," Quinn said.

Out of the corner of my eye, I noticed the burly fellow from the parking lot. He had lugged in that piece of equipment I saw him taking out of that too small car of his.

"Who's that?" I asked.

Quinn peered over my shoulder and then said, "Oh. That's just Orrin. He's kind of the supply, 'fix it' guy for our office. Brings in copy paper, repairs the printer, phones, stuff like that. We even have him haul records from the station down to storage."

I turned and watched him go off into the break room. I wasn't sure if it was just my imagination, but I could've sworn he seemed awfully interested in Quinn and myself, but then again, it could just be that I was a strange new face in town. He's obviously known by these officers.

"Hey, Guilliame. How long has Orrin been around?" Quinn asked.

Brett Guilliame looked up from his computer screen. His face said he was annoyed that we were bothering him with what I could only imagine he saw as a mundane question, but he answered, "Old Orrin's been around a couple years now. His dad used to run the business, Robicheaux Cartage or some such shit as that. Before your time, Quinn." He turned his attention back to whatever was on his computer screen. I was betting it's a game of solitaire.

"And there you go," Quinn said.

"Alright, I've got to hit the road. We're going to scoot down to Alexandria."

"Will you be coming back through tonight? To go over, our, uh—"

"You bet," I said, "providing it's not too late."

"Cool. At least now you can actually call me and let me know." Quinn smiled again, and I turned and headed out. I walked past the break room and could see the large fellow adjusting the equipment he was returning. He was one big son-of-a-bitch. Yet there was something else about him. I couldn't put my finger on what, so I chalked it up as nothing.

I hopped back into the SUV. Dale was still asleep. No surprise there. I cranked up the Tahoe and got us back on the road to Alexandria.

CHAPTER 51

ORRIN HAD STARTED watching the old man just as soon as the black SUV pulled into the police station parking lot. Their arrival was unexpected. *Did they follow me?* The question made sense, but Orrin felt that he hadn't been compromised just yet. But there were still some unanswered questions: *Who are these guys? What are they doing here? Are they cops? They certainly could be. High-ranking cops, maybe? Come to look into the disappearances of the girls?*

Orrin had no desire to mix it up with the cops. He didn't want to taunt them or play some high-stakes, cat-and-mouse game with them. He didn't want fame. Orrin's only care was just to stay a few steps ahead.

For Orrin and his desires, fame would *kill* the dream.

Anonymity was how he maintained his way of life. He took his time pulling the fax machine out of the backseat, giving the old geezer time to shuffle on into the building ahead of him.

Orrin made his way inside the police station; then it made sense. The old bastard didn't follow him here. He was here to see the lady *piggy-piggy*. What were they cooking up together? Orrin made his way into the break room, taking his eyes off them just in time before the old man turned and peeked at him. He fumbled around inside the break room, buying time. It seemed the old man would be at the lady piggy-piggy's desk forever. Finally, the old coot left, and Orrin caught a glimpse of him over his shoulder as he headed out.

Orrin stepped out of the break room and walked over to Brett Guilliame's desk.

"Hey, Orrin. How's it goin'?" Guilliame looked away from his computer and the game of solitaire he had been playing.

"Things are alright. Just returning the fax. It's set and ready to go now, boss."

"Thanks, Orrin."

"So, uh…who's the new guy? The old guy that was just in here? He some kind of high-level boss man?"

Guilliame let out a chuckle. "That old fart? Heck no. He's some PI from Chicago. Came down to ask a few questions about somethin' or another that happened up in Alexandria."

"Oh," Orrin chuckled a bit. "Just curious is all. You all have a nice day."

Private investigators? Private investigators from Chicago? Well, well, well, they weren't cops then. That's for sure. That changed things. Boy, did that change things. *They weren't invited to play in my sandbox. They certainly weren't invited into my business, not by me! There's a price to pay for that.*

Orrin made his way back out to Jolie Everson's Hyundai. He leaned into the passenger side window where the frail Emily Robicheaux sat, with the seat lain down into the back. "Send me them pictures you took, baby girl. I'm goin' to call up Billy and his brother. They owe me a favor, and I know just how they can pay it back."

CHAPTER 52

Alexandria, Louisiana

WHEN DALE AND I arrived at the police station, we were once again greeted out front by Captain Freere and Officer Williams.

It seemed the captain was in need of a cigarette. He actually had given up the habit he told us, but after the day's events, he felt he needed one. I probably should've asked to bum one off him. I was not a cigarette smoker myself, but it had been a day. We followed the two officers inside once the smoke break was over.

When I had spoken with Paul on the phone earlier, I said we'd be interested in knowing exactly what happened. The words spoken were not good.

"It was Aryan Nation who jumped him. Five guys, the prison report says." Captain Freere invited us into his office. It was a tight fit, but there was room enough for all four of us.

"A kid that size, I'm sure it took every one of them," Officer Williams said.

"Do we know what happened?" I asked, taking a seat in front of the captain's desk, although I was pretty sure I already knew the whys and hows on this one.

"It appears one of the guards at the prison let slip that he was the suspect in the McAllister girl case—" Freere began.

I cut him off, "You don't have to finish. I know the rest. Let it slip? Let it slip? How in the fuck is that possible?"

"Look. It wasn't us, okay? I'm just as livid as you are," Captain Freere assured me. "I've already asked the DA to spearhead an investigation. I want the son-of-a-bitch who leaked it to pay."

"What really are the chances of that happening?" Dale had his cynical tone working. Freere didn't appreciate it, going by the look on his face. Dale didn't care. He went on, "Look. How bad is he?"

"Bad," Paul Williams said. "His jaw is broken, several rib fractures. He's got a concussion, with many other bumps and bruises. But what's got the docs most concerned is he was shanked three times. One strike punctured his spleen. His liver was injured too."

"Jesus," Dale said. His face turned red with anger.

"You said it, bubba," Freere went on. "Now look, you two. You got to know, even though I think this kid is guilty, I believe he deserves his day in court. This wasn't supposed to happen."

THE RETIRED DETECTIVES' CLUB

I said, "Well, I hope the plan is to put him into protective custody going forward?"

"I'll be talking with Ozzie about that. I agree. It's what we need to do."

"Otherwise, gentlemen," Dale spoke up again, "he won't make trial. The Aryans will kill him."

It took everything in me not to spill the beans about what Dale, Quinn, and I had been investigating. Quite frankly, it's because it's still not enough and I didn't want to bring any unnecessary heat down on Quinn. Her boss was a surefire asshole. She didn't need me stirring the pot before we had some meat to dump into it.

I was hoping we'd get a chance to talk to the DA, but Freere had already confirmed that Ozzie wouldn't be able to meet with us this evening. That worked out fine. After finishing up with the captain and Officer Williams, we were able to ride back out to Pollock at a decent hour and catch up with Quinn.

Like Dale, I didn't believe that the DA was going to investigate what happened to Curtis. Nor did I believe he'd acquiesce to protective custody. I felt we were under pressure before, but now I was really feeling it. We had to solve this thing in a hurry, or someone's going to kill this kid.

Part Six

THREE'S COMPANY

CHAPTER 53

Pollock, Louisiana

WE GOT BACK out to Quinn's place around 9:15 p.m. She had taken the liberty of running out to one of the local BBQ establishments and bringing back brisket sandwiches and fries for us. I had to admit I was surprisingly pleased by the brisket. It was tender and flavorful, just the way I liked it. The fries were a bit greasy and smothered in BBQ sauce. Lord knows I need to cut back on the grease, but I got through half of the little baggie they came in before giving up.

Quinn supplied the beer again, but this time, I was smart enough to grab the rest of the Blanton's from my room in Alexandria before we headed back out to her place. She immediately noticed the difference.

"Guess I just learned something new tonight, huh?" she said after the first sip.

"It's a big world of bourbon out there, Quinn. You're welcome." We exchanged another playful glance. I didn't know what *it* was, but I knew what *it* wasn't. She certainly wasn't interested in me like that. Was she? Why would she be, right? My feelings for my wife (I still didn't know if she's my ex) aside, there's not much I could do for her anyway. I could pop the little blue pill, yeah, sure, but I might have a heart attack. Then again, if you gotta go, that might be the way. Just the same, I was too old for her, and I knew that. And while it was nice to daydream for half a second, that's not why I was here.

I put those thoughts out of my mind, and once everyone was done stuffing their faces, the three of us got to work on our case. The mysterious Emily who had responded to Quinn on You Trade It was a prime suspect. But whomever she was, she not only did not show up to our meet but apparently had already dumped the cellphone that was used. While Dale didn't want to exclude any other possible responses we could get on the app—and rightfully so, in my mind and Quinn's as well—we believed this had to be our suspect.

We kicked around a few more ideas in between shots of Blanton's and Miller Lite (funny how the Miller Light helped so much with the Jim Beam the other night, but seemed, in a way, inadequate for the Blanton's). Quinn checked her phone. "I got another response, guys, someone looking to offload kittens. I'm guessing it's worth a shot."

"It is, my erstwhile officer. It is," Dale said with a slight twinge in his voice. The Blanton's was doing its work on him. Pretty soon he'd start spouting off every five- and ten-dollar word he knew.

Knowing my limit, and the fact that we had about a half-hour's drive ahead of us, we bid Quinn good night. The meet was set for tomorrow for the kitten, and we'd see if this one would show up. That would put us further than we got today, further and hopefully closer to finding out what happened to Cecilia McAllister and the other two missing women on Quinn's wall. As a bonus, that might get us closer to getting Curtis Wakefield out of prison. We damn sure needed to get him out before he recovered. I just knew those assholes were going to throw him back in gen pop with a target on his back.

Quinn walked us out her front door and onto the porch. I fished the keys out of my pocket. "Thanks ag—"

Three gun shots rang out, piercing the night, before any of us knew what had happened.

CHAPTER 54

DALE HIT THE deck. I pulled Quinn down out of the doorway, shielding her body with mine. The bullets splintered the wood of the banister on her porch as they made impact. One of the front windows of Quinn's home was blown out as well.

Wood chips and shattered glass rained down on top of all three of us as we lay as flat as we possibly could. Had those shots been either a few inches higher or better placed, that's possibly two dead private detectives—and maybe one dead cop to boot.

My reflexes were a little slow, but after a few seconds of groping around, I had my SIG P250 in hand and returned fire on a pickup truck that was in the middle of the street. I heard the report of Dale's Kimber 1911 .45 ACP as he let off three rounds in quick succession shortly after. The hard plunking sound of multiple rounds striking metal could be heard. We also heard a man howl in pain. One of our rounds had found its mark.

Tires peeled and screeched, the pickup's headlights popped on, and the vehicle took off into the night. I ran (sort of) down the steps and tried to line up another shot. The darkness of night combined with the distance and my bourbon-blurred vision wouldn't allow me to get a bead on them, and then they were gone. My heart continued to pound in my chest. I felt shaky from the adrenaline flowing through me.

I got back up on the porch, nearly out of breath. "You okay?" I asked Quinn.

"Yes. Yes, I'm fine. Thanks. You?"

"I'm good." I holstered my SIG. "You good, Dale?"

"I'm good, Bobby. I'm good. Where the hell did they come from?"

"I didn't see. Were they there the whole time?" Quinn asked no one in particular, but all three of us were wondering the same thing.

I pulled out my cellphone. "It's time to call in Ashe."

CHAPTER 55

Chicago, Illinois

CENDALIUS ASHE, AN imposing figure at six four and a muscular 240 pounds, pulled his cellphone from his back pocket. It looked like a child's toy in his large hand. He looked at the number and name that popped up on the screen. He'd given thought to ignoring it, but only because he was in the middle of something.

It had been just three weeks ago that a comrade in arms, a fellow marine, had reached out to him. Most of Ashe's old unit knew that he became a Chicago police officer after his discharge from the military. Yet, only one knew that he had since left the force (under less than optimal circumstances) and became a private investigator. That was Moses Miller. Ashe and Miller not only served in the Marines together; they were best friends. Their bond had been forever sealed the day that Moses saved Ashe's life.

During a battle in Fallujah, Ashe had taken a bullet. The impact of the round dropped him on the field of battle. Though he fought to pick up his M1 rifle, Ashe was out in the open—exposed. That's when PFC Moses Miller went into action. He took two rounds himself, but he managed to drag Ashe back behind cover.

Fallujah!

Just the name of that place echoing in his mind made Ashe flash back over memories, memories of the roadside bombs that tore through many a Humvee and many a soldier, the bullets whizzing by in various fire-fights, making a distinct hissing sound when they were close and a sharp cracking sound when they were fuck-ing close.

He had memories of the nights he spent on patrol, nights on the hunt for Al-Qaeda operatives. He had memories of close quarters combat, hand to hand even, where the techniques he learned in the Marine Corps Martial Arts Program (MCMAP) were put to the test—and allowed him to come out on top.

In the end, both he and PFC Miller made it home alive. Those valiant actions on the battlefield had cost Moses Miller the full use of his left arm and leg—and earned him a medal. It also earned him Ashe's undying respect, friendship, and loyalty. It was through that bond that Ashe found himself face to face, so to speak, with a man known by the nom de guerre Eightball that very night.

Three weeks ago, when Moses Miller came to Ashe with his problem, that bond forged on the battlefields of Fallujah made it a no-brainer that he'd help. Miller's twenty-three-year-old daughter, Dinah, had a problem. She was hooked on heroin. Dinah had been trying her best to kick. She really was. But every time she found herself back in the neighborhood, her former (and, by all accounts, current) dealer, Eightball, would track her down, entice her with a free sample, and get her hooked again. Threats from her father did little to dissuade Eightball. After all, what could a gimp with a useless arm and a leg that was barely better ever do to him? Every chance he got, he looked to put Dinah back under his spell.

A tearful Moses Miller had reached out to Ashe and found a listening ear. More importantly, he found a willing participant in a radical intervention.

"You do understand what you're asking me, right?" Ashe had asked.

Through a few forced sniffles and tears, Miller responded, "Yeah, my brother. Yeah, I do. And if you're willing—"

"It's not a question of if I'm willing. You already know there's nothing you can't ask me," Ashe replied. "But I do need to know that if it goes that far, you'll be—"

"Okay with it?" Miller interrupted. "You damned right I will be."

"Then that's good enough for me."

The two men embraced. "Give me a couple weeks. I'll have it handled by then."

"Ashe, I really can't thank you enough for helping me with this." Miller found himself still having to fight back tears. His left arm dangled loosely beside his body.

"You don't owe me any thanks," Ashe replied. "We'll get Dinah better. We'll do it together. I promise."

That promise echoed through Ashe's head as he looked down at the ringing phone and then back into the face of the man seated before him. Eightball, a freshly minted, mid-level dope dealer, woke up not too long ago to find himself bound to a chair with duct tape, in an abandoned house on the south side of Chicago, in the heart of Englewood, *his* territory. Yet, here he was being held hostage, after being severely beaten.

"One moment, please," Ashe said to his captive. He stepped away from Eightball and answered the phone, "Robert Raines. What can I do for you?"

"Things are getting a bit hairy down here in Louisiana. It'd be great if you could join us," he heard Robert say.

"I'll be on the next flight out. Have some of that good bourbon waiting on me." He ended the call and returned his phone to his pocket. In that moment, he felt a rush of the Chicago night air flow through the window of the abandoned building. It had been hot earlier in the day, but the temperature had cooled to a comfortable eighty-two degrees. The humidity wasn't all that bad, but he still had managed to work up a sweat dealing with his captive.

Ashe reached into the small of his back and produced a Glock 19. He stood in front of Eightball. "I'm kind of pressed for time suddenly, so I'm going to need an answer from you, now. Can I trust you to leave Dinah Miller alone?"

The badly beaten and bloody Eightball had come out second best when things got physical. He looked at Ashe through his one open eye, snarled his lips, and spit blood onto Ashe's shoe.

"Man, fuck you and that hoe! You better kill me, muthafucka. You understand that? 'Cause if you don't, I swear I got hot ones for that bitch, her daddy, and for you!"

"I was actually hoping you'd say that," Ashe said. He reached into his pocket and removed a suppressor that he screwed into the barrel of the Glock. Ashe placed the barrel against Eightball's forehead. "See I didn't trust your worthless ass anyway."

Eightball didn't have a chance to blink before Ashe pulled the trigger twice, putting two bullets squarely in his forehead.

CHAPTER 56

Alexandria, Louisiana

I AWOKE THE NEXT morning to knocking on my hotel room door at 5:15 a.m., a full two hours before my alarm was to start squawking.

Given what had taken place last night, I picked my SIG Sauer up from the nightstand by the bed. I slowly made my way to the door. A round was already chambered in my gun, and I placed the barrel flush with the door. I stared out the peephole. It was Ashe.

"Jesus!" I opened the door and let him inside. "I was expecting you later in the day. How'd you get here?"

"Good to see you too, Robert. I told you I was taking the next flight out. Once I got here, I rented a car. And here I am." Ashe walked in. "Where's the bourbon?"

"Are you kidding me? It's five in the morning."

"And for me, it's been a long day already."

"You get that personal matter taken care of?" I asked.

"Yes, I did. Thanks."

I moved over to the dresser. There's maybe a shot of bourbon left in the Blanton's bottle. I handed it over to Ashe.

"Well, I can see you guys have been enjoying your time down here," he said and then proceeded to drink the remnants straight from the bottle.

"We'll get some more later," I promised.

"So what's going on?"

I filled Ashe in on our case. I told him about the missing McAllister girl. I also informed him about the women who had previously gone missing here in Alexandria several years ago and how those abductions suddenly stopped and that none of those women were ever found. I got him up to speed on Curtis Wakefield as well. The attack on the kid by the Aryan Nation struck a particular nerve with Ashe. As a black man, he'd seen his share of discrimination and hate aimed his way just because of the color of his skin.

I went on about the thin connection Dale and I had made down in Pollock and that we had hooked up with a young female officer down there to investigate. Then, my final reveal—my piece de resistance:

"We were shot at last night."

"What? Are you guys alright? Why didn't you get me down here sooner?"

"First off, Ashe, we're fine. Other than my pride, at how slow my reflexes have become, no one was hurt, well, not one of us. I think we clipped one of the guys who was shooting at us. I'm pretty sure I heard a bullet hit meat. If I hadn't been drinking—"

"I know," Ashe said. "They'd be dead."

He's probably right. Sober, I was an accurate shot.

"Just the same, it's good that you winged one. That will make it easier for me to find them. I'll see about getting a line on them. See who put them up to it. Obviously you two stumbled onto something; otherwise, why would someone make that play?"

"I was thinking the same thing."

"And I don't believe in coincidences."

That was something the two of us had in common—no such thing as a coincidence. And now Ashe was going to put his *particular set of skills* to work for us down here. If he wanted to find someone, they're as good as found. And if he had to get information out of someone, well, let's just say they'd be best served to be as forthcoming as possible—and fast. Ashe was asked to leave the force due to some of the…excessive nature in which he worked. After all that he'd seen during his three tours of duty, maybe he never should've been in the force. I didn't know I couldn't make that call.

I didn't personally see him use excessive force, and the day I offered to bring him on, I did ask him about it. He looked me directly in the eyes and calmly said, "Have I ever used excessive force? I would say no. But the official reviews deemed it excessive. Therefore, it was." Simple as that. What I did know was that Ashe was a good man. He's fair. And he got things done. That's why I hired him on. I felt a hell of lot better now that he was here.

I gave him Dale's description of the vehicle the shots came from—an older model Chevrolet pickup, either red or maroon. Dale had a partial license plate too—well, actually a partial-partial as he could only make out the first two numbers, "19." Ashe was confident that the make, color, partial-partial, and the bullet holes would be enough for him to track it down.

"If they're dumb enough to still be driving it," I said.

"Well, if they wanted to ambush you two, they could've waited until you made it down the stairs. You would've been easier targets, with less cover. In the very least, these aren't pros. I'll take my chances on that."

I went over to my duffle bag; and after my hands came upon the familiar shape of my Glock G43, I pulled it from the bag and handed it, along with two extra clips, over to Ashe. He's actually not supposed to carry, given the tricky circumstances of his dismissal. We're still working our way through and around that particular set of circumstances. Just the same, after we were shot at last night, no way was I letting him walk around unarmed.

"Thanks, Robert. Speaking of no coincidences, did you pull the files from the old Alexandria cases?"

"No. We weren't sure there was a connection. Captain Freere doesn't seem to think there is either," I said. My interest was now piqued however.

"Maybe there isn't. Pull them anyway. Cross-reference them with what you have on your current case. Maybe, just maybe—"

"It's worth a shot," I said.

Ashe turned and headed for the door. "Good. I'll be in touch."

"So what are you going to do now?" I asked.

Ashe flashed a bit of a smile and said, "Go hunting."

CHAPTER 57

Pollock, Louisiana

THE SUN CAME creeping stealthily over the horizon. Dakota Quinn hadn't slept at all, and now it was just about time for her alarm to start screaming that it was time to get up.

It had taken several hours before her adrenaline rush finally subsided and her body returned to its normal, pre-being-shot-at levels. She hated that jacked-up feeling of not knowing if you were coming or going, but now that it had melted away, she felt spent. She had promised both Robert and Dale that she was okay, but that was just so they'd get on their way. She was far from okay, then and now. She'd never been shot at before. Hell, only once in her five years on the job had she ever had to pull her own weapon.

Hearing the cracking sounds and the heavy thuds as the bullets struck her porch, she freaked. No two ways about it, she flat out panicked! Regardless of the number of times Robert tried to console her, telling her that was a perfectly normal reaction, she couldn't accept that. Oddly enough, she'd found herself imagining, on multiple occasions, how she'd react to just such an event. She didn't even come close to how she had envisioned. If Robert hadn't reacted when he did and pulled her down, she might have been killed last night.

That was the part that had kept her up all night, the part that made falling asleep impossible. She didn't react. She just froze. All of the training she'd gone through over the years went right out the window when the shit hit the fan. *What else did Robert say?* "Doesn't matter how much time you spent on the range. Paper targets don't shoot back. A live situation is always different. It's your first. Don't be so hard on yourself."

She gave him an A+ for being supportive. But that didn't change the facts. That "first" easily could've been her last. *Almost bought the farm, Dak. You almost bought it.* There'd be no more trips to visit Mom in Monroe. Nope, that would've been over, and their final communication would have been a simple *Hey, have a good day* text. She had concluded it with *I'll talk to you later.* Sitting on her sofa, a half-smoked cigar in the ashtray across from her, she realized "later" almost became never.

She felt paralyzed by that realization. *Later* almost turned into *never* in a split second. She felt a wave of panic wash over her. *What if they come back?* She looked over at her Smith & Wesson M&P nine-millimeter that sat beside her on the sofa. She pulled it closer and rested it against her thigh.

See, baby girl? Her father's voice echoed in her head. *Do you see why I told you to meet you a good man, settle down, and have some babies? That's what you'd be good at. This police business with guns is man's work. Man's work is best done by men, not women who want to play like they belong in a man's world.*

Quinn stared at the picture her mother and father had taken with her teenage self. Her father hadn't smiled when that picture was taken, but he seemed to be wearing a self-satisfied grin now, as if he was saying, *Told you so.*

Is this what failure feels like? Quinn had never considered that possibility in the past. Why would she have? She didn't consider it when she was sixteen and first decided to embark on her law enforcement journey, but in this moment, self-doubt ruled.

What if, she thought, *that lack of reaction cost either Dale or Robert their life?* Had Robert taken a bullet trying to save her, she didn't think she'd be able to forgive herself. And what would this mean for the future? How could she become an FBI agent if the only thing she was good at was wilting under pressure? When it's all or nothing, could she get it done?

The birds began chirping outside. The morning was officially beginning. Quinn took a deep breath. *Robert said this reaction is normal, right?* "Learn from it," was something else he had said. Only one of two things to do, she thought, pull your shit together and move forward or quit.

Quit! She heard her father's voice say.

"Fuck that."

Quinn got up from the sofa. She put on a pot of coffee and headed for the shower. It was time she started getting ready for work.

CHAPTER 58

EMILY ROBICHEAUX HAD been in the kitchen, cooking a breakfast of eggs, hash browns, and bacon, when Orrin lumbered in behind her. He gave her a hard slap on her rear end as his way of saying "Good morning."

She couldn't tell if he was in a good mood or a bad one. Then again, it was always like that. In her mind though, as long as he wasn't beating or cutting on her, he was in a great mood. And whether he truly was or wasn't, she certainly was. She began setting a plate for him and then asked, "How did it go? Is that new problem solved?"

Orrin pounded his fist on the kitchen table. "How do you think it went?" He growled at her. "Those two assholes missed! And one of 'em managed to get shot in the process!" Emily quickly got his breakfast plate on the table, being careful not to brush too close to him. He was in a bad mood for sure. She watched as he flopped down to the table and began to shovel forkfuls of eggs and hash browns into his mouth. She made her way over to the refrigerator. She trembled as she poured him orange juice (OJ). She set the glass of OJ next to his plate and snatched her hand back quickly. She didn't think he'd bite her hand like some rabid pet, but she wasn't going to take the chance either.

He was angry alright, angry at Billy and his brother, so much so that he hadn't bothered to share with her what their next move was to be. *Plans have to change*, was all she'd been told. She knew she needed to ask. God, she didn't want to. But she had to know…

"S-s-so what are y-y-you gon' do, now?"

"Do?" Orrin yelled. "Do? What am I gon' do?" his voice continued to rise. "I'm gon'—" Just when it seemed Mount St. Orrin was about to blow, the big man paused, a reflective look—something Emily had never before seen or at least couldn't recall seeing—came across his face. "Mama's jewelry," he muttered.

"What?"

"You're gon' place an ad on another app, this time for Mama's jewelry, no more pets. And we won't use the same app more 'n twice. By the time anybody gets on to it, we'll be done already, on to the next. We gotta improvise, just like Daddy always said."

"When should I post an ad?"

"Today!" Orrin yelled, sending bits of egg and potatoes spewing into Emily's face. "Dammit, girl! Do I have to do all the thinkin'? And get Daddy some breakfast while you're at it."

"Yes. Yes, baby. Of course." Emily scurried back to the stove. He hadn't hit her, but every time his voice rose, she thought he was going to.

She would hurry and get a plate prepared for his father and then, before 10:00 a.m., have an ad prepared, an ad that embellished the description and value of his mother's jewelry—which was little more than costume jewelry trinkets—but any potential buyer didn't need to know that. No, that wouldn't do at all, especially when all she needed to do was steal an image of a nicer-looking piece of jewelry from another webpage and just paste it into her ad. As she had in the past, she'd only respond to women.

Orrin had a plan to continue his passion, his *obsession*, as she'd come to recognize it. It was more important to him than anything. She never had to have a conversation with him about it to know. She'd already lived it herself. And if that obsession was going to continue to provide her *some* peace, a continued respite from the beatings and torture that she had endured, she was going to see to it that he was successful, no matter the cost. See this was about her survival as much as anything.

CHAPTER 59

Alexandria, Louisiana

AFTER ASHE HAD left, I found that I couldn't go back to sleep. Those two hours had been lost, lost to the place where all unclaimed sleep hours went to be forgotten, never to be taken advantage of again. By 8:00 a.m. Dale was at my door. I filled him in on Ashe's arrival and the fact that he was already out looking for the assholes who took shots at Quinn and us.

Speaking of Quinn, I had already spoken to her prior to Dale's arrival. She was more than a little shaken up by the whole thing—and rightfully so. She had said it was her first time being shot at. That could be a bit... unmooring, to say the least. It wasn't the first time I'd been shot at, not that I'd been shot at bunch of times either, mind you. Having bullets flying your way was one of those things that if you made a habit of it, odds were long that one's going to have your name on it.

I convinced Quinn not to inform Sheriff Noblise about the incident. The fact that Dale and I let off our guns in the street was sure to get his attention. That was something we didn't need right now, not when we were possibly getting close to having all the answers. She made up a story. I didn't press her as to what and left us out of it.

While Dale was making breakfast plans, I decided I'd follow up on Ashe's suggestion and put in that call to Captain Freere for the files on the previous Alexandria abductions. The tone his voice took on after my initial question told me he probably wouldn't be on board. And why would he be? He believed Curtis Wakefield was their man after all.

"Just why would you all be interested in those old case files, Mr. Raines?" he asked. His voice was still pleasant, but there was an undertone. I got the impression that he didn't have the time, or patience, to entertain my request.

After he had been so accommodating before, I wondered what had changed.

"We'd just like to review them, on the off chance that there are any similarities, even in the smallest details," I said, trying to sound hopeful.

"Look," Captain Freere's tone softened just a bit. "I'm sorry. Didn't mean to seem standoffish about it. You guys can take a look at the files. Only one problem, though."

"Oh?"

"I'm short on man power at the moment. A lot's gone on the last two days. I don't have anybody who can pull the files for you just now."

"If it's okay with you, Dale and I have no problem pulling the files ourselves if you can just point us in the right direction."

"Good. We've had four db's dropped in our collective laps over the last two days."

"Sorry to hear that, captain."

"Four homeless victims in two days. Based on the mutilation patterns to the bodies, at first glance, the doer appears to be the same. Could be a serial. If life hadn't kicked these poor folks around enough already, we've got some bastard out there slicing their throats and their femoral arteries and their—"

"Left pinkie finger is removed," I said cutting him off, finishing for him actually.

Captain Freere nearly choked. "How do you know about that?"

I could feel my blood running cold. "Captain," I said, "we need to talk."

CHAPTER 60

I DECIDED TO SKIP breakfast. I no longer felt like eating—not after the news given to me by Captain Freere. I had Dale drive us over to the police station. This subject required a face-to-face conversation. My mind was racing a hundred miles an hour, taking me back to 1998, when I was still on active duty. That year I was handed one of the cases that haunted me right into retirement.

When I started snooping around in the basement at the precinct, feeding my obsession and costing me my marriage in the process, I deliberately avoided one case in particular. While actively working that case, I took it as far to conclusion as I could. At the time, I believed we had an accurate profile, but we had no physical evidence. We also never had a witness who could describe the suspect beyond what he wore.

When the dust had settled, the murders of thirty-six homeless citizens were attributed to this elusive nutjob.

Thirty-six lives snuffed out. The scary thing was there were probably more. There's the possibility that there were some bodies that were never found, some victims unidentified as his. And while there was an uproar in the midst of the investigation, it quickly subsided. There were only a handful of families who came forward to say they had a missing loved one who had been homeless. Only seven bodies were claimed. The fervor over what the police were (or, in the public's mind, *weren't*) doing to solve the assault on the homeless community died down as the calendar continued to turn. Different stories began to dominate the news cycle. People forgot.

I didn't. I stayed on the case as long as the department allowed me to. After a while though, the case officially got kicked down to cold status. New crimes occupied my mind, but I always wanted to catch the son-of-a-bitch who murdered all of those people. It said nothing good about our society, in my mind, that some people could just fall through the cracks and go to their graves unmourned and forgotten.

When we arrived at the station, Captain Freere was very helpful. He quickly told us where we could retrieve those records we were after. Assuring me he could handle it on his own, Dale was off to the races.

Captain Freere then turned to me and said, "Okay, then, Mr. Raines. Let's you and me have that chat."

I followed him into his office. We both took a seat, and he got right to it. "How did you know about the missing fingers on my victims?"

I swallowed hard. "Because it was my case, back in Chicago."

Freere's eyes grew wide. "How's that?" he asked.

"Twenty years ago, we had a serial killer in Chicago who was stalking our homeless community. The killer slit their throats, sliced through their femoral arteries, and took a trophy with each kill. He removed the pinkie finger from their left hands. We never caught him. To be honest, we never got close to catching him."

We did have a suspect who came onto our radar at one point. There were multiple assaults on his record. But what had him in our crosshairs was that he had a prior arrest for attempted murder—of a homeless person. Most of those assaults in his jacket, they were against the homeless as well. Initially he looked good for it—solid, even. But extensive digging into his whereabouts at the time of several of the murders gave him the perfect alibi. He was already locked up in the county jail. So he wasn't our guy. The solid image of him as a suspect turned into sand and fell through our fingers.

Once again, we had nothing.

Freere's hand went over his mouth. His face became pensive.

I continued, "I got the case in '98 and worked it the better part of six years. Our last known homicide had occurred in '02, but the chief of Ds let me stay on it an extra two years before they kicked it to the cold files. I hadn't looked at it since."

"And here he is now, after all this time, in my city. Why?"

I thought about telling Freere that on the occasions I had found myself thinking about this case and our unknown suspect, I'd just assumed—hoped, actually—the guy was dead, or possibly locked up, doing life. That's usually how it happened when a serial killer suddenly dropped off the map.

He was too much of a gentleman to say it, but the look on the captain's face said he thought this recent spate of murders in his city was my fault somehow—that I should've caught this bastard long before he crossed the Louisiana state line. He's probably right. He'd get no argument from me. There was no point in me telling him about my hopes of this killer's demise. Of course I could just be projecting, because I certainly did feel responsible.

"I have no idea why he'd be in Alexandria, now, captain," I said.

Captain Freere's brow furrowed, and then after a moment, he asked, "Do you think he followed *you* here?"

"Followed me?" I allowed myself to consider the possibility for one moment and then said, "No. For one, the odds of him knowing that I ran that investigation twenty years ago are slim. What's more, I didn't even know I'd be taking the McAllister case. As much as I hate to say it, because I don't believe in them, but our being here at the same time is, for lack of a better term, a coincidence."

"Well, coincidence or not, I'm in full scramble mode on this one," Captain Freere said. "So I best get to it. Need to head over to—"

"Captain," I interrupted him, my voice trembling just a bit, "let me help you catch him."

CHAPTER 61

I ALMOST WANTED TO take the words back just as soon as they'd crossed my lips. This was not why I was here. All the cold case sleuthing I'd done aside, I was hired to do a job, not come down here and assuage my wounded ego over things left undone.

Yet, I couldn't stop myself. I imagined my face had the wounded puppy dog look that Elena always said I used on her when I was trying to play nice to get my way, because after he'd frowned and groaned at my request, Captain Freere finally said, "Look. You can advise, for now. I'd like to know everything you know about this suspect. Get me a copy of your old profile if you can manage."

"That I can do, captain."

I made a quick phone call to Dale first, letting him know that I'd be abandoning him for a bit to get the captain up to speed on everything I knew about the man we in Chicago had dubbed the Street Life Killer (SLK). He assured me it was no issue and that he could shoulder the load in the meantime. "Besides," Dale said, "if I actually need some real detective work done, Ashe is in town." He hung up on me before I could reply. It was Dale being Dale. His mind was made up to pull all those files and start digging into them alone. He wasn't one to dwell on it. It's one of the reasons we got along so well.

My next call was to an old friend of mine who was still riding a desk at the twelfth back in Chicago. Detective Abner McNamara—we all called him "Mac"—went way back with me. He's about three years shy of retiring himself, but it wouldn't surprise me if he held on just a bit longer. Since his wife died ten years ago, he'd always talked about how he had nothing to retire to. I got the distinct impression he'd determined to hang on to the job as long as he could.

"McNamara," his grizzly bear-like voice came across the phone.

"Hey, Mac, it's Raines."

"Raines-ey! What's shakin', pal?"

"I need a favor, Mac."

"Speaking of favors…you still married to that pretty girl of yours? If not, maybe you can give me her number. I might have a shot," he said and immediately broke into a laugh. Cop friends—we were some sick bastards sometimes, but I would guess that's most friends. If they couldn't give you grief when the chips were down, what's the point of being friends?

"Still a prick, I see. Trust me. If you have a shot at all, it's coming from my SIG." I chuckled.

"Alright, you mean old bastard. What can I do for you?"

"I need you to go by my house. The spare key is still in the usual place. Look in the bottom drawer of the file cabinet that's in the living room. There'll be a file marked SLK-2002. I need you to same day that to me."

"Same day? You know how much that costs, Raines-ey?"

"I'll refund you, you miser. Just get it done for me. Will you?"

"Yeah, yeah, yeah. Where am I shippin' it to?"

I gave him the address to the Alexandria police station. After which of course I had to answer a few questions as to why I was down here and why I needed these notes so bad. I gave him the CliffNotes version, and after reminding him once again that I needed him to tend to this now, I hung up.

I walked back into Freere's office. He's pouring over coroner reports. As much as the reappearance of the "Street Life Killer" was on my mind, so was something else.

"Captain? How's Wakefield doing?" I asked. "Has he regained consciousness?" I was hoping to have heard about Curtis's condition by now. Given that I hadn't, it was a perfect time to ask.

"No. Not yet, I'm afraid. Last I heard, his condition is about the same. That's probably for the best, though."

"How's that?" I asked. Freere's words and his tone of voice had me worried.

"I talked with ol' Ozzie. He said, and I quote, 'Once that boy wakes up, he goes back in gen pop,' unquote."

"Son of a—" I was as mad as I could recall being in some time.

"Yeah, I didn't agree with that myself. An' that ol' public defender Wakefield has, I don't think he has the stones to argue with Ozzie on this, so…"

"Thanks for the update," I said as I managed to calm down just a bit. I was going to be burning the candles at both ends. At my age, that's a really short candle. But finding Cecilia, which could free Curtis Wakefield, and finally putting an end to the SLK—well, that'd be worth whatever damage was done by going at it this hard.

I looked the captain in the eyes. "And thanks for letting me help on this."

CHAPTER 62

Pollock, Louisiana

FIRST ORDER OF business for Ashe after he had left Robert Raines at Motel 6 was to check the crime scene. He rode over to Officer Dakota Quinn's place, and though they hadn't met, he recognized her when she walked out of her home.

Ashe sat parked three doors down from her house on the opposite side of the street. It gave him a clear look at her porch. If it was dark out, and he were sitting in a running vehicle, he doubted that he would've been noticed.

Raines had described Dakota Quinn down to a "T." The fiery-red hair that ran down the sides of her face with the remainder pulled back in a ponytail was unmistakable, as was her Pollock Police Department uniform. But it was the look on her face that gave away just as much information as the things Raines described. She wore the look of someone who had just had a harrowing experience mere hours ago.

Her eyes darted back and forth when she stepped out onto her porch. Her right hand was firmly against her right hip, fingers ready to grip the handle of her service pistol. She was hypervigilant, a common condition suffered by those who went through traumatic experiences. Almost having your ticket punched by a bullet as you walked out of your front door qualified as traumatic. Ashe had seen that look many times before on the faces of men and women he had served with in the Marines.

He watched her take very slow steps, looking around with every pace, to her car. She got in and put her head in her hands for a moment before seeming to gather herself. She started her car and pulled off. Ashe then got out of his rental. He made his way across the street and took a good look at the bullet holes that lined Quinn's wooden railing. If their attackers had been brazen enough to pull this off in the daytime, his friends would've probably been dead. Truth be told, if their attackers were good marksmen at all, Raines and Gamble would've been dead when it happened at night. The darkness was the perfect cover, for someone who knew what they're doing, anyway. He was now even more convinced that these men did not. But they came close. They came damn close.

Ashe returned to his rental vehicle. As he walked back around to the driver side, he noticed a pile of cigarette butts. It appeared someone had been waiting there for a while. And that someone liked unfiltered cigarettes—another clue to add into the pile. Satisfied

Quinn's area told him all that it had to tell, Ashe headed off. He planned to grab some breakfast, maybe even take a nap in the car, and then get back to his search.

Ashe spotted a few red Chevy pickups along his way to get a bite; however, when he maneuvered to get along the passenger side of the vehicles, none had bullet holes in them. It's not possible that anyone would be able to get the damage fixed this fast. None of these were the vehicle he was looking for. There were a couple of bars he passed by also. They weren't open yet, but they'd be good places to check a little later in the day. Maybe he'd see something, or maybe he'd hear something—either way stopping in should be worthwhile.

As he sat and enjoyed a breakfast of eggs, ham, and sausages with a large coffee, Ashe recalled the story Raines had told him about the young black college kid, Curtis, the basketball player with dreams of going pro who had been identified as the prime suspect in the missing McAllister girl case. The worst part of the story was that he was badly beaten by the Aryan Brotherhood prison gang some hours ago. The prison report had said he was beaten by five men. Ashe thought of the horror, the helplessness, the despair, and the pain this young man had to be going through in that moment. It made him angry. Someone was going to have to pay for that. It was just a matter of finding them. But that's what he did. He always had—in Fallujah, in Chicago, and now in Louisiana. He'd find *the* someone. And they would pay.

CHAPTER 63

Alexandria, Louisiana

JUST ABOUT TWENTY minutes or so past noon, my FedEx package from Chicago arrived at the station. I had been sipping coffee since my arrival this morning, so I was amped up.

I sat across from Freere in his office and tore into the packaging with abandon, like a kid opening a Christmas present. We spent several hours covering my notes, the theories that had developed during my investigation, as well as thoughts on the murders that had just occurred. While I wasn't a board-certified or degreed psychiatrist, or psychologist for that matter, the techniques I learned at Quantico were invaluable. The department took full advantage of both myself and Dale having gone through the training. I'd always been confident my work was spot-on.

As I thumbed through the pages and pages of notes that I had taken during my six years working the case, I realized just how bad my handwriting was. I had trouble making out a few things I'd jotted down, but I was still able to give an accurate detailing of the profile we had put together of the "Street Life Killer". It was only the second profile I had done at the time, putting that FBI profiler training to the test.

In 1998, we felt we were looking for a white male, between the ages of eighteen and twenty-four. He would be a loner, most likely from a broken home, and probably working a menial job—something low profile, just to get him by.

I recounted the few eyewitness reports we did have; witnesses reported seeing a slim man between 5′11″ and 6′1″, dressed in black from head to toe. A hoodie was always pulled up over his head and cinched in tight; it was hard for anyone to make out his face.

We'd found bodies along Lower Wacker Drive near downtown Chicago. There were bodies found in the Chicago River and bodies found on the west and south sides of the city. There were a few bodies found further up north, so we knew he was mobile. He had his own means of transportation. Then, out of the blue, he just quit. I never knew if he felt any heat coming down on him because quite frankly, I didn't ever feel that we had put any heat on him. It was one of the reasons that I thought (hoped, really) that he met his end falling over into the river or maybe being hit by a speeding train.

"What makes a man do things like this?" Freere asked.

I was sure it was a rhetorical question, but being that I was fully engaged, I couldn't help but answer. "Serial murders generally aren't committed for obvious reasons like greed, jealousy, profit, or revenge," I said. "Most cases, the killer is deeply disturbed. They have a compulsion to kill that just eats away at them. These urges are driven from inside, not some external stimuli. To put it another way, you never truly know the 'why' behind what they do—but they feel they have to."

"In other words, he's just a sick son-of-a-bitch," Freere offered.

I nodded in agreement.

"One who takes pinkie fingers as trophies," he added.

"The severed digits allow him to relive the murders over and over again. They allow him to experience whatever feelings of joy, euphoria, or contentment he feels when he takes them."

"Jeee-zus! You think he still has them…all the ones from Chicago, I mean?" Freere cringed.

"I'd be willing to bet he does, captain. They're every bit a part of his ritual as the murders themselves. I don't think he'd part with them. I would imagine he found some way to preserve them or someplace to store them for safekeeping to visit anytime he wants. They'd be just that important to him."

"Well, either way, he's ahead of the game. Psycho killer 4, Alexandria PD 0," Freere said as he reached for some of my notes. "Based on your original profile," Freere began again as he stared hard at the papers in front of him, "you had him between eighteen and twenty-four years old?"

"That's right. Given that twenty years has passed, he'd be between thirty-eight and forty-four now," I said.

"A white male, at that age. Great. He'll just blend right in," Freere said.

"That's it, captain!" An idea hit me. "He *has* to blend in. And that's one advantage that we have this time."

"How's that?"

"In Chicago, he could commit his crimes and then walk right back into his normal, everyday life, blend in as Joe Citizen—Chicago born and raised. But he's not from around here, and he's just left the starting line. We're not too far behind this time. Now, the first thing he would've done was found a place to stay. If the rest of my profile stands up, and he's set up shop here, he'll be working a minimum-wage job, something that pays just enough to cover his rent and immediate expenses; so he'll be looking to rent on the cheap—hotels, motels, low-end rent apartments."

"Or he could be sleeping in his car," Freere countered.

"Not impossible," I said. "But when you hear hoof-beats, think horses, not zebras." The look on Freere's face seemed to indicate he didn't follow that, admittedly age-old, idiom. "I'm just saying let's start with the simplest possibility and work our way from there."

I figured my idea ultimately made sense to Freere. His mood seemed to pick up, just a bit, and he nodded his head in agreement.

"I know a couple of landlords and motel managers who would fall into that category. They rent to transients mostly—cheap too. Sounds like the type of places our boy might like to try to hide out in."

"If they're renting to a white male in that age range who just hit town, in the very least, you'll have a person of interest. Nothing concrete obviously, but a start."

"Thanks for the input," Captain Freere said as he stood up at his desk and extended his hand. The handshake meant it was time for me to go. It's an active Alexandria PD investigation after all. Just the same, I was glad he let me help in the manner I did. It'd ease my mind tremendously if they caught this bastard. I shook the captain's hand.

"Mind if I hold onto these?" he asked, pointing at my collection of notes.

"For as long as you need to, captain."

"I'll set up a canvas and make a few phone calls," he said. "If anything interesting pops up, I'll let you know."

"Thanks again. Good luck."

Freere was kind enough to arrange a ride for me back to Motel 6. It was time I got back to work on the case I was actually being paid to investigate.

CHAPTER 64

Pollock, Louisiana

"*I NEED YOU TO* come with me," Trina McNair, already dressed in a tan scooped neck camisole and white pleated sun skirt, yelled from the bedroom. Her stark-white tennis shoes completed her ensemble. During the prior twenty minutes, while she was putting herself together, she had called out several times to her boyfriend (actually fiancé now), Kyle Young, to get ready.

He dutifully ignored her. He sat in the living room in front of the television watching one of his favorite reality shows, *Rocky Mountain Law*. He was sipping a Michelob Light and intently watching a police chase come to its conclusion, just as one of the pursuing officers performed a pit maneuver, spinning the fleeing vehicle 360 degrees before it came to an abrupt stop, trapped in a ditch, when Trina entered and stood directly in front of the screen.

"What? Hey, wait. I was watching that!" he said.

"Kyle, you're supposed to be coming with me."

"Coming with you where?"

Trina shoved her cellphone in his face.

His eyes scanned the screen quickly. "So? And who's Emily?"

"You don't see that? That is a sterling silver, one-carat diamond tennis bracelet."

"You know you can't afford it. I sure as hell can't afford it, so what's your point? And I'm missing my show, now."

"You don't see the price? This Emily girl is practically giving it away. It's only two hundred dollars."

"Two hundred dollars? Well, maybe it's not real then. Or, Trina, maybe, just maybe, she's plannin' on rippin' you off."

"Well, that's why you're goin'."

"An' just where are you gonna get two hundred dollars from anyway, huh?"

"Well, if he knows what's good for him, my fiancé is gonna buy it, especially since he agreed to it when we were layin' in bed after he had just got off top of me!" She gave him a stern look.

In that moment, Kyle remembered, fresh from a heart-pounding round of sex that started in the laundry room and wound its way to the bedroom, that he did agree to buy it. She shoved that cellphone of hers in his face (much like she had just done now) and mentioned how someone was getting rid of some nice, fancy jewelry for cheap. She mentioned the two hundred dollars, and he blurted out, "Sure, babe. Anything for you."

Funny, now that he's all rested and sexually satisfied, Kyle found himself wishing he'd kept his mouth shut or that her legs had stayed shut.

"Fine!" he finally blurted out. "I'll get ready. Where we goin' anyway?"

"I got the address. It's out in the boonies a little bit, but if we get movin', we can be there and back before dark."

"Why can't she meet us someplace?"

"Because, just like us, she and her husband only have one car. And he's out. Now c'mon. Get ready."

"Stupid Craigslist," Kyle muttered and then headed into the bedroom to find his clothes. Deep down, he knew he was doing the right thing, not just buying the bracelet because he said he would, but in going with Trina. The world's a crazy place, full of psychos and assholes. She didn't need to go alone.

Unfortunately for Kyle Young, that good deed would cost him his life.

CHAPTER 65

AROUND 6:00 P.M., Kyle drove his Chevy Blazer onto Orrin Robicheaux's property. He actually had been saving to buy a new vehicle—well, relatively new, nothing fancy, just something more recent than the relic he owned from 2002.

Whenever he thought about it, he realized the amount of money that he'd spent in repairs on this vehicle could've been used to buy a new one by now, which was why he tried not to think about it often.

Yet here he was, borrowing from his "new" car fund to buy this bracelet that Trina just simply had to have. Oh, well, what was that thing they said, *Happy wife, happy life?* He figured he'd better get used to making sacrifices. It's what he was signing up for after all—a lifetime of it. The Blazer came to a stop a few feet from a large tree that sat out in front of the house. The sun had just begun showing signs of calling it a day. That tree seemed to cast a giant shadow over nearly the entire property.

Kyle and Trina looked around. There was no one in sight.

"Isn't she supposed to be waiting on the porch or something?" Kyle asked.

"Yeah, that's what she said." Trina pulled out her cellphone and called the number she'd been texting back and forth with ever since she responded to the ad on Craigslist earlier in the day. She got no answer. She reached for the door handle.

"What are you doing?" Kyle asked incredulously.

"I'm gonna get out and ring the bell."

"No, no, we're not doin' that... Ain't you seen *Deliverance?* Or *The Texas Chainsaw Massacre?*"

"Oh, grow up, Kyle. You're not gettin' outta buying me that bracelet that easily." Trina hopped out of the Blazer before Kyle could protest further. He watched as she made her way up the stairs and rang the bell.

She stepped back away from the door. There was no answer. She turned and looked at Kyle, throwing her hands up.

"Okay. That's it then. Let's go." Kyle opened his door and leaned halfway out. "We're not waiting around here, Trina. It's about to get dark. Usually when something seems too good to be true, it is."

Trina knocked on the glass partition in the door, a last desperate and frantic act. She really wanted that bracelet. There was still no answer. She turned and reluctantly began walking down the stairs and back over toward Kyle, who had sat back inside the Blazer and dropped it in gear.

As Trina got to the truck, she heard from behind— "Oh, hey! I'm sorry."

Trina turned around to see a scrawny, dingy-looking woman with what could best be described as dirty blond hair. The skinny woman was coming from behind the house. She was removing gloves from her hands.

"You must be Trina, right? You here about the jewelry? Don't mind me. I was just doin' some chores out behind the house."

Slightly stunned by the woman's appearance, Trina stammered out, "Uh…yeah, yeah. We're here for the jewelry."

"We?" Emily asked. She stopped in her tracks. A look of shock crawled across her face.

"Yeah, me and my fiancé." Trina turned and pointed to Kyle who had again opened his driver side door and stepped halfway out.

"Oh, hi!" Emily hastily flashed her crooked smile.

Kyle returned a weak smile and gave a half-hearted wave.

"Well, let me just run in and get the bracelet. You all have the money, right?"

"We sure do." Kyle shut off the Blazer's engine and stepped out.

He reached into his pocket for the cash, walking toward Trina, when the drab blond woman said, "I'm sorry. I don't mean to impose, but can I ask a favor?" Emily turned back and forth, looking at Trina and Kyle as if not sure to whom she should direct her question. "I was chopping some wood out back. One of the pieces my husband brought back is just too big for me to get on the block. I could really use the help of your big strong man here. I just need to borrow him a sec."

"Why can't it wait for your husband to—"

"Of course, Kyle can help you," Trina cut him off and shot him a look. She mouthed, angrily, *The necklace!* at him.

Exasperated, Kyle slapped his hands at his sides, "Fine. C'mon. Let's get it over with."

"Thank you. Thank you so much. It's just right around back here. Won't take you but a moment." Emily then flashed that awkward and crooked smile again.

CHAPTER 66

KYLE MADE HIS way around to the back of the house first, a few steps ahead of the two women. Just as he cleared the house, he heard a loud cracking sound, and the world suddenly turned black. The darkness only lasted momentarily, as the world came back quickly, in flashes at first. Then his eyes found their ability to focus. He could hear loud screaming and shrieking. Then it hit—the pain.

He realized why the world had gone dark. That loud cracking sound he'd heard was of a hard, blunt object being smashed across his head. The shrieking, that was Trina. He knew that voice anywhere. After a moment, he realized that when he was hit, he had crumpled to the ground. He looked up to see a very large man standing over him.

Upside down, he could just make out that the large man was pointing something at Trina, yelling at her, "Get the fuck on the ground, bitch!"

Kyle's vision cleared enough for him to make out that the man was holding a shotgun. As the big man stepped over him, moving closer to Trina, Kyle sprang to his feet. He was still woozy and nearly went pinwheeling feet over head and back down, but managed to catch his balance.

"Run, Trina! Get in the truck!" Kyle shouted. As the large man turned toward him, Kyle rushed at him; and with all his might, he grabbed the shotgun and forced the barrel end up into the air. The big man was strong. Entirely too strong for Kyle, although not a small man himself, he was no match strength for strength. The big man flung him into the side of the house. The impact dropped Kyle to his knees.

The big man then turned back and saw Trina hop into the vehicle that they had arrived in. He took a step in her direction, and Kyle again sprang to his feet and launched himself at the big brute. The impact of colliding with the man's body sent a jolt of pain through Kyle. The big man however barely even budged. He raised the shotgun about as high as his head and then brought the butt of it crashing down on top of Kyle's head.

Kyle dropped to his knees. The big man raised one massive boot and kicked him hard in the chest. Kyle fell to his back, the wind knocked out of him. He gasped for air. His eyes opened wide when he heard the big man rack in a load in the shotgun.

In the next moment, the big man pulled the trigger. A gaping hole was opened in Kyle's chest. He let out a gurgling, hissing sound as he breathed his last breath.

Kyle Young was dead.

CHAPTER 67

TRINA MCNAIR RAN for her life. Her mind was having the damnedest time believing what her eyes were seeing.

When the savage big man struck Kyle across the head, with the sound it made, she thought he was dead. *Dead? Just how is that possible? He was just helping this lady before she sells me the tennis bracelet.* The tennis bracelet meant absolutely nothing now. She didn't even know why she wanted it in the first place. She froze, but when Kyle yelled, *Run!* that got her moving. She heard screaming as she ran and, after a few moments, realized it was her own shrieks and cries that she was hearing. Somehow they seemed to be coming from someone else, somewhere else. This entire event seemed to be something she might have been watching on TV.

Trina got to the Blazer. She fumbled with the handle on the driver side door for a moment before she was able to open it. That was when she heard that blood-curdling sound—the explosive bang that echoed around the property, bouncing off the trees and back toward her ears. She felt it in her bones. Trina turned and looked. That big son-of-a-bitch had just shot Kyle. Now, he *was* dead! *Dead? Yes, he's dead! He just got shot because YOU had to have that fucking tennis bracelet! Now, get out of here!*

Trina reached for the ignition, but the key was not in it. She patted her pockets. "Keys! Keys! Oh, God! Where are the keys?" She screamed frantically. The realization that the keys had to be in Kyle's pockets and that the big man wielding that shotgun, along with his scrawny, frumpy little friend, was walking toward her sank in. She locked the doors. The windows were already up. Thank God!

The large man, with the skinny, odd-faced woman in tow, walked over to the driver side. The big man rested the shotgun casually across his shoulder and said, "C'mon out, girlie. We ain't got time for this. You come on outta there, now!"

"Just do like he says. Just do like he says is all," Emily yammered.

"Fuck you!" Trina screamed. "You killed Kyle!"

"Why'd you bring—" Emily began before the big man cut her off.

"I'm only gonna tell you one more time, tramp. Come on outta there, now!"

"No!" Trina managed through her tears and in between sobs.

The big man lowered the shotgun from his shoulders and, in one mighty thrust, rammed it against the driver side window. Shards of glass rained across Trina's face. She could feel some of it land in her hair and seem to cling there, not wanting to drop to the floor. The big man continued to knock out the loose bits of glass from the windowpane, ignoring Trina's increasingly frantic screams. Once satisfied, he reached one of those large meat hooks he had for hands inside and grabbed a handful of Trina's hair. He clinched his fist tight and pulled. She tried her best to resist, grabbing hold of the steering wheel. But the big man was strong. She'd never felt anything like it. And she knew her hair and scalp would pull away before she broke that iron grip of his. Within moments, he drug her out of the truck through the window and dropped her like a sack of dirty laundry on the ground. Before she could blink, he'd taken the butt of that shotgun and gave her a good whack in the head with it. There was nothing but the deep, dark black that was unconsciousness for Trina McNair after that.

"What now, Orrin?" Emily asked.

"What now?" Orrin raised a hand and slapped Emily hard across the face. She dropped to the ground. "What now? I ought to beat you somethin' fierce! That's what now! What the hell were they doin' here?"

"I didn't know she was gonna bring him, Orrin! I swear I didn't know. I did just like you said. I told her it would be just us girls."

Orrin grew even more incensed. He yelled, "What were either of them doin' here, Emily?"

"You said…you said…we needed to change our plans. I thought… I thought—"

"Are you crazy? You invited her to our house? What were you thinking? They could've told somebody they were coming here! I don't like it! I don't like it at all! Lucky we were able to get him to come 'round back. Goddammit!"

Orrin continued to stare angrily at Emily. After a few minutes, his breathing had slowed down, and his anger subsided just a little bit. He said, "You drag her down into the cellar. You should be able to handle her. Get her strapped in good for me. I've got to get rid of this car and his body."

CHAPTER 68

Alexandria, Louisiana

BEFORE MAKING MY way back to the motel, I had the officer giving me a ride drop me off at Edna's. It was a small eatery just three blocks from Motel 6. Having skipped breakfast and lunch, I was starving and needed to fill the tank before doing any more work.

The place had a rather extensive menu, but the bacon cheeseburger was calling my name. It was simply incredible. Without exaggerating, it was probably one of the best burgers I'd ever eaten. There were Cajun spices of some sort in it, along with cheddar cheese and a ton of bacon. It had been cooked perfectly. The fries were hot and crispy on the outside, but soft on the inside. I savored every bite and washed it all down with an ice-cold Coke. As a rule, I tried not to drink too much soda, but it went perfectly with my meal.

I could only gather that having waited so late in the day to eat my blood sugar must've been low. At least I told myself that was the reason I ordered a dessert. Then again, after the beignets the other day, I'd guess that sweet tooth that I always said I didn't have was growing.

The tarte a la bouille piqued my interest. I was rewarded for my curiosity with a delicious orange- and ginger-flavored tart that wasn't too sweet but fit the bill of what I was looking for in the moment.

After settling my tab, I walked the three blocks to Motel 6.

As I expected, even though evening had rolled around and the sun had begun to show the faintest signs that it was preparing to set, it was still hot and muggy outside. I just had to knuckle up. A three-block walk in this heat wasn't going to kill me.

It did require me to take a quick shower after I got in my room, though. A romp in the cold water and a fresh change of clothes did wonders for me. I worked in a quick call to Officer Quinn. As more hours had come between her and the time of the shooting, she had settled down and was getting back to her old self. That was good to hear, but I had figured she'd get there sooner than later. I was right.

After talking with her, I headed over to Dale's room.

We chatted a few minutes about where I left Captain Freere with the man we knew in Chicago as the "Street Life Killer". I appreciated Dale allowing me to split my time with another of my old cold cases. He knew how much this case had eaten at me over the years and how hard it was for me to get past my failure with it.

After getting him up to speed on where that stood, he walked me through the work he'd done so far on *our* case. Dale had worked through the morning and into the evening, after he had gotten back to his room, combing through the files that Captain Freere was gracious enough to let us take a look at.

"Some of those poor women," he said, "didn't even have a family member or friend file a missing persons report on them. It looks like the cases just kind of fell into Alexandria PD's laps through employers, bill collectors."

How depressing was that—to go through life and when it came down to it, nobody even noticed you were missing—other than your job or Visa and Mastercard? It makes you wonder. Would anybody notice if I just up and disappeared one day? I'd like to think so. Sadly, not everyone apparently could say the same.

I grabbed a few files and dug in.

CHAPTER 69

THE ABDUCTED WOMEN in the original case—all eight of them—varied in age and occupation. It didn't appear that any of them had run in the same circles, though four of them, it turned out, did attend the same church. However, nothing indicated that any of them knew each other on any personal level.

Two of the women were married. Of course, their husbands were prime suspects at first, before they were cleared. That's just the nature of this particular beast, although I was sure neither husband appreciated being put under the microscope, essentially accused of harming the love of their respective lives. Who would?

Immediately disappointing was that the MOs didn't match between our case and the cold cases. With Cecilia McAllister and two of the cases Quinn had, those women all were connected by using a trading app. Each young lady had answered an ad, looking to buy a pet. It appeared that's how they were lured into whatever trap befell them. And it seemed that trap might have been sprung at various times during the day.

The women abducted in Alexandria starting eight years ago, all of them, based on the evidence gathered, had been taken at night. And all were taken after having been out at a bar or some other social gathering. It seemed there were some blitzkrieg attacks. Some of the women were taken from parking lots and at least two in their own driveways, which told us they were being watched, stalked, hunted.

"As much as I hate to say it," I looked over at Dale who was lost in a pile of photographs, "these Alexandria kidnappings seem more old-school."

"Old-school?"

"Exactly. I figure an older fella wouldn't be using an app to lure anybody. He'd get out there, out in the streets. It's the way he would've had to do it when he got started eight years ago. The thrill of the hunt was what was motivating this first guy."

"Whereas a younger fella would be a little more tech-savvy and know that's the perfect way to set up a meet and greet with somebody these days," Dale added.

"That's where I'm going with it."

"You know, Sherlock, the only younger suspect we have is Curtis Wakefield," Dale said with trademark sarcasm.

"And that's why, Watson, I've only shared that thought with you for the time being."

"Good man."

"I can't wrap my mind around the end game, though," I said. I set the file I had been perusing down. Undoubtedly, I was beginning to burn out. Soaking in all of this information and not having it lead to any substantial conclusions was frustrating me.

"End game, Bobby?" Dale stared at me for a moment. He tossed the file he had in his hands back into a pile on the bed. "Try this. Ten will get you twenty, we're dealing with a psychopath, someone who sees these women, not as human beings, but as objects, things that have no meaning whatsoever. It's about power, or reclaiming power in some way because of some past issue or perceived sleight."

"Mommy issues?" I offered.

"Possibly. It could be any stressor. It could be the death of a loved one. His actions now are giving him the power of life and death over his victims," Dale said. "What he's doing once he has them, that's anybody's guess right now. But these abductions are how he's taking back the power that he feels he lost."

The conversation didn't help. I was burned out. My eyes were starting to feel strained and heavy. I needed a break and was overdue for some coffee. "I'm going to make a coffee run. You want anything?" I asked.

"We're out of Blanton's, as you know. Maybe see if you can find that, or something similar while you're out."

"Will do."

I grabbed the keys and my SIG P250 from the nightstand and headed out.

As I was getting into the truck, I caught a glimpse of something in the backseat. I almost ignored it, but figured I'd better take a look now anyway. My memory wasn't what it used to be, and I just might forget it was back there.

As I opened the back door and leaned in for a closer look, I couldn't help but yell, "Holy shit!"

Dale rushed out of the motel room, his Kimber 1911 in hand. I hadn't realized just how loud I had been.

"What in the hell?" Dale looked around, pistol in the low and ready position, expecting some sign of trouble.

"This," I said. I held up a large manila folder.

"What the hell is that? And where did it come from?"

"It was in the backseat. I guess it must've been in between boxes instead of inside of one. And there's something else."

"What?"

I handed Dale the folder. He read the name across the label. "You've got to be kidding me."

We both agreed—the coffee and the Blanton's would have to wait.

Part Seven

CLOSURE—OR SOMETHING CLOSE TO IT

CHAPTER 70

Pollock, Louisiana

EMILY STRUGGLED LUGGING the newest addition to Orrin's collection, Trina McNair, down into the cellar. The unconscious woman probably outweighed her by a solid twenty pounds, but as dead weight, Emily thought the woman had her by thirty plus easy.

By the time the two had reached the cellar steps, Emily was winded, and her back began to hurt. She set Trina's body down; leaned against the cellar doors, hands on knees; and sucked in hard. The heavy, sticky, Louisiana air was hot going down in those huge gulps she took. There was only one way she was getting Trina down into the cellar, dragging her in feet first. Emily grabbed her legs and pulled. Trina's head bobbed hard against the wooden steps on the way down. She stirred, but didn't wake.

After getting Trina's limp body down the steps, Emily needed to catch her breath again. She paused for a moment, gathering her strength. That was when she noticed the eyes, eyes staring at her from the cages, the other women she'd helped Orrin lure into this putrid pit—this hellhole out in the backwoods. None of them said anything. They didn't have to. The looks on their faces—those looks of fear and despair—said it all. As Emily dutifully dragged the unconscious Trina over to the gurney, those haunting looks reminded her of the first time *she* had met Orrin.

All those years ago, when she was simply Emily Loreanne Peters. She was just thirteen at the time, an innocent, wide-eyed, gullible teen. That gullibility combined one fine day with her penchant for skipping school and brought her face to face with Willie Robicheaux.

Spotting her as she strolled around an empty park, Willie slowly pulled over in the very same van that Orrin used to this day. He introduced himself, quickly gaining her trust, asking about a *lost* puppy. She had no fear or trepidation as the older man calmly put his van in park and exited. Willie described in detail what the dog looked like, as he slowly moved in closer and closer to her. Before Emily knew it, he was upon her, striking her viciously across the face and tossing her limp body into the back of the van. The previously sunny, easy-going day had turned dark for Emily. It was the day her innocence died.

She lay, in a state of shock and confusion, as he held a wet towel over her nose and mouth. It had been soaked in chloroform she would come to learn years later. She remembered him sitting in that van, holding her tightly until she drifted off into darkness.

When Emily awoke later that day, with a rag tied around her mouth, she was being dragged into this very cellar. On the way down the stairs, she saw a large pimply faced kid. She had no idea what was to transpire next.

Thinking about her first day with the Robicheauxs, as she struggled with all of her might to lift Trina from the floor and onto the gurney, Emily remembered that there was a woman who was locked in one of these very cages. *What was her name?* Iris? Carla? Ingrid? Wait… It was Irene. *Irene!* That was her name. Emily remembered Irene screaming something about keeping her eyes closed. It was a shame that she didn't remember the names of any of those other women. Oddly enough, and unbeknown to Orrin, she herself had uttered those same words—*Keep your eyes closed, honey. Don't look at him*—to the women who had recently become residents of the cellar, when he's not around of course; otherwise, he'd beat her *something fierce!*

The next thing she remembered occurring on that fateful day was a young Orrin Robicheaux, no more than fourteen or fifteen years old himself, leaning in over her while she was strapped to the gurney. Emily remembered him saying something about *having fun.* Then the cutting began, followed by the rape, the first of many, many rapes, over and over again. Cut, beat, rape, repeat—the brutality went on for years. She had seen many women— tormented by his father—come and go. She'd lost count as to just how many it had been—lost count or just gave up on remembering their faces. That was a burden in and of itself, after all, remembering the faces of all of the victims, past and present.

Pouring through her mental rolodex, Emily flashed back one day in particular, just about a year ago now. Orrin was incredibly brutal with her. He stormed into the cellar in a rage. He unshackled Emily—she wasn't *lucky* enough to have her own cage—she found herself chained to the wall in the corner where a worn-out mattress lay on the cellar floor. He slapped her hard across the face. She let out a whimper. The look on his face said it wasn't loud enough, not near loud enough at all. Orrin bawled up his fist and punched her in the face and then the gut. She let out a rather loud yelp then.

He grabbed her by the throat and began to squeeze. Her eyes began to roll back in her head; then without warning, he brought a straight razor across her thighs (those poor, tortured thighs). The cuts weren't deep, superficial actually. But Emily was hurt just the same. He then brought the razor across her chest, slicing into those breasts that had been scarred since her arrival. She winced even now at the memory.

As she screamed and writhed in pain that day, he dropped his pants and pulled out his hard penis. He used the straight razor to cut her panties off and then rammed himself inside of her. He began to thrust violently in and out, in and out, and back and forth. On and on he went. Choking her, striking her across the face, he rocked back and forth inside of her. Her cries for help only made him more vicious.

Orrin went at her for hours and hours while he worked out whatever was going on in that perverted, deviant mind of his. Later in that same brutal, violent day, he asked her to be his "wife," taking his last name and all. It wasn't a traditional coming together before God to be joined in some holy union deal that Orrin was after. She didn't even know if he believed in God. (*How could he, after all?*) It was just something else that he had decided in his head he wanted to do.

Fearing he would hurt her more if she didn't agree to it, she said yes.

CHAPTER 71

THAT SAME DAY, after Emily had accepted his *proposal,* Orrin paid a visit to the women locked in the cages in the cellar—his father's *playmates.*

Emily recalled that he stood before them and, in what she thought at the time was an oddly calm and serene voice, said, "Ladies...my daddy can't play with you all anymo'...and since yer no use to me..." his voice trailed off, and he closed his eyes as if he were going to pray.

Emily remembered watching him pull a gun from his waistband. She didn't know what kind it was, but she knew it was big. She watched in horror as, after what appeared to be a silent prayer, he opened fire. He mowed down each woman in her cage. Orrin fired multiple rounds until they were all dead. She distinctly remembered wondering, in that moment, if that was what had happened to Irene. Was that why she was no longer a prisoner here?

Was she taken outside and shot? Put down like a lowly animal?

But what Emily remembered most about that day was that the vicious beatings, the torture, and the rapes all stopped. Well, there were no beatings as long as she made Orrin happy and did what he said.

Otherwise, there were beatings galore!

She just no longer had to endure those horrors on a daily basis, not like this new batch of women. They all had a heavy price to pay. In some ways, Orrin had worse than his dad ever was. And as he told her on that day, "It's my time now. Daddy can't do it no more. You're gonna have to help me."

She remembered in the aftermath, Orrin staring over his handywork. He examined each of the deceased females, taking mental notes, admiring their crumpled, bleeding corpses. He then turned back to her and said, "That's why I had to get rid of them. Those were Daddy's playthings. You, you gon' be my wife now—and you gon' help me get *my* playthings."

Emily remembered readily agreeing to that proclamation. And that was before Orrin raised that same handgun and pointed it directly in her face. His expression, previously calm and serene, was twisted and contorted in an angry expression. His voice was nearly a growl as he said, "And don't you ever try to fuckin' run away from me, Emily. Do you understand? If you ever try to run from me, I swear to God I will fuckin' kill you! Do you hear me?"

She meekly muttered "yes," and in a flash, his rage was gone. He promised her that day that things would be different for her. Being honest, she'd have to admit that for each girl she'd helped him kidnap—this latest chickie-pie made five now—his violence toward her had subsided, somewhat, unless she screwed up, of course.

Like that time he wanted three ice cubes in his drink and she gave him two, that earned her an upper cut and a few boots to the ribs while she was down on the floor. Or that time she was helping him strap down that young girl, Dahlia—lucky victim number 1—Emily didn't properly secure the girl's hand, and that goddamned Dahlia managed to scratch Orrin across the face. She clawed him good. Emily paid for that one as well, receiving a savage beating and ending the night raped by her *husband*, up front and in the back. That was a particularly painful night.

But she learned her lesson. You would bet she did. None of the other girls taken since had ever gotten a chance to fight back—to kick, scratch, or claw at Orrin again. Emily just could no longer take the beatings or the brutal sex acts or the cutting—especially the cutting. She'd do anything to make it stop. While at first it pained her to help him in his evil quest, the fact that her torment stopped made it worthwhile.

She began tightening the stirrups around Trina's ankles, and though she fought hard against the inclination clawing at the back of her conscience, she couldn't stop herself from turning and looking at the women in the cages again. Those eyes—those goddamned eyes staring back at her, blank, lifeless almost—for the first time, began to tear at her. And they made her remember…

For the first time in a long time, she remembered that her name was Emily Peters.

Not Emily Robicheaux, Emily Loreanne Peters, god-damn it!

Emily remembered the helplessness and the pain, especially the pain. She remembered everything about the horrors that she had gone through, the same horrors that these women were going through, daily. Emily felt faint. Her legs got weak and felt rubbery but heavy at the same time. She steadied herself against the gurney, breathing in deep the scents that haunted the cellar…she nearly vomited. It crossed her mind—though she (more likely her fear of Orrin) quickly ruled it out—to release them all, right now. No! That's just not possible…but…

She slogged over to the cellar steps and staggered up them. Emily made her way outside, visions of the abused women rapidly flashing through her mind. Another thought, a question, really, danced across her mind, interrupting those horrible images. *Is the new girl strapped in securely to the gurney?*

Emily didn't care to go back in and check.

CHAPTER 72

Alexandria, Louisiana

THE NAME SCRAWLED in black marker across the top of the investigative file that I had found in the back of our SUV read "Emily Peters."

"The person Quinn was supposed to meet the afternoon before we got shot at identified themselves as Emily," I said.

"Could be a coincidence," Dale offered. The tone in his voice suggested to me he didn't believe that though.

"Actually, earlier today, I would've dismissed that possibility out of hand," I said.

"Right. Before you found out SLK was in town," Dale offered.

We made our way back inside the motel room. We opened the file, and right away two glaring differences from the women in the other files jumped out at us.

"This girl was just thirteen when she was taken," I said.

"And it appears she's believed to have been taken during the daytime, not at night like the others."

"This doesn't fit either profile, not the old cases or anything we have now. Maybe this case file was bundled with the others accidentally."

"Well, the victimology is certainly different, but let's not jump to that conclusion just yet." Dale continued to read the reports of young Emily Peters's abduction.

"I'll call Captain Freere. First things first, let's find out if this Emily Peters case is still open or if she's ever been found."

I couldn't see his face when I asked the question, but the long pause before he responded told me that Captain Freere was taken by surprise when I asked about Emily Peters.

"My god, I haven't heard that name in some years," the captain finally responded.

"Was her disappearance part of your investigation into the missing women in Alexandria eight years ago?"

"No. Our task force reviewed the case, but the MOs didn't match, didn't fit the profile. There was a separate FBI investigation set up for that girl, what with her being under age and all."

"Any luck with this one?" I asked.

"None," Freere said. "We had everyone from our local PD, church groups, the feds, and the National Center for Missing and Exploited Children (NCMEC) searching high and low for that girl. It's not only one of our cold cases. Both the feds and NCMEC still have it open too. It shouldn't have been mixed in with those other files. Most likely it got filed incorrectly and just so happened to be in the bundles your associate grabbed."

"What about her family?" I asked. "Has anyone spoken with them lately? Find out if they've heard from her?"

"Her mom had passed before her disappearance. That left just her dad as her only living relative in Alexandria. He passed two years ago, probably from a broken heart. Lord knows what it's like to lose a child."

"Uh...yeah." I swallowed hard. "Thanks for the info, captain."

"Sure. No problem."

I was just about to end the call when something else that had been on my mind, pushed into the background by this morning's news, leaped back into the forefront.

CHAPTER 73

"*CAPTAIN? YOU STILL* there?"

"Yes?"

"One more thing. Might be a weird question, but does your station contract to have supplies like copy paper delivered, machines repaired, stuff like that?" I asked.

"Yeah, sure. We use McMillian and Forester. They're relatively new, but they outbid our former contractor and besides that they provide some digitization services that we didn't have before."

"Oh, really? And who was the former contractor?"

"It was a one-man operation, a guy by the name of William Robicheaux. Think he called it Robicheaux Cartage or something like that. Why?"

"I was just curious. I ran across a rather large fella by the name of Orrin Robicheaux the other day. He does the same type of work for the PD down in Pollock."

"Pollock? No shit, you took a trip out to the sticks, huh? Well, as far as the guy you came across, Orrin, as I understand it, William is his dad. I heard he took ill, so it stands to reason his son would pick up any contracts he had left to keep the business going."

"Okay. Thanks again, captain," I paused. The entire time I had Freere on the phone I was doing my best not to ask for a follow-up on SLK. I was hoping he'd offer one. He had said he would. It simply could've been that there was nothing to update. Just the same—

"Before I let you go, how's your search coming, captain?"

"I've made some calls. Still waiting to hear from the property owners," Freere explained. "There's still a couple of individuals I need to reach out to."

I was hoping for better news, but at the same time I was just relieved he didn't tell me to piss off. It was my case back in Chicago some twenty-years ago. It's not mine now. He didn't have to share anything with me.

"Understood. Thanks," I said.

"Sure thing. Now, a question for you." Freere's voice seemed to carry a more serious tone than what I had previously heard from him.

"Shoot."

"This SLK thing aside… Wakefield's in prison. Looks like he's taking the weight for the McAllister girl. I talked to the family. There's not much more they're expecting from you. May I ask why you boys are still in town?"

"Just tying up some loose ends, captain," I said. It was still too early to divulge anything more substantive than that. I still had to play this one close to the vest. "The McAllisters paid good money for our investigation. Just want to make sure all of the Is are dotted and the Ts are crossed."

"Fair enough," Freere said.

I didn't think he bought it, but at this point, it seemed reasonable enough that he had to accept it.

"Well, if you need anything, you let me know."

"Will do. Thanks, captain."

I ended the call. Dale looked up from the Emily Peters file. "Case is still open," I said. I excused myself and headed over to my room and returned in moments with my notepad. I sat at the desk with my notes as well as some of the case files scattered about. It was like a puzzle. All of the pieces were there, but they weren't fitting, not just yet.

Then it hit me like a ton of bricks—my "ah-ha!" moment.

"Oh my god. I just thought of something." I scrambled through my notebook. "Something Captain Freere said to us the day we met him."

I flipped through the pages and found the notes I took when we first sat down with the captain. When I jotted it down, I did so reflexively. I had no idea at the time why, since it seemed more an offhand comment from the captain than anything else. I found what I was looking for. "Yeah, he said it was like whoever committed the crimes was sitting in the bull pen with them, getting an update."

"So?"

"When I took Quinn her phone back the other day, I came across a guy who delivered supplies and did small repairs for Pollock PD. His name was Orrin Robicheaux. Talking to Freere just now, there was a Willie Robicheaux who did the same kind of work for them 'til about a year ago. You've seen their office. He would've been right on top of them."

"Having access to the Alexandria PD offices could explain how he stayed under the radar. He could've been aware of what they were looking for," Dale said.

"Exactly. Just like this Orrin character being in the Pollock office. You know, the whole time, I thought he was staring at Quinn, but he had to be looking at her board."

"There was a picture of Christa Miller on that board."

"Along with other clues, details, Quinn jotted down." A new thought streaked across my mind. "The app. She wrote about the thing-a-ma-jig... That's why we were stood up."

"Holy shit." That reflective glaze I'd grown accustomed to seeing rolled across Dale's face. "The timeline matches up. The father stopped working a year ago, and there weren't any new kidnappings in Alexandria. His son picked up, but he's partial to Pollock. If that's all true, we have a father and son serial kidnapping tandem."

"What's the age-old question about psychopaths? Are they born or bred?"

"That would also explain the different MOs. Two different people. Looks like there is more to the family business than just deliveries and repairs."

I nodded in agreement. It was beginning to make sense. Some of the puzzle pieces were beginning to fit together.

"One question"—Dale raised a finger—"if the Emily from the file is indeed the same Emily whom Quinn was supposed to meet, how do you suppose she got to the point where she decided to work with her kidnappers? How do you square that circle, Bobby?"

I wasn't sure about that just yet. I had to admit I had not gotten that far in my theory. I hunched my shoulders and said, "Not sure how she'd get there, but it's not unheard of." I paused a moment and then offered, "Stockholm syndrome, maybe?"

"Well, it happened to Patty Hearst," Dale replied.

There was still some conjecture here, but certainly enough circumstantial evidence that it warranted checking out. After all, circumstantial evidence had Curtis Wakefield in a prison hospital right now.

"Just the same—"

My cellphone rang. It was Ashe. I put the call on speaker. "Ashe? Go ahead."

"Have you two come across the name Orrin Robicheaux?"

CHAPTER 74

Pollock, Louisiana

THE SEARCH HAD lasted into the evening, but Ashe had finally found *the* Chevy pickup truck he was looking for.

Aside from his breakfast stop, and a well-deserved nap after, he'd been on the hunt since leaving Robert's motel room. That he was able to get comfortable, at his size, and get some solid sack time in the Traverse he had rented came as a pleasant surprise. Long hours on his previous *investigation*, with the late-night flight into Louisiana tacked onto the end, made a nap just what he'd needed. He awoke just after one in the afternoon, refreshed. The hunt resumed.

Tracking required patience. It's not a sprint; it's a marathon. It was just about 6:30 p.m. when that patience paid off. Ashe drove by the Look Elsewhere bar, and the dull, sun-beaten, red Chevy pickup truck parked in its lot caught his attention immediately. Ashe whipped his vehicle around making a quick U-turn and pulled into the lot. He parked three spaces down from the pickup. He got out of his rental and walked over for a closer inspection. It was just a matter of whether or not this vehicle fit the description given to him by Robert. At first glance, the pickup checked the first box on his list; it was an old beater—made up of more rust than metal now.

A look along the passenger side of the vehicle checked box number 2. There were three nickel-sized holes along the cab and two more dime-sized holes in the passenger door. No question, they were all bullet holes. Ashe examined them closely. He judged them to have been made by forty-five-caliber and nine-millimeter rounds. He moved to the rear of the vehicle. The license plate number began with "19." Box number 3 checked, Ashe was satisfied. There was no doubt in his mind that this was *the* truck he was looking for. It only stood to reason then the men he was looking for would be inside.

Ashe made his way inside. He stood in the entrance way and scanned the room. Two men in particular stuck out like a sore thumb among the sparse crowd. They were seated directly across from the bar. One had his right arm in a sling. His t-shirt sleeve was rolled up over his shoulder revealing bandages that ran down to his elbow. The other man with him, in between swigs of his Pabst Blue Ribbon, puffed away nervously on a cigarette. Ashe stole a glance at the pile of butts in the ashtray as he walked past them. It was unfiltered—jackpot.

He made his way over to the bar, positioning himself within earshot of the men's table. He ordered a shot of bourbon. Of the available options, he chose Jack Daniel's. Ashe knew that at this point, it would be a waiting game. They needed to make the next move. He didn't mind though. Ashe was used to being patient. The scenario reminded him of being on over watch in Fallujah. There were plenty of days his quadrant didn't see action, but he had to be patient so as not to give up his position. He had to wait until the action rolled his way. And when it did, he unleashed hell from his M40A6. He didn't have a sniper rifle this time, and Pollock, Louisiana, sure as hell wasn't Fallujah; but the waiting—that was pretty much the same. He'd have to wait them out—and then unleash hell.

Ashe was just happy that the wait was in a bar. In between making small talk with the bartender and knocking down several more shots of Jack Daniel's, he was able to pick up on bits and pieces of the conversation between the two men. At one point, they whispered and gesticulated wildly back and forth. He couldn't make out what they were talking about, but he had a pretty good idea. The rest of the time, when their voices were audible, there was a lot of inane banter between the two, sophomoric and idiotic to say the least. But Ashe continued to exercise patience.

It was another hour and a half or so before the twosome Ashe thought of as *Heckle and Jeckle,* decided to leave. Ashe squared up his tab and headed out after them. He sat in his rental and waited for the Chevy pickup to pull out of the lot. Ashe turned and reached in the backseat for his duffle bag. He rummaged inside and produced black latex gloves and slid them on. He also retrieved rubber slipovers for his shoes. His breathing had slowed and his muscles relaxed. He was at peace, just like anytime he found himself staring through the scope of his sniper rifle, lining up the perfect shot.

After a few minutes, he pulled out of the parking lot too. The two men were easy to keep in sight, even in the fading sunlight. They were in that raggedy red pickup, after all.

The bullet-riddled Chevy truck pulled into the driveway of Billy Coogan's home. His brother, Wade, groaned as the truck lurched to a hard stop and he bumped his injured arm against the passenger side door.

"Easy, goddammit!" Wade growled.

"Sorry, Wade," Billy said, his head swimming from all of the hooch he and his brother downed at the bar.

He ambled out of the vehicle, nearly falling over the hedges that lined the side of the driveway. "Whoops!" he hollered out. "Almost took a tumble, Wade. You see that?"

"Naw," Wade replied, equally inebriated. "I didn't see—"

A loud thud could be heard, and then Wade crumpled in a heap. Billy's vision was a little blurred, betraying him just a bit as he tried to focus. He was sure he could see someone, a black man no less, standing over on the other side of his truck where his brother had been.

CHAPTER 75

"*HEY!*" *BILLY REACHED* for the door of the truck.

"Uh-uh. Don't do that," Ashe said. He leveled the Glock used to knock Wade unconscious at Billy. Billy froze, his hands shot straight up in the air. "That's more like it," Ashe said. He nudged Wade with his foot. Wade moaned but otherwise didn't move. "Any weapons in the truck?" Ashe asked.

"Yeah. My rifle and a revolver." Again, Billy reached for the Chevy's door handle.

"Don't worry about those. I'll get those." Ashe opened the passenger side door. He checked the glove box and found the revolver, a .38 snub nose. The rifle was harnessed across the pickup's rear window. He removed that as well. "Whose house is this?"

"Mine," Billy answered, struggling to keep his feet.

"Anyone inside?"

"No. It's just me that lives here."

"Okay, tell you what. You come over and get your friend up. Carry him into the house."

"But he's heavy," Billy protested.

Ashe stepped back away from Wade's prone figure, with the revolver now levelled at Billy. "Well, be sure to lift with your legs then."

After Billy struggled for a few moments to get Wade up and across his shoulders in a fireman's carry, Ashe motioned for them to head into the house. Once on the porch, he fished the keys out from Billy's pocket and opened the door. Ashe entered behind the two men, setting the rifle down by the door. Inside, Billy nearly collapsed under Wade's weight and dropped him to the floor.

"Pick him up. Sit him on the sofa. You take a seat right next to him," Ashe instructed. "Who is he to you anyway?"

Billy complied, getting Wade onto the sofa, and then said, "My big brother. Look, mister. We ain't done nothin' to you. I mean we're cool... We're cool with the blacks, y'know. I got like two black friends."

Ashe held up a finger. "Stop *like* talking." He tucked away Robert's Glock.

"C'mon, man. Seriously now, what's this about?"

Ashe slapped Billy hard across the face. "I said stop talking. Now's the time you're going to want to listen. Nod yes, if you understand."

Billy nodded in the affirmative.

"Good. Last night, you and sleeping beauty over there took some potshots at two older gentlemen and a young lady. Before you tell me you didn't, just know the bullet holes in your truck and in his arm tell me different."

A deer-in-the-headlights look flashed across Billy's face. The rather large man—armed with *his* revolver—in front of him, was demanding an answer to a question he'd rather not answer, not at all. After a few moments of hesitation, he said, "Uh…yeah, mister. Yeah, that was us, but…those guys…"

"Again, stop talking and listen. I know somebody put you up to it. And this may be where you feel compelled to lie to me. You're thinking, out of some misplaced sense of loyalty, that you don't want to give that somebody up. But I assure you you don't want to lie to me."

"We just—"

Ashe struck Billy hard across the face with the revolver and then jabbed the barrel into Billy's throat, striking his Adam's apple. Billy doubled over, coughing, hacking, and struggling to catch his breath.

"Easy, now. Easy. Breathe in deep, nice and slow," Ashe said calmly. He helped Billy sit up straight. Billy coughed hard and swallowed a few more times before he was breathing normally again. He patted at his forehead and then looked at his hand. It was covered in blood.

Ashe leaned in close to Billy, nearly nose-to-nose, and said, "Let's try this again. Before you get to going on about how it was just you and your brother behind this, understand something—I've only been around you a few minutes, and I don't believe the two of you are capable of organizing a trip to the men's room without help. You follow what I'm saying to you? Now, this doesn't have to be any messier than it already is. I'm going to ask you, again. Who put you up to this?"

Wade began to stir.

"One moment," Ashe said and then stepped over to Wade. He whacked him across the head with the butt of the revolver. The impact made a harsh, thudding sound. Wade groaned but was out again. "Continue, please."

The cut on Billy's forehead continued to ooze crimson. His throat was raw and sore, but he forced the words out, lest he get hit again, "His name's Orrin... Orrin Robicheaux!"

"I'm going to need an address."

"Sure." No point in holding back now, Billy understood that. He put the name out there. He might as well be all in.

"Well, anytime now," Ashe said.

"Don't you want to get pen and paper or somethin'?"

"I don't need it. The address. Let's go."

"He's out at 1012 Glenmora Road. He'll be the only property once you get a quarter mile in off the main road. Lot of forest and creeks 'round there, gators too. You'll want to be careful, mister."

"Thanks. Your concern is touching. See now that wasn't so hard, was it?" Ashe stood up.

"What? You mean...that's it, mister?" Billy began to relax. Any problems he and his brother might have in the future with Orrin could wait. This guy was the problem now.

"That's it," Ashe said and made for the front door. He stopped in his tracks when he reached the door. "Oh, shit. You know what? There is one more thing."

"Yeah? What's that?"

Ashe picked up the rifle, turned back around, and said, "You almost killed two friends of mine. That was a mistake." He leveled the rifle at Billy and fired twice, hitting him square in the chest. Wade stirred at the sound of gunfire, just in time, it turned out, to receive two shots, one in the chest and one in the head, from Billy's .38. Ashe walked over to Billy's body, being mindful of his steps, and placed the revolver in Billy's hand. He sat the rifle on the couch next to Wade.

He took out his cellphone and dialed a number. "Raines? It's Ashe."

CHAPTER 76

Alexandria, Louisiana

HEARING THE NAME Orrin Robicheaux from Ashe made a chill come over me. This was it. It had to be. The pieces fit anyway.

Cecilia McAllister responded to an ad on that Trade whats-a-ma-hoozit; and it's our belief she got our girl, Emily, the same Emily who, according to mine and Dale's theory, was kidnapped by Poppa Robicheaux all those years ago—and now found herself helping his son. They drove her car back to Alexandria, which was why no one had seen Cecilia, not to mention no cameras in the area; and then they scooted back down to Pollock and no one's the wiser.

Unfortunately, for Curtis Wakefield, he picked the wrong time to act like an asshole and send those threatening texts. He walked into the perfect storm, and it got him imprisoned and waiting to stand trial. With any luck though, we'd just found his get-out-of-jail free card.

"Yes," I replied to Ashe's question. "I actually saw him just yesterday."

"Well, he's behind those two shooters from the other night," Ashe said.

"He realized we were on to him. Quinn's board at the police station is my best guess," Dale said.

"Makes sense to me too," Ashe was convinced. "I'm also thinking about paying him a visit. You got a pen? I'll give you the address if you want to join me."

"You're still in Pollock?" I asked.

"Yes, about twenty minutes away from this Robicheaux character, if GPS is to be believed."

"We're heading out from the motel, now." Dale and I raced out to the SUV. I hopped behind the wheel and fired it up and handed my phone to Dale.

"I'll get there ahead of you two and do a little recon," Ashe said and then disconnected the call.

I looked over at Dale. "He's not going to wait for us, you know."

"Yeah, I know. Let's get out there in a hurry, Bobby."

CHAPTER 77

SILAS CARRENS HAD bigger dreams in life than just being a landlord.

Those dreams had run the gamut from wanting to become a policeman as a child to a pro baseball player as a teen to a restaurateur in his early twenties. He wasn't good enough to be a pro ball player; point of fact, he was awful. His foray into the restaurant industry ended with him filing for bankruptcy and losing two properties. He seemed to lack the knack for that endeavor as well.

When the opportunity arose a little over two years ago, right after his fiftieth birthday, to buy the rundown apartment building that its previous owner had lost to foreclosure, he jumped at the chance. It was an opportunity, after all, an opportunity to try to climb back up the ladder from the gutter he'd allowed himself to get washed down into.

The building needed all manner of work done, from tuck-pointing to painting. The windows also needed replacing, and the roof was in dire need of repair. And that was just on the outside. Inside the floors creaked and cracked with each step. The stairways and banisters that ran up between floors seemed ready to give way at any moment and send anyone traipsing up those steps spiraling down to the basement, not to mention there was a rat and bug infestation that needed addressing as well.

He had faced facts some time ago—the building probably should be demolished and rebuilt from the ground up. Right now however, there's no money in the Silas Carrens budget for a project of that size and magnitude. For the time being, the Band-Aid repairs that he managed to accomplish on weekends would have to suffice.

The big break for him was that his tenants didn't complain much. They just weren't the report-the-landlord-to-the-city types. Besides, given that he didn't do credit or background checks on renters, that was sort of a trade-off. Anyway, what would be the point of complaining when you're paying only thirty-five bucks a week for what amounted to little more than a one bedroom closet? The folks he tended to rent to were walking into the situation with their eyes open. Most were people on the fringe who either were down on their luck or had something to hide and were just in need of a place to lay their heads.

That was why the call Silas had received from Captain John Freere of the Alexandria PD—asking if he'd added on any new renters in the past few days—

didn't strike him as odd. Cops were always looking at somebody around here anyway. Besides, he had no illusions about his tenants. Most of them had done *something* they probably shouldn't have. That's just the nature of this particular beast.

The description Freere gave fit his latest tenant to the proverbial "T": white, male, and possibly between the ages of thirty-eight and forty-four. What's more, he fit the other criteria that the police captain had inquired about. The new guy was from out of town, new to the Alexandria area, new to Louisiana in general as a matter of fact.

After telling Freere he could drop by, though said tenant was out at the moment, Silas Carrens decided he'd take a quick look-see into his newest renter's apartment and see if he couldn't sniff out just what had the captain's hackles up.

He had always wanted to be a cop since he was a little kid after all.

CHAPTER 78

THE CURRENT SHIFT could not end soon enough for Wayne Casey. If he wasn't stocking or restocking shelves, greeting the assholes at the door who came into this dump to shop, or picking up after their ill-behaved children who just had to touch every toy, or item that looked like a toy, and set it down some place that it didn't belong, he was stuck listening to his stupid co-workers bitch and moan about their respective lots in life.

Don't ever let me catch you sleeping out on the streets, he thought, *because I'd put an end to all of your complaining, all of your suffering.*

He checked his watch every five minutes, as if that would somehow make time go faster. It didn't. And Shelly from electronics didn't take the hint when he rolled his eyes into the back of his head. Neither did Angela from housewares. On and on they went about the deadbeat fathers of their children (multiple children) and who at this stupid store was sleeping with whom, as if he could possibly give a shit.

Wayne Casey escaped to the men's room for about forty-five minutes before Joe Ingle, the shift manager, came in and chased him out. It was a brief respite but well worth it, even with Joe yelling in his ear about how he wouldn't get paid for the time and that he needed to be more responsible—and professional.

Professional? I'd better not catch you out on the streets at night either, Joe Ingle, he thought. *You'd see just how professional I am. Oh yes! You'd see, alright. You'd be raising your stupid voice, but it would be to scream in pain!*

Wayne made his way back onto the floor and endured another two hours of brutally banal conversations. He checked his watch for probably the thousandth time; and, mercifully, it was finally checkout time. He nearly yelled *Hallelujah!* aloud. He raced for the door, bumping past Angela as she tried to say goodnight or something other. He wasn't quite sure. He didn't care either.

His emotions were high. He was amped up, revving like a high-toned engine. The other day, when the angel of death paid a visit to those three homeless sheep sleeping underneath the I-49 overpass, he thought maybe he'd been greedy. He changed his mind on that score, when, the following night, taking a single victim left him feeling empty—unfulfilled. While listening to Angela and Shelly, his mind wandered. *One was too few, and three, well…that did work out just fine the other night, didn't it? How about four this time?*

In between his co-workers inane rants, he gave serious thought to the number 4. It was an even number, after all—ambitious, yet dangerous. Wayne knew that the longer he was out on the streets, the odds of being spotted—identified, even—increased exponentially. But after a day like today, it seemed like that was just the type of thing he needed to do just to calm himself down, to make the world seem sane again.

Times like these made him wonder just how did he survive his prison sentence, not that there weren't days, many days, where he thought about taking the bedsheet exit. He gave that serious thought many times—although he found himself wondering more often about why he stepped outside of his wheelhouse anyway. That was why he'd gotten caught—credit card fraud, of all the stupid, stupid things. He had no experience with it. Sure, the money was nice—very nice, actually. Just the same, it just goes to show stick with what you're good at. What was it his dad would say? *Stay in your lane.* Check that, it's what his dad *used* to say. Just the same, that was exactly what he would do going forward—stay in his lane. He never had a goal to be the most prolific fraudster in world history; no, that was not the plan. He would leave that to the Jordan Belforts and Bernie Madoffs of the world.

What he was good at, plain and simple, was murder. Like many things in life, it only made sense to specialize, and only bad things could come from ignoring the gift that made you special. Aiming for another purpose when yours had already been laid out, he had learned, did not end well. But his masterpiece, his magnum opus, would end just as he wanted it to, with him given the glory and the attention he so richly deserved—when the time was right, that is. He didn't want to be discovered too soon. That just wouldn't do.

In the meantime, four—yes, four—sounded like the perfect number for this night. That's exactly what Azrael would be shooting for, so to speak.

After he arrived at his apartment, he quickly clambered up the stairs, being sure not to step where he realized the wood was weak. It would do no good to end up in the hospital himself. As he approached his door, he noticed it slightly ajar.

What's this? No way the law is on to me yet, he thought. *No way!*

He cautiously crept inside. There were no uniform-clad officers scattered about his place, rifling through the few belongings he had. There was a visitor however, that creep—*what's his name?*—the landlord. His back was to Wayne as he advanced on him. The landlord was bent over the vacuum sealer, poking and prodding at it, completely ignoring what was going on behind him. Azrael slowly unsheathed the karambit and then grabbed a handful of wispy thin hair, catching the sniveling, sneaky landlord unaware, and brought the curved blade up in a thrusting motion just below his ribs. While it wasn't his normal fare, the landlord might have already seen too much.

Apparently, there would be five victims tonight.

CHAPTER 79

Pollock, Louisiana

THE VOICES SEEMED to be calling—no, screaming—to Trina McNair, from some faraway place. There
were so many voices. She didn't know just how many
there were, but each of them seemed to be getting pro-
gressively louder.

She wasn't sure exactly how long they had been
shouting at her. She wasn't sure of much of anything
right now. Trina wasn't even sure of where she was at.
Nor was she sure why her head was throbbing the way it
was or why she couldn't move.

The dark haze that had enveloped her was beginning to clear. Bits and pieces of what had happened
were coming back to her. *The tennis bracelet!* She and
Kyle had left their place to meet up with some woman
about a—

Wait. Where is Kyle? She blinked furiously. Her vision began to clear, and the women's voices became clearer as well.

"Wake up! C'mon. Wake up!" the voices were saying in unison.

But...where's Kyle?

"Wake up! One of your arms," a woman yelled. "The restraint! It's loose! You can get out!"

Kyle? Oh my god! Kyle!

The memory came back hard and fast. It was of the big man—that awful big man who was waiting behind the house. *That no good skinny bitch sent us back there!* The big man, he had hit Kyle in the head with a shotgun. They fought and struggled. She had made her way back to the truck before realizing she didn't have the keys, and it was then when she heard that awful sound—the sound of the shotgun blast that killed Kyle!

That's right! That's where Kyle is. Kyle is dead!

"Come on, lady! Please!" one of the voices yelled again.

Next, Trina remembered the big man pulled her from the Blazer like a rag doll and then brought the butt of that shotgun down, violently, across her head. And now, here she was. She realized why it was that she couldn't move. She could see that she had been strapped to a gurney. But those voices, where were they coming from?

She turned, and to her right she saw the cages. There were eight cages set up in the corner of the cellar. There were five women, each in their own cage. She could only imagine, given her current circumstance, that she was meant to take up residency in one of the empty cages. Her heart began racing, pounding even harder than it already had been. The women looked to be in terrible shape. As bad as her experience had been since she arrived, one look at them told her theirs had been much, much worse. A pungent odor filled the air. There was no doubt in Trina's mind that scent was coming from the women in the cages.

"See if you can get your right arm free," one of the women said. She was in the cage closest to the gurney. "Can you hear me?"

Terrified, unsure of herself and still uncertain of what was going on, Trina managed to eke out a response, "Yes…yes, I can hear you."

"Your right arm," the woman said again, her voice calmer now that she seemed to have the latest arrival's attention. "See if you can get it loose. I don't think she pulled the restraint all the way. It looks like you might be able to wriggle free. Hurry! You don't want to be tied in when *he* gets in here."

"Yes! Hurry! You got to get out of here and get help for us!" another one of the women yelled out. The women in the cages carried a look of fear and desperation on their faces that was not lost on Trina. She had lost enough already, in her short time here. She didn't want to lose what they had as well.

She began struggling, squirming, and yanking away with her right arm. The woman in the first cage was right. While Trina couldn't move her left arm at all, she felt a lot of give on the right side. The restraint had not been buckled properly. As she worked furiously to free her arm, another memory burst into her consciousness. It was of the skinny, blond woman. She had literally dragged Trina down the stairs into the cellar. Trina vaguely remembered the woman struggling to get her up onto the gurney. The woman was flustered and out of breath while she strapped her in. After that, Trina's mind had gone dark again until she woke to the caged women screaming their heads off.

The restraint began to rub the skin on Trina's right wrist raw, but she could feel freedom was near. She continued working her wrist back and forth and up and down. The chaffing began to draw blood, but with another good yank, she was free!

Trina rolled as far as she could over on her side and undid the restraint on her left arm. She then quickly moved on to the restraints at her feet.

"Listen," the woman in the first cage said. "My name is Dahlia Movane. You run, now. Run! And please, please send back help! We have to get out of here!"

"My name is Jolie Everson," the second woman said. The remaining women took turns identifying themselves.

"Erica! Erica Graham! Please get help!"

"I'm Christa Miller," another shouted, her voice cracking.

"Ce...Ce...Cecilia. Cecilia McAllister," the last caged woman said. Her voice was low, almost a whisper. It was as if she had to force herself to speak up at all. All of the women carried their suffering on the face, but there was something about that last girl. It was her look that terrified Trina most of all.

Trina slid down off the gurney, and her knees buck-led, nearly giving way. It was quite possible that she was concussed, but at the same time, the fear that ran through her body right now made her weak—as if she couldn't feel her extremities at all. But she knew it was now or never. She summoned all of her courage and slowly made her way toward the stairs.

Taking one last look at the caged women, she said, "I will send back help. I promise."

And with that, Trina McNair ambled up the stairs and out of the cellar.

CHAPTER 80

TRINA MADE HER way out of the cellar and back around to the front of the house. Kyle's Blazer was gone. She cautiously crept around to the opposite side of the house. Kyle's body was gone as well.

She wasn't certain what time it was now or how long she had been out; but the sun had gone down, retired for the day, and it was dark out. That meant she was going to have to make her getaway in the thick, black veil of night, with only the moon to guide her. Under normal circumstances, the thought of traipsing around in this wooded area at night would have terrified her. But these weren't normal circumstances. No, sir, not by any stretch. They were anything but, and by the looks of the women caged in that cellar, terror was what she would experience if she didn't get a move on.

Just as she had steeled her nerves to move ahead...

"What are you doin'?" a voice spoke out from behind Trina. It was that woman's voice—the skinny, hard-faced blonde who lured her and Kyle out here in the first place. Trina wheeled around, shocked but angry at the same time. When she focused on Emily Robicheaux in the moonlight however, those feelings changed to complete fear.

Emily stood before her wielding a large butcher knife.

"What are you still doin' here?" Emily asked, looking around frantically and keeping her voice low. "I thought you'd be gone by now."

"What?" Trina was more than confused. Moments ago, this crazy woman had just lured her and her fiancé into a trap. Now, she was asking a question that made no sense at all. The knife Trina saw in her hand made the situation even more baffling.

Emily took a short, choppy step toward Trina. "You don't have much time. You hear? You don't have much time at all. You better get moving."

"What?" Trina staggered back. Every instinct told her to run, but her legs wouldn't cooperate. This had to be a trick. Of course it did. No way could she trust her. Could she?

Emily turned the knife handle up and held it out toward Trina. "Here. Take this. You'll need it. Take this and go. Get some help out here. You're the only hope for those women down there...all of us... You're our only hope."

Trina stared at the scrawny woman in utter disbelief. "What? You got my boyfriend killed. You know that?" Her voice was shaking.

"We don't have time for this right now," Emily said, the knife still outstretched toward Trina.

An unmistakable voice bellowed out from behind the women.

"What in the hell?" Orrin yelled.

Trina peered over Emily's shoulder. The sight of the big man lumbering toward them made her blood run cold. Her knees got weak. She thought to run, but she couldn't shake the feeling he'd catch her.

"Take this!" Emily said again, shoving the knife toward Trina. "And hit me!"

"What?"

"Hit me!" The look in Emily's eyes pierced the fog of fear that had held Trina in place. That look told her everything she needed to know. It wasn't her best punch. Lord knows it wasn't the way her dad had taught her to throw a punch; but Trina, after taking the knife from Emily's outstretched arm, reared back and delivered a solid blow. Emily dropped in a heap.

"Now, run!"

Still in a daze, Trina ran. Bolting past the fallen Emily, she ran toward the house. She bounded up the front steps and slammed the door shut behind her.

"No!" Emily whispered. "You're going the wrong way."

CHAPTER 81

ORRIN ROBICHEAUX STORMED over to Emily. With each step he took, Emily swore she felt the ground shake. She struggled to get to her feet. He was seething, frothing at the mouth almost.

"What the fuck was that shit? Huh? What the hell happened?" Orrin yelled.

"She...she...she got out somehow," Emily stammered out. Her eye and jaw throbbed and ached as she spoke. As soon as she gained her feet, Orrin reared back and slapped her hard on the other side of her head, dropping her in a heap again. Trina had landed a solid shot on her, but the blow from Orrin made her head swim. She saw stars.

"I give you the simplest, easy thing to do, the easiest. You hear me? And you can't even do that right!"

"I'm sorry, baby! I'm sorry! I don't know how she got out."

"Well, she got out, though, didn't she?"

"Yes."

"I'll deal with you later, and you better believe it's gonna hurt. I guess I just been too nice to you lately. You don't know how to obey no mo'!" Orrin yelled.

"I'm sorry! I swear, Orrin. I didn't mean—"

"Not as sorry as you gon' be, girl. I can promise you that. Now, c'mon inside. Let's put this bird in her cage."

Orrin and Emily made their way up the steps. Orrin turned the door knob—the door was locked.

"Dammit!" Orrin bellowed. "Well, girl? Where's your key?"

"Inside," Emily said meekly.

If looks could truly kill, Emily's life would've ended from the stare that Orrin laid on her. She might have even burst into flames. He shook his head from side to side in disappointment and then rammed one of his large shoulders into the door—it immediately gave way.

Orrin rushed in, his eyes darting around the living room. There was no sign of the woman. Emily slowly stepped inside behind him, trembling with fear. She could only hope the girl was smart enough to keep moving.

Orrin eyed their bedroom door. It was shut. The door was never shut.

"Listen here!" Orrin shouted. "You in the bedroom, you only making this worse on yourself. You hear me?"

There was no reply from the bedroom.

"Have it your way, girl. You want me to do you in there instead of in the cellar? That's fine by me, this time. Next time, we play with the knives. Get ready to hurt, whore!"

Orrin began massaging between his thighs, the thought of hurting Trina arousing him. Orrin slowly walked over. He put a hand on the doorknob and twisted it. He pushed the door open a crack.

The blade of the butcher knife flashed out, and Trina brought down in a slashing motion, scraping along Orrin's face. The cut wasn't deep, but the knife had drawn blood and caused the big man to bellow in pain. Trina quickly slammed the door shut again.

The bulge that had grown in Orrin's pants had immediately went as limp as an empty banana peel. "What the—? How come you didn't tell me she had a knife?" he yelled at Emily.

Emily cringed, expecting that Orrin would make her pay for that transgression by slapping her across the face again—or worse. Instead, he stormed past her and into the next room. He returned with his shotgun. His Beretta was tucked into the front of his overalls as well. He loaded five slugs into the shotgun and racked a load into the chamber.

"You hear that, girly? Huh? Knife-havin' whore! I got my shotgun out here. You want to play games, we gon' play then. You really only making this worse on yourself! You hear me?"

There was no answer.

"I'm comin' in now, whore! You swing that blade at me again, and I'll blow your ass clear across that room. You hear?"

Again, there was no answer from inside the bedroom.

Orrin kicked the door open; it nearly splintered into a thousand pieces along the frame from the force of his impact. He leveled the shotgun and stormed inside. The room was empty. The bedroom window was wide open.

"Goddammit! Goddammit!" Orrin raced out of the room past Emily. He nearly knocked her over. "This is all yo' fault, girl! This is on your head! You know what's comin' out tonight? The knife, that's right. You earned it. Now get out here and help me find her!"

Orrin ran out onto the porch. "I'm gonna find you, girl!" he yelled into the warm Louisiana night. Orrin stepped down off the porch and fired off a round from the shotgun. The deafening blast pierced the otherwise quiet night. "And that's what you gonna get when I do!"

Orrin and Emily set off into the night.

CHAPTER 82

RUN! RUN, GODDAMMIT! Run! Trina exhorted herself over and over again. She had felt something pop in her leg—it felt like a strain or a pulled muscle—when she hopped out of the bedroom window, but she had no time to worry about that now. Her legs were heavy, and her head somehow felt detached from her body, as if it couldn't communicate with her limbs, but over and over she shouted to herself, *Run!*

She wasn't even sure if she was running in the right direction. *What if you're running away from the main road? What then?* Kyle had driven them onto the property, and her eyes were fixed squarely on her cellphone on the ride up. Every sound she heard, the snap of a twig, the chirp of a cricket, sent waves of fear through her. He had to be right behind her by now—the big man who killed Kyle. He had to be gaining on her. Branches slapped her in the face, and twigs reached out for her legs as if to trip her, as she barreled ahead as fast as she could get her legs to move.

She heard the big man yelling out for her. He was angry. "I'm gonna find you, bitch!" she heard him holler several times. She couldn't tell if his voice was moving in closer or if she was actually putting distance between herself and him. Then she heard the report of the shotgun echoing all around her. Her heart leapt into her throat. Trina immediately thought of when Kyle was shot. She had to cover her mouth with both her hands in order not to let out a scream. *Don't you dare scream!*

Tears streamed down her face, and her vision blurred just a bit. She felt her feet leave solid earth for a split second, and her body spilled forward. She got her arms out just in time to avoid face planting on the ground. She landed with a thudding impact. She could feel the burns from skinned knees and elbows as the sweat that trickled down her body rolled over her new wounds. It was only then that she realized something else.

In her haste to open that bedroom window, she put the knife down on the bed, the knife that she used to slash the face of the big brute who killed Kyle. And that's where it remained. She'd left without it. She obviously wouldn't be able to surprise him again, but she'd certainly rather have it if...

No time to worry about that, now. Get up! You have to get up and keep moving!

Trina felt like she was trying to pull herself out of quicksand. She got her arms under her in the push-up position. Then she managed to get to her knees. The trees seemed to be closing in around her. And was that… *It's nothing! Get up. Come on, girl. Get up and run!*

With all the energy she could muster, Trina sprang to her feet and took off running again. She didn't hear the big man yelling and screaming after her anymore. *Is it because he's close? Is it because he already can see you?*

Trina did her best to put those thoughts, those fears, out of her mind. She just kept telling herself over and over again, *Run!*

CHAPTER 83

ASHE FOLLOWED THE GPS instructions to Glenmora Road. The headlights of the rental revealed that Glenmora, beyond a certain point, wasn't paved.

It was a rutted dirt road that led back into the woods and presumably to the Robicheaux property. It made sense to go on foot from this point, following the directions given—reluctantly—by the late Billy Coogan.

Ashe crept up the path, moving as quickly and quietly as he could, shielding himself in the high grass and along the tree line. He'd been walking up the road about ten minutes when his phone began vibrating like crazy. It was Dale Gamble.

"Ashe, we're just a few minutes out."

"You'll see my rental parked where the paved road ends. Hang there. I'll give you a call if I need—"

A loud bang pierced the night.

"What was that?" Dale asked.

"It's gunfire, most likely a shotgun," Ashe said.

"Ashe, stay put. We'll be there shortly."

"I don't think I can do that, Dale," Ashe said. "Pull up to my vehicle and sit tight. I'll be in touch." Ashe ended the call and continued up the path. He could vaguely make out that someone was shouting. He wasn't quite clear on what was being said, but it was definitely a male voice that he heard. He also heard…panting— panting and quick, padding footsteps. Someone was running directly toward him.

Ashe crouched down along the side of the road, partially shielding himself in the shrubbery. He listened as the footsteps grew closer. They quickened in their pace. Then as the speeding target approached, he lunged forward from his hiding spot and grabbed…*her!*

Trina McNair attempted to scream. She flailed wildly. *It had to be him! He was ahead of you all along!*

"Shhh!" Ashe said as he held his hand over her mouth. He made sure the young woman looked him in the face. "Calm down. I'm going to remove my hand from your mouth. Don't scream."

"Help me! You've got to help me!" The woman was frantic. She was covered in sweat. Her heart was pounding hard in her chest. Ashe could feel each beat.

"What's going on?"

"My name…my name is Trina. My fiancé…he's dead! There's a man back there… He's…he's trying to kill me!"

"Okay, okay. Listen. Go straight down this path, and I mean straight. When you get to bottom of it, you'll see a vehicle. It's mine. Get in. Two older gentlemen will be along shortly. They're associates of mine."

"Are you the police?"

"Not exactly." Ashe pulled out his cellphone and called Dale. "Listen. I'm approaching the residence. I just found a young woman running through the woods. She says someone is trying to kill her. I'm sending her down the trail. She'll meet you at my car. Keep her safe."

"You got it, big guy. We're just a few minutes out."

"And…and…there's other…women, other women being held in the cellar," Trina managed. She seemed on the verge of collapse. "You have to help them!"

"Did you hear that?" Ashe asked Dale.

"Yes, I did."

"This is the place. Time to call in the cavalry."

CHAPTER 84

ASHE CONTINUED UP the trail. The shouting he'd heard earlier had faded. The closer he got to the house, the further away the voice got. The shouter was headed in the opposite direction than where Trina had run. That was good.

Ashe drew the Glock as he approached the house. He could see the shutter doors leading to the cellar on the left side of the home, just as Trina had described. The doors were already opened. A dim light emanated from the cellar, and as he got closer, a pungent smell wafted up and out into the Louisiana night air. It hung thick.

Ashe made his way inside. The moment he became visible, the caged women went into a frenzy. Shouts of "Mister! Get us out of here!" and "Please! Help us, please!" came from the cages.

"Shhh!" he cautioned. "I'm going to get you out of there."

Ashe looked around. There were knives, hammers, screwdrivers, leather belts, and chains, however, no bolt cutters. He didn't see a hacksaw around either.

"Come on, mister! What are you waiting for? That lunatic will be back anytime now!"

They had a point. By the time he found the perfect tool, there'd possibly be more than just the locks on the cages to deal with. He needed to get the women out of those cages fast and down the path toward Robert, Dale, and the Pollock PD.

There's no point in playing it quiet now.

"Step back, all of you. Get as far back in the cages as you can." As he approached the cages, getting a better look at the women brought a pained look to Ashe's face. He could see they had been tortured. He didn't have to be told they had been raped too. It was obvious to him that they had been made to suffer God knew what indignities during their captivity. The deplorable conditions that they were forced to live in made his blood boil.

He raised the Glock 43 and, one by one, shot holes in the locks along the left corner, snapping the locking mechanism in each. He snatched each cage door open. One by one he assisted the women out, some needing more help than others, and then said, "All of you, with me. Now!"

The women began racing up the stairs; but one, the one Ashe recognized, made a beeline for the workbench.

"What are you doing?" Ashe asked.

"This!" Cecilia McAllister let out a guttural cry as she picked up a hammer from the workbench and brought it crashing down, violently, repeatedly, on the record player sending shards of vinyl and bits of the machine flying across the room. The Chordettes would haunt the cellar no more.

"Enough." Ashe grabbed her and took the hammer from her hands. "Let's go."

Ashe escorted the women out of the cellar, pistol in hand and at the ready. He led them over to the dirt trail. "Listen to me. Go straight down this road. In less than a quarter mile, you'll run into friends of mine; and with any luck, the police will be there too."

"Why aren't you coming with us?" Cecilia McAllister still had fear in her voice as she asked the question. She didn't want to be left alone, not with the monster, Orrin Robicheaux, still around.

"I'm going to have a look around, make sure there aren't any other women being kept here."

"What about Orrin?"

"The police are coming," Ashe said. "Now stick together. Get on up the trail. Go!"

Ashe watched the women scurry up the trail until they melted away into the darkness of night.

He then headed back into the cellar to wait.

CHAPTER 85

ORRIN ROBICHEAUX HAD grown weary. Though still highly agitated about Trina McNair's escape, he had to face the fact that she obviously didn't head in the direction he'd chosen.

With the head start she had, she could've easily made it to the main road by now—made it to one of his neighbors, even. They could be calling the cops at this very moment as he stood outside in the dark, dicking around in this fruitless search.

This was no good. No, sir, no good at all. A major mistake had been made. His mind began to race. *What would Daddy do? How would he handle this? Actually, Daddy never would've left Emily in charge of that new piece of pussy. That's where Daddy wouldn't have made the mistake.* He turned and looked at Emily, her silhouette framed by the moonlight. He gave serious thought to killing her right then and there. A major mistake had been made, after all. And it was made by her.

His emotions raged inside of him. There might not be any way to recover from this. This might be the end. If that whore made it to the cops, it's definitely the end for this group of girls. It would be time to do for them what he'd done for his father's girls after the stroke. Just like a fire sale, *everything must go!* All of his dad's hard work, all of the planning, the time spent being as careful and cautious as possible, had been ruined in less than an hour.

Pure carelessness—that was the problem with Emily. She was just too goddamned careless. Orrin thought about the scar that would inevitably be left behind on his face from the knife slash he received earlier—that was Emily's fault too. She'd really gone and made a mess of things. He stared at her again. More and more it made sense to just get rid of her. Yes, that's it. He would get rid of Emily. She's nothing more than a liability these days. First, bringing that couple out to their home, that was a no-no. Then to add insult to injury, somehow, she let the woman escape.

His mind was made up.

After putting a bullet in the back of Emily's head, yeah, right in the sweet spot, the plan would be to hop in the van and take a ride around the area. Maybe that tramp who ran off got lost in the woods. It's highly possible, after all. She's not from around here, and roaming around in the dark of night, it's easy to get turned around. There just might be a way to salvage this whole thing after all. That's the hope. Orrin was not near ready to give up his playthings in the cellar.

Orrin and Emily arrived back at the house and headed over for the cellar. Emily, who'd been walking behind Orrin the entire time during the search, was more than a little apprehensive when Orrin stepped aside and said, "After you."

"Orrin… I'm… I'm sorry," Emily stammered out.

"Go on. Get on in there!" he said.

Emily made her way past him, and he reared back and struck her in the back of the head with the butt of the shotgun. Emily whipsawed ahead and fell face first, unconscious, to the cellar floor.

Orrin slowly made his way down into the cellar. The only thing left to decide now, big decision number 1 on the night, was whether to send Emily packing with the Beretta or the shotgun. The big man's eyes grew wide when he reached the bottom of the stairs and got a glimpse of the back of the cellar. All of the cages that housed his playthings sat *empty* now. The only person left in the cellar was a tall, large, black man. And Orrin noticed *that nigger was pointing a pistol.*

"You're going to want to put the shotgun down, Orrin," the large black man said.

Orrin grinned and asked, "An' jus' who the hell are you?"

CHAPTER 86

"*IT'S NOT REALLY* important who I am," Ashe said. "What's important, Orrin, is that you put that gun down."

Orrin grinned and then said, "An' what if I don't?"

"I'll put two in your chest and one in your head before you get that shotgun pointed in my direction," Ashe calmly explained.

"Well, sure then. Easy, mister. No need to be all hostile." Orrin still had that broad grin across his face. He set the shotgun down on the floor.

Ashe gestured at the Beretta. "And the pistol you got tucked away there. Slow and easy."

"Oh yeah. This." Orrin slowly removed his trusty Beretta pistol that he had tucked in his overalls. He sat it on the floor, next to the shotgun. "Didn't know you saw that. Now, you mind tellin' me, fella, what you're doin' on my property? See I don't allow niggers on my property, y'know, not the bucks, anyway." Orrin continued to grin.

Ashe said nothing.

"Didn't you hear what I called you, boy? I said darkies ain't allowed on my property. Now, what you think about that?"

"You think I give a damn about anything you said, hillbilly? For all I know, you're up to no good out here in the middle of nowhere because Daddy diddled you as a little boy."

"Don't you talk about my daddy!" Orrin yelled. That self-satisfied grin had disappeared from his face. He took a half step toward Ashe, but then glanced down at the Glock pointed at his chest and stopped cold.

"Struck a nerve with that one, huh?" Ashe chuckled.

"You still ain't told me what you doin' on my property," Orrin continued, hands in the air.

"Right now, I'm giving you an opportunity, just one chance and I do mean *one* chance to surrender. Turn yourself in."

"Well, ain't that just sweet of you, whoever you are? But I decline! Now, where are my girls?"

"They're gone, Orrin. I don't think you were treating them any better than that one on the floor there, so I sent them on their way."

"Those are my girls! I treat them how I want! I do what I want! You understand that?"

"Oh yeah. I understand. I understand that you're the guy who likes to kidnap and rape women. That sound about right?"

"That ain't all I was doin' to them, friend."

"Really?"

"You put your gun down, and maybe you'll get to find out firsthand." Orrin lowered his hands down to his sides and balled them up into fists.

Ashe dropped the clip from the Glock and ejected the chambered round and then said, "I was hoping you'd say something like that."

Orrin charged, moving his massive frame at full speed toward Ashe. Ashe calmly sidestepped and, in a roundhouse motion, brought the empty pistol crashing against the back of Orrin's head. Robicheaux crashed hard to the cellar floor. He turned and looked up at Ashe, enraged; he hopped back to his feet.

Orrin charged again, this time finding himself struck by Ashe's fists—first a left, followed by a lightning-fast right. He was staggered momentarily, but managed to rear back and strike Ashe across the face with a meaty right hand. The two men exchanged thunderous blows back and forth.

Ashe parried the larger Orrin Robicheaux's next attempt at a punch and then, with his left hand, grabbed a firm hold of Orrin's right arm. With his own right hand, he whipped a firm grasp around the back of Orrin's neck and shoulder and, in the same motion, pulled the big man forward ramming his knee up into Orrin's midsection. The force of the blow knocked the wind from Orrin and collapsed him in a heap to his knees.

"Need a minute?" Ashe asked. He stood over the fallen big man. "Take your time. Catch your breath."

Orrin staggered to his feet. He was still gasping for air when Ashe struck him again, first with a straight left-hand punch that landed directly on the bridge of his nose, breaking it and sending blood spraying from his nostrils. The follow-up shot was a palm thrust to the throat that landed with a nasty crunching sound. Orrin collapsed in a heap again, struggling to catch a breath.

"Come on. Where's the tough guy? Where's the guy who likes to beat and rape women, the guy who sends a couple of assholes to shoot at two old men? That's who I'm here for," Ashe taunted his fallen foe. "You know your friend, Billy? I think that's his name. Who gives a shit, right? Well, before I put two bullets in him, I overheard him and his brother talking about you. I mean it's like they were terrified of you, like you're some badass boogeyman type. But you know what, hillbilly? You haven't shown me shit."

Orrin spat blood and then sucked in as much air as he could, trying to catch his breath. He shakily made it back to his knees. "Jus…just…just a minute, boy. I'm… gonna…fuck you up," he yammered.

"Actually, we're probably going to have company soon. I think we're out of time. I do have a question, though. You ever choke one of your victims to death? Have them gasping for air, trying to cling to life? You ever wonder what that felt like?" A wave of what could only be described as hate raged through Ashe. Thinking of all evil Orrin had visited upon those women drove his blood to a boil. *He had the chance to surrender—to turn himself in. He should've taken it.*

Ashe maneuvered behind the kneeling big man and got his right arm firmly cinched under Orrin's chin and around his neck. He brought his left arm behind Orrin's head and pushed it forward.

Ashe then began to squeeze.

CHAPTER 87

MINUTES LATER, EMILY awoke. She could still feel the throbbing in her head and taste the fresh blood that was pouring from her nose and mouth after her fall.

She touched her hand to the back of her head. It was wet as well. She didn't have to look, but she did anyway and confirmed that her head was bleeding. The last thing she remembered was Orrin being angry with her. She figured he was angry enough to kill her; and for a moment, when she first opened her eyes, she thought he had and that she was waking up in hell. But it was the cellar on the Robicheaux property, sure enough, which just might be the same place.

Emily staggered to her feet, leaning against the gurney (that goddamn gurney) for support, half-expecting to be hit again. When the hit didn't come, she allowed herself to look around. Orrin was gone. Not only that, she noticed that—and for a moment felt a burst of sheer panic—the women (*Orrin's playthings*) were gone also. Emily's mind raced: *How long was I out? Where's Orrin? Where's the women? Did he give them what he and his dad had called a proper send-off? Is he coming back to kill me?*

That last question, the all-important question of Emily's survival, kicked her into high gear. She had no idea if that Trina actually escaped. And if she did, would she just be glad that she got out alive, or would she actually send help? If life had shown her one thing, people wouldn't do the right thing, unless it's the right thing for them.

Regardless, she had to leave. If Orrin was on some murderous rampage, if he killed those women in the cages, then it was a safe bet that her bony ass was next. She didn't know where she was going or, short of walking, how she'd get there; but she was leaving right now, with just the dingy clothes on her back and blood smeared across her face. She turned to make her way to the steps. When she looked up, the sight before her caused her to stagger backward and fall down again.

A large, menacing figure stood at the top of the steps. It wasn't Orrin, though. No, this was some fella she'd never seen before. She trembled as the large black man before her made his way down the cellar steps. She trembled even more when he spoke and said, "Hang on there, little lady. You and me are going to have us a chat. I want to know about everything that went on here. And I mean everything."

"You have no idea...you have no idea, what I've been through," Emily managed.

"Enlighten me."

"What about—"

"Orrin? Don't worry about him. It's just me and you now."

"Well, then, mister... I'll tell you whatever you want to know."

CHAPTER 88

WE HAD ARRIVED at the location, Ashe's parked vehicle anyway, shortly after he and Dale had gotten off the phone. A call into Captain Freere along the way, who checked public records for us, revealed that William Robicheaux had a wife die roughly eight years ago. That could've been his stressor, his inciting incident.

William Robicheaux's stroke was just over a year ago which most likely would've set off the junior Robicheaux. This *was* it! We were right. The elation that I'd felt from that paled in comparison to the joy I felt when the young woman, Trina McNair, whom we found hiding out in Ashe's rental told us one of the girls she saw locked in the cages up at the Robicheaux place was named Cecilia and that she was alive, along with the missing women whom Dakota Quinn was looking for.

I put in a call to Quinn and gave her the address. It was time to wrap this up. Not long after ending that call, a stream of five women came running up the dirt trail, screaming for help. Dale and I directed them over to our vehicle. I recognized Christa Miller from the photo that Quinn had. And I immediately recognized, "Cecilia?"

"Yes...yes, I'm Cecilia." Frightened and looking worse for wear, she nearly collapsed in my arms as I helped her into the truck. Unlike the bright, smiling visage on the "Have You Seen Me" flyers her parents and the citizens of Alexandria were passing out and posting in storefront windows, this girl looked emaciated, a shadow of her former self.

"My name is Robert Raines. I'm a private investigator. Your family sent me looking for you. They're going to be so happy to get you back home."

Cecilia burst into tears. The other women followed, each crying one by one in a chain reaction. I could only imagine their ordeal. Even in the dark of night, I could see scars and bruising on their scantily clad bodies. They obviously weren't kept well. They looked gaunt and dehydrated and probably hadn't properly bathed since their disappearance. Tears began welling up in my eyes as well. I looked over at Dale. It was an attempt to pull myself together more than anything else.

"This was good work, Bobby," he said.

This time, I didn't mind him calling me Bobby. I didn't mind at all. "Yes, it was, buddy."

"Can you take me home?" Cecilia asked. Tears were still streaming down her face, but the heavy, stuttered sobbing had stopped.

"We're going to get you home as soon as possible, all of you."

We could hear sirens blaring in the background. Dakota Quinn was first on scene from the Pollock PD. I studied the look on her face when she got an eyeful of the women huddled together in our vehicle. I thought she might break down and bawl right along with them. Of course, if she did, there wouldn't have been anything stopping me either.

I just thought, we needed to be an anchor for these women. We had to stay solid, so that they knew, in this moment at least, they were alright now. They were safe. Two more squad cars pulled up shortly after Quinn had arrived. When her fellow officers Guilliame and Faraday arrived on scene and got a look at the tortured, beleaguered women huddled together in my SUV, their jaws dropped as well.

"A lot of this is the result of Quinn's work on these cases," I said, being sure that they understood my statement directly implied that they did nothing. And "they" included their dickhead boss. Maybe it's not the best timing on my part, but truth was there's a lot that would've been missed if Quinn wasn't already working those disappearances the way she did, so I wanted her to get that credit. She'd earned it.

The Pollock PD officers pulled out their long guns and prepared to make their way up the road to confront the women's captor. They were taking over tactical command, and rightfully so. This was their scene. A familiar figure cut through the darkness just as they'd finalized plans. It was Ashe.

"It's okay. He's with us," I said.

"About a quarter mile up, you'll find the home of Orrin Robicheaux—you won't find him though. He managed to slip away in the darkness. Headed off into the marsh I suppose. Emily Peters is there though, along with one Willie Robicheaux. Emily can fill you in on all the details, but you're going to want to reach out to the Alexandria PD. It appears those eight women abducted from Alexandria—well, from what she told me, there's a mass grave a few hundred yards from the property. She also told me that there's more than eight bodies."

Ashe filled us in on the details recounted to him by Emily Robicheaux—Peters, actually—how, when she was just thirteen years old, she herself had been abducted by Willie Robicheaux as a plaything for his son. She told how she not only was raped and tortured herself by Orrin but was at times forced to watch as Willie did his thing to the women whom he had kidnapped from Alexandria, how, when women tried to escape or if they fought back, they were given what the Robicheaux men called a *proper send-off* and someone new was grabbed to take their place.

She told Ashe that when the elder Robicheaux had a stroke, Orrin killed those women who were caged at the time, burying them on the property. He then put her to work luring in other women in order for him to keep his father's sick tradition alive. She said she didn't have a choice. She had to help. Ashe left her crying in the cellar. He told the officers that the crippled William Robicheaux was in his bed in the house. He also mentioned that any bruising they found on the man was there when he arrived.

The Pollock officers advanced on the house to collect Emily and Willie, while the three of us waited on the ambulances that were coming to take the victims to the hospital for exams before the eventual reunions they'd each have with family and friends.

After the officers were out of earshot, I pulled Ashe and Dale to the side. "Ashe?"

"Yeah?"

"What really happened to Orrin Robicheaux?"

"I offered him a chance to surrender, to turn himself in," Ashe said matter-of-factly. "He declined."

"And?" Dale asked.

"If gators don't make a meal of him and anyone should happen to find his body out in the marsh, it will appear he died from a self-inflicted gunshot wound to the head, using a Beretta nine-millimeter."

Ashe handed me my Glock back. "And who's to say he didn't?" I said.

"Exactly," Ashe said. "Who's to say he didn't."

I had just tucked away the Glock 43 returned to me by Ashe when my cellphone began buzzing. I recognized the number immediately. It was Captain John Freere of the Alexandria PD. "Captain, great news! We found her!"

Freere's voice was full of shock, "The McAllister girl?"

"Yes. We found her. She's alive!"

"That's fantastic."

"It was the Robicheauxs, captain, the father and the son. They were involved in multiple abductions and murders, including the ones from your cold case files. It's a real mess, captain."

"My god."

"There's still a lot to sort out here, but based on what we know so far, it's not good news."

There was a long pause from the captain. "I'll get someone out there, hook up with their office, and we'll get to sorting out what needs sorting out. I'll get Ozzie in the loop too. We've got an innocent man to set free."

"Indeed you do."

"Say," Freere continued, "the reason I called you is I was wondering if I could ask a favor."

"Anything, captain. You name it."

"One of the landlords called me back, guy by the name of Silas. He runs a little fleabag apartment complex, thinks he has someone who matches the description I put out."

"Really? That's incredible."

"Thing is my officers are spread pretty thin at the moment, running down a few other leads. I'm about to take a ride out there. Thought you might want to join me. Maybe give me your read on the fella after I sit down and talk to him, if I can pull you away, that is."

I was elated beyond words. It was the first tangible lead I'd ever had on SLK. There was no question I was rolling. Any homicide detective who said they're not excited about times like these was a liar. We had a potential suspect and we're coming for him, and he didn't know it. I loved it.

"Pollock PD is on site," I said. "My team can finish up with them. Text me the address, captain. I'll meet you there."

CHAPTER 89

Alexandria, Louisiana

BY THE TIME I parked the Tahoe out in front of the apartment complex, Captain Freere was already standing outside of his vehicle. He'd only been waiting on me for a few minutes. There's nothing like having a lead foot.

"I tried calling Silas twice in the last twenty minutes," Freere said. "I haven't been able to get hold of him since I told him I'd be stopping by."

"What about the tenant? The new guy, is he around?"

"He wasn't when I talked to Silas earlier. I got a name, probably an alias. Apartment is on the third floor. I was just about to go inside and check it out. Care to join me?"

"Lead the way."

I followed Freere into the rickety old apartment building. This definitely would fit the bill, based on my profile. Our suspect would be looking for an inconspicuous place to lie low. If everyone you're surrounded by carried the appearance of lying low themselves, you would look less suspicious.

"What's your play?" I asked as we moved inside.

"I'll just say we're canvassing the neighborhood for information on a hit-and-run from the other day. I'll try to get some general information out of him. You listen in. Tell me what you think."

"Done."

We stopped by the manager's office first, looking for Silas Carrens. We didn't get a response when we knocked on the door. Captain Freere eyed the staircase. I nodded in agreement. We made our way up the stairs to the third floor. I found myself praying with every step that the wood didn't give way and collapse. That would end this trip on a really bad note, really fast. We got a win, finding Cecilia, worse for wear, but alive. Saving those other women was an unexpected bonus. Ending the reign of terror of the Robicheauxs was game, set and match. At this point, I was just hoping to give Captain Freere any additional insight I could to help him catch SLK before we headed back to Chicago—not plummet twenty feet or so into a concrete basement.

There were three apartments to a floor. We reached the third landing, and Freere pointed to the right, "Should be this one, here."

We approached the door and heard shuffling sounds as we got closer. Someone's home. That's for sure.

Freere knocked. The shuffling quickly stopped, and the apartment went silent. He waited a few moments before knocking again.

"Alexandria police! Open up please," he announced.

We could hear the sounds of a safety chain being unlatched before the door slowly creaked open. Staring at us from the other side was white male. He stood about six one or so. He was rather thin but looked fit and strong just the same. There was a slight amount of gray in the stubble that grew on his face. I put his age around forty-four or forty-five. His eyes darted back and forth from Freere to me and back. He seemed a little nervous. He didn't open the door completely. He held it open just enough that we could get a partial view of him, but none of the apartment.

"I didn't call the police," the man said abruptly.

"No, you didn't," Freere replied. "We're canvassing the area, talking to all of the neighbors. There was a hit-and-run accident a few nights ago. We're trying to find any witnesses, get as much information as we can."

"Oh," the wiry man said. He seemed to calm down a little. "Well, I didn't see anything. I work pretty late."

"Working man. I understand that," Freere replied in a calm and friendly tone. Getting the man to settle down would be the key to get him talking, hopefully.

"Whereabouts?" I added over Freere's shoulder.

"And you are?" the man asked.

"He's one of my detectives," Freere responded.

"Detectives?" the man seemed jumpy again.

"Hit-and-runs are serious," I offered, looking to keep the man calm. He hadn't relaxed his grip on the door, and he certainly hadn't opened it any further. He looked as if he were ready to slam it shut at any moment.

"I s'pose they are," he said. "I work at Walmart."

Freere took out a little notepad and pen. "I'm sorry. I didn't get your name."

"Well, what do you need to know that for, officer?" the nervous tenor in the man's voice increased. His eyes were doing that thing again, darting back and forth between me and Freere.

"Just for my report," Freere countered. "I have to make a note of anyone I've spoken to." That answer seemed to calm the squirrely man once more.

"Wayne. Wayne Casey," the man said.

"Okay then, Mr. Casey, just a few more questions and we'll be out of your hair," Freere had begun before we heard a muffled thump coming from inside the apartment.

Mr. Casey turned his head back inside the apartment, then turned back to us, and blurted out, "Now wait a minute. When did this accident take place?"

"It would've been last week, Tuesday," Freere responded.

"Well, that settles that. I just got in town three days ago. Nothing I can help you with. Now I've got things to do, if you'll excuse me." Wayne Casey abruptly slammed his door shut. We could hear the safety latch being drawn across its track.

We exchanged a glance. "He seem a little jumpy to you?" Freere asked.

"Just a little," I said.

"Just arrived in town. It's thin, but he may fit the profile. He'll bear watching. I'll run the name Wayne Casey, see what pops. I guess we'll have to wait and see what his next move is."

I was set to offer an opinion, but something on the door that was just slammed in our faces caught my eye. I couldn't believe what I was seeing.

"I don't think you need to wait, captain." I pointed to the door. There, staring back at us, were two bright-red fingerprints.

"Is that—"

"Yes, it is," I replied. "That's blood."

Freere drew his pistol.

"Think maybe he's cutting up a chicken or some steak?" I said.

"Well, if he is, then I owe him an apology—and a new door."

I nodded and pulled out my SIG. Captain Freere reared back and kicked in the fragile door. The wood around the frame splintered and cracked, and the door went down in a heap. He cautiously stepped inside. I followed.

CHAPTER 90

COPS! THERE ARE fucking cops at the door! Wayne Elliot Casey had panicked—a direct contrast to the calm and cool demeanor he displayed when on the prowl as Azrael.

Slamming the door in their faces as he did gave it away. *Face it, bubba.* He simply wasn't expecting this visit, not yet, anyway. It was too soon, and he just wasn't prepared. He looked over at the body of his landlord which had slumped to the floor from its upright position against the refrigerator. The sound made when that sleazy, snooping douche bag tipped over had spooked him. He lost his shit at the door, and he saw it on their faces—the cops—they knew something wasn't quite right. He wouldn't have much time at all. He needed to move.

He kicked the motionless body of Silas Carrens as he maneuvered over to the kitchen counter to retrieve his karambit. When he reached for the curved blade, only then did he notice the magnitude of the mistake he had made. Of all the ridiculous errors he could possibly make, this was not only the silliest but the most sloppy and amateurish. This was worse than his decision to get involved in that fraud scheme down in Florida—much worse.

This cemented his legacy, not as a killing machine worthy of the nickname the night stalker, but as a bungler, akin to a fat, stumbling drunk tripping over his own feet. Self-doubt washed over him in a wave that tightened his stomach in knots. He hadn't felt this insecure, or this level of anxiety, since his first kill over twenty plus years ago.

He stared down at the blood smeared on his hands in disbelief.

It was his first test, and instead of having nerves of steel, he wilted. If he'd taken his time, composing himself, before rushing to the door, no way this would happen. His dream was in jeopardy, and he had no one to blame but himself. If only—

His front door caved in with a crash. The sound roused him from his pity party. This was it. The time for sniveling was over. He'd always known that his reign wouldn't last forever. But there was more to do, so much more. And that was all ruined now. *The wolves are at the door!* If this was going to be the end, it would be an end worthy of Azrael. There was nothing more Wayne Elliot Casey could do here. There was only the angel of death.

CHAPTER 91

CAPTAIN FREERE HAD moved in ahead of me. Guns drawn and leveled, we walked slowly down a blind hallway that opened to the left and right. We reached the end of the hall; in a flash, I could see a blade swing down, catching Freere across the wrist. He dropped his gun. Blood squirted from the wound. The cut had been deep. He instinctively grabbed the injured wrist with his free hand and found himself in the clutches of the madman Wayne Casey, who quickly put that blade up to the captain's throat and shielded himself from me using the captain's body.

"Whoa! Whoa! Easy now, Mr. Casey," I called out and raised my SIG Sauer.

"No! You take it easy, or I cut a smile in this motherfucker's neck!" He cinched the blade tighter against Freere's skin. Blood continued to flow freely from Freere's wrist. It began pooling on the floor.

Out of the corner of my eye, I caught a glimpse of a man lying motionless on the kitchen floor. He didn't appear to be indigent.

"Not your normal target. What's that about?" I asked, hoping to engage him and get him to concentrate on me instead of Captain Freere.

"Caught him snooping… Wait. What do you know about my normal targets? Who are you?"

"I'm a retired detective from Chicago. And I know you're the street life killer."

"Street life… God! I hate that fucking name. I am Azrael, the angel of death!"

The tone in his voice was different than before. He didn't seem to be the nervous, deer-in-the-headlights creep who had answered the door previously. He was more confident, now.

"Either way, I know you prey upon the homeless."

"What are you doing here, anyway?" he asked and then cinched up on his hold of Freere. "Chicago? Are you following me, after all this time?"

"No, I wasn't. As much as it pains me to say it, our being here at the same time is just a coincidence, but I did work your case back then."

"Fine job you did too, pops. Yes, I prey on the homeless, because no one gives a shit about the homeless! People care more about stray cats and dogs than they do about *stray* humans. Ask around. You think the homeless problem is even in the top five things people think are wrong with society? I'd bet it's not even in the top twenty. You know why? Because they don't belong to anyone! They're a disposable waste of human life!" He was becoming more agitated.

"That's where you're wrong, Mr. Casey. I care," I said, keeping my voice level like Dale would, trying to talk him down.

"Bullshit! Nobody cared when *my* family was homeless!" he railed. "Where was all the care and concern when my mother and father got addicted to heroin? Nobody cared when they shot up or smoked away everything we owned. Where was the care as we spent cold winter nights on the streets? Do you know what that's like for a child?"

"I'm sorry to hear that your family had it rough, Mr. Casey. But that doesn't excuse what you've done. Where are your parents now? What would they think of all this?"

"Oh, well, don't feel sorry for them, Mr. Retired Detective. When they proved to me that all they cared about was getting their next fix and were willing to neglect their only child and any other responsibility in life, well, I did for them what the drugs were already doing. Only I did it quicker. I made a bit of a mess, though. Cut off my mom's pinkie finger by accident. But I kept it. It was a nice reminder."

"And you've been keeping fingers ever since," I said.

"That's right, fat man. I kept them all, from Chicago to Florida to Louisiana! And when I'm done killing this cop…and you… I'm going to add those to my collection too!"

Freere tried to shake free, but Wayne had a good grip on him and slid that blade across his throat a little, drawing a trickle of blood. "Keep still, damn you!" he shouted.

"Easy, captain. I've got you." I made eye contact with Freere. I didn't want him making any sudden moves. "Wayne, right? This is your last chance. Put the knife down and release the officer. Then get down on your knees with your hands on your head."

"Oh, what? You think you got a shot on me, fat man? You'll probably scatter this cop's brains all over the apartment before—"

The report from my SIG Sauer startled both Wayne Casey and the captain. One shot—it was all I needed. I might have retired from the force, but I never retired from the range. I spent a great deal of time there. I was always an accurate shot, but one thing I knew for certain—shooting was a perishable skill. I didn't let my skill perish. And I was sober today.

The entire time Casey was talking, I was getting down on my front sight. I sent a round through his clavicle area which was exposed. The beauty of that shot—when it's on the money—was that aside from it hurting like hell when it shattered the clavicle, it ruptured the brachial plexus. With those nerves fried, he had no control over that arm, no feeling in his hand. The blade fell harmlessly to the floor before he did. If I said I'd practiced that shot ten thousand times during my career, I'd know I was low on that estimate. Even so, you never knew what path the bullet would take once it hit the human body and struck bone. But it worked out just fine today.

To my surprise, Wayne Casey, or Azrael, whatever he called himself, writhed around on the floor, screaming and hollering.

"You shot me! You actually shot me!" he wailed. "It hurts! My god! It hurts!"

"Shut up, you big baby," I said as I rolled him over onto his belly and pulled his arms behind his back. I reached over for Freere's cuffs and locked Casey in them, tight. He moaned again.

"That's for calling me fat," I said. I looked over at the captain. Blood was still streaming from his wound. I moved into the kitchen and checked the body of the man on the floor for a pulse. It was low and thready, but there. We might have gotten to him just in time. I found a towel and returned to the captain and wrapped it tight around his wrist. I could feel him trembling.

"You okay?"

"Better now. That's Silas over there. How is he?"

"He's in trouble, but he's still with us. I'm going to get a bus rolling this way, get you both taken care of."

"That…that…was one hell of a shot, Mr. Raines, one hell of a shot."

I took out my cellphone and called for an ambulance. I could feel my adrenaline still pumping through me. I took a deep breath. Captain Freere was right. That *was* one hell of a shot. It's been one hell of a day too.

CHAPTER 92

I FOLLOWED THE AMBULANCE to the hospital, to check up on Captain Freere. I was a little worried about him myself. He never lost consciousness, but he did lose quite a bit of blood. He got stitched up, and the doctors decided to keep him overnight for observation because of that blood loss, but all indications were that he would be fine. Silas, the landlord, was rushed into surgery. SLK had been cutting on him pretty good before we got there. The doctors were taking a wait-and-see approach with him.

Officer Paul Williams, along with Acossi and two other patrolmen, met us at the hospital. Williams would be placing Wayne Elliot Casey in custody once he was out of surgery. I told him to feel free to accidentally unplug the morphine pump once that SOB was cuffed to his bed. It was a load off of my mind to know he was in custody, even more so knowing I was able to help. He had been my failure, after all, a failure that had haunted me for years.

I was thrilled he's off the streets and would face justice for his vile acts. Louisiana would end up getting first crack at him since he's already in their custody. I knew for a fact Chicago wanted this guy. He mentioned crimes in Florida before I shot him, so I could only imagine he'd end up on their docket as well. Needless to say, he'd never see the light of day again. He's going to die in prison, and he had me to thank for that.

As I left the hospital, heading back to Pollock to catch up with my team and wrap up our involvement, it crossed my twisted cop mind that on some level, meeting SLK had been a letdown. I thought I had been chasing the boogeyman. Maybe I'd thought all those years ago that if I came face to face with him, it would somehow be a battle to the death.

He was a monster to be sure. There's no way he could commit those atrocities and not be a monster. Hearing him speak on his childhood, it became clear that all of those homeless victims were surrogates for his parents. He hated them and what they had become, so with each additional homeless victim, it was as if he got to murder his parents over and over again. He wasn't going to stop. When that bullet struck him however, it seemed like he was that helpless child he had described all over again—lost, lonely, and afraid.

One surprising thing about him, however, was that after he'd gotten over the initial shock of being shot, and his adrenaline leveled off, he became a talker. I probably couldn't have paid him to shut up. While waiting for the ambulances to arrive, he told me of his grand plan to return to Chicago and his desire to become number 1 on the all-time serial killer list. He felt he was competing with a Columbian known as La Bestia. He went on to explain to me, as I wasn't familiar, that La Bestia was a serial child killer with a confirmed body count of 172, but estimates put the figure well over three hundred.

He even directed me to where he stashed his trophies. I'd seen few things worse in all my years in law enforcement. I didn't take an accurate count. I figured I'd leave that for the Alexandria PD and their evidence techs, but guessing, I'd say there were just over a hundred pinkie fingers, vacuum packed to keep his memories alive. We might have stopped him before he reached his ultimate goal, but that's no consolation for the hundred-plus victims of the street life killer.

The neglect of a child by his parents, and the perception that being homeless meant being a throwaway, led to this macabre desire in him. In the midst of his rambling, it dawned on me why he was talking so much. He was getting his story together, working out the kinks, practicing for his fifteen minutes. He knew it was coming. I knew it was coming. I guess he was warming up, testing the story out on me same as he warmed up and tested his method of killing on his parents. He wouldn't get the title he was after, but his name would be on the national news. It's hard to say if we'd ever know the names of all of his victims, but *his* name— that'd be on everyone's lips. Ain't that a kick in the head?

By the time I arrived at the hospital in Pollock, my thoughts and focus shifted from SLK and his takedown. He'd gotten enough of my time. I was only thinking about Cecilia McAllister, her family, and the Robicheauxs's other victims. That we found Cecilia and those other women alive, I felt even better about taking Dale up on that idea of his. I was proud of the whole team and what we were able to accomplish.

Reflecting on how the night's events unfolded, I found myself asking if it's in some way a moral dilemma having Ashe as part of our team. On the one hand, I could see why it would be. Allowing Ashe to go up to that house alone, figuring who and what we were dealing with in the person of Orrin Robicheaux, it's really a question of would I have expected any other outcome.

Dale, Ashe, and I left the hospital after there were no more questions for us to answer. We headed back to our motel. As we were more than overdue, we stopped and picked up a bottle of bourbon along the way. We were in luck. We found a bottle of Blanton's. Everyone congregated in my room, and it wasn't long before that bottle was running on empty. After the day we'd had, the bourbon was just what the doctor ordered, so that was to be expected. Ashe filled us in on the fate of my and Dale's would-be assassins. Again, what did I expect? I figured he had to do it. The more I had talked to those women, though, and heard the stories of what they endured, well, let's just say I couldn't bring myself to give a shit about what happened to Orrin Robicheaux and those two assholes who tried to kill us.

What I did care about was that we saved those women. We managed to save six lives, although unfortunately there was nothing anyone could do for the other women and that one young man who fell victim to that freak show of a family. We saved whom we could.

That would have to be good enough.

CHAPTER 93

OVER THE NEXT two days, the Alexandria and Pollock Police Departments and the respective prosecutors for both Rapides Parish and Grant Parish began sorting through the cross-jurisdictional nature of the mess left behind by the Robicheauxs.

Recovering Cecilia McAllister and the story she told of her abduction was more than enough to get Oswaldo Cox to drop the charges against Curtis Wakefield and get him released, and not a moment too soon as he was set to be transferred back into gen pop.

I was glad Captain Freere, on the mend and up and about, allowed Dale and I to be the ones to deliver the news to the young man, who was awake and on the rebound himself, that he was free to go—and that Cecilia had been found alive. He hugged us so tight I thought both Dale and I were going to need a hospital stay.

The McAllister family, needless to say, was thrilled, not only because we found Cecilia but because when they thought a suspect was in custody, and most likely that their daughter was dead, we didn't give up. I was glad too.

The media also swooped in. The story commanded headlines in both Pollock and Alexandria. One such story, with pictures of the Robicheaux property as the backdrop, was titled, in bold, black letters: THE HOR-ROBICHEAUX! *Local Family Responsible for Twelve Deaths! 17 Abductions!* Somehow, the fact that both Robicheauxs had access to the police departments in both towns and practically carried out their crimes right under the nose of officers was also leaked to the press. There was fallout from that.

Sheriff Noblise was heavily criticized in Pollock, and rightly so, for his handling—one journalist called it bungling—of the case. It looked like he might have a tough time with that upcoming election after all.

The prosecutor in Pollock, in collaboration with Ozzie Cox, decided on a reduced sentence for Emily Robicheaux. They took into account her age when she was kidnapped and brutalized and what that must have done to her mental state. It's beyond me how she was able to go along with Orrin's plans; but then, when it's about survival, people had done all sorts of things. She received four twelve-year sentences, minimum security, but they would all run concurrently. She'd be eligible for parole after two years. My understanding was that she's receiving psychiatric care as well. I had mixed feelings about Emily Robicheaux, or Peters, not sure which she'd go by; but in a lot of ways, I did wish her well.

Willie Robicheaux, the monster who spawned this freak show and groomed his son to be just as evil and debased as he was, found himself sentenced to life in prison without the possibility of parole. We'd see just how he enjoyed prison in his current physical condition. And as for Orrin, well, needless to say, he wouldn't be hurting anyone again—ever.

There were a lot of distraught women (not to mention the anguish their families had gone through) left in the wake of the Robicheauxs's carnage. Luckily, a trial was avoided, and they didn't have to relive their nightmares in front of an audience. There's a lot of healing that families in both Alexandria and Pollock would have to do, the communities themselves even, now that everything had been brought to light. I wish them the best.

In the aftermath of it all, I found myself wondering: *What drives men like the Robicheauxs? What drives them to be what they are and to do the things that they do? How is it that they can not only think up their evil deeds but then be driven to carry them out? How do people get this fucked up in the head?* I don't know that there are any answers to those questions, none that are satisfying anyway. I had no further to look than SLK to know that.

But there's a simple truth that I believe, and this case only seemed to further cement that belief. This is a wicked world, with wicked people in it. And wicked people do wicked things. We're all just playing the odds that we, or someone we love, won't be the next victim. A bleak outlook I know, but it's honest and it worked for me.

CHAPTER 94

Alexandria, Louisiana

AFTER ALL WAS said and done, Ashe flew back to
Chicago. He needed to check up on that personal matter
he was working before I dragged him down here. The
first chance I got when I was alone, I took the opportunity to do something that had been on my mind the
entire time that I had been in Louisiana.

I called my wife.

I was surprised that she answered the phone, so
much so that I had almost forgotten what I had called
to say. After stammering and making small talk for a
moment or two, I got it out.

I told her that I loved and missed her. I told her
that I wanted nothing more than to work things out. I
admitted my fears and my faults, especially the obsessive
behavior about the job. I also admitted something else,

something I suspected she had been feeling, but never brought up. I admitted that losing our son did cause me to be distant with her. I'd wrestled with that demon for years and finally was able to pin it down and get it off my chest. Finally admitting it allowed me to deal with it. I felt it could allow us to deal with each other.

We talked for a solid hour and a half. After I'd said what I needed to say, my wife said the only thing she could say.

No.

It just wasn't in her anymore, to try to make this thing work. She appreciated my honesty. She appreciated hearing what I had to say, but she said something to me that was even more profound than the words of that profiler a long time back. She said, "Sometimes, Robert, you have to realize that just because you want something doesn't mean you should have it."

The words hit me hard, but I honestly did understand. And I could appreciate her position. *I* allowed her to grow apart from me, to fall out of love with me. I pushed her there and fought all of her attempts to return from that place. That's on me. Sometimes, even if it's for what we feel are the right reasons, you just don't get a do-over with something like that.

It turns out you can't be the screw-up in a relationship your entire adult life and then when you got old, say, never mind those things. It's funny it took until now for me to understand what it was I had heard in her voice the night she left me, that thing that made her voice sound so odd and foreign to me. It was resignation. That didn't happen overnight. She was doing what she needed to do for her. I could only respect that.

The beautiful thing to come out of that phone call, however, was that she did agree to work on us being friends. I liked that. I'd take it.

CHAPTER 95

DALE AND I had packed up and checked out of the Motel 6 we'd stayed in. We were ready to go when a familiar face came driving up in the parking lot. Dakota Quinn pulled into the parking space next to our SUV.

"You boys taking off?" Quinn asked from the driver side window of her Buick LaCrosse.

"Quinn! Fancy seeing you here," Dale said.

"Yes. It's about time for us to hit the road," I said.

"Awww! I thought you boys were going to join me in New Orleans to listen to some jazz and enjoy a little bourbon?"

"I've got to get back home to my wife, before I get in trouble," Dale said with a slight chuckle.

"Where's Ashe? I only got to meet him briefly," Quinn said, looking past us as if the big man would magically appear from out of nowhere.

"He headed out yesterday. Had some pressing matters back in Chicago he needed to tend to, which is just as well. Ashe is not one for goodbyes anyway," I said.

"What about you, Robert? Maybe stick around a few days? I even hear the incumbent sheriff in Pollock might have a hard time with his campaign this year. You want to run for sheriff? You'd get my vote."

"No. I'm definitely still a big city boy. I'll be heading home. How about you, Quinn? Why don't you run?"

Quinn shut off her engine and stepped out of her car. "Because…" She began and handed me a letter. I opened it. It was from the FBI. She had been accepted into the academy in Quantico.

"Congratulations, Quinn! I'm happy for you."

"Good job, whippersnapper," Dale joked.

"Thanks, old-timer. I already gave notice. I head to Virginia in three weeks."

"You've got great instincts, Quinn. Always listen to your gut," I told her.

"You sure I can't get you stick around?"

I looked to Dale. He simply shrugged. "You can handle the drive back?" I asked.

"Don't worry about me, Bobby. I'll be fine."

I tossed Dale the keys to the SUV. I went around back, opened the tailgate, and retrieved my bag. Quinn opened her trunk.

"Three days," I said. "I can hang out for three days, and then I'll rent a car and drive back to Chicago."

Quinn frowned. "Drive?"

"You haven't put it together? Bobby's afraid of flying. That's why we drove down here in the first place."

"I'm not afraid of flying," I said defiantly. "Crashing, on the other hand, terrifies me. And you do know the best way to avoid dying in a plane crash, don't you?"

Dale sighed. "Do tell."

"Don't be in one," I said with a wink.

Dale threw his hands up. "You're impossible. Well, Quinn, he's yours for the next few days."

"Cool beans!" Dakota Quinn beamed. She turned to me and said, "You are gonna enjoy the food and the music! Trust me. You won't regret it." Quinn did that thing again, where she cut her eyes in a flirty way—at least I think it could be flirty—and flashed that beautiful smile of hers. Regardless of what it was, or wasn't, it still felt nice. I'd found in my lifetime that it never hurt when a pretty woman smiled at you. Then, just as I had earlier, I dismissed the thoughts in my head and tossed my bag in her trunk.

What else did I have to do anyway? I had always wanted to go to New Orleans, and Quinn was fun, so I'd have a kick-ass guide to boot.

We watched as Dale hopped in the SUV. He waved goodbye and then headed off back to Chicago. We got on our way to New Orleans. I'd enjoy the next three days and use them to take my mind off this case, losing my wife, and everything else that'd haunted me on this trip. I was going to drink a lot of bourbon; and no doubt, with Quinn in the lead, I'd end up smoking a cigar or two, as well. Then I'd head back to Chicago and see what's next on our plate.

Maybe we'd even shoot that commercial too.

The Retired Detectives' Club

Will Return

in

Shawn Scuefield's exciting upcoming novel

SIMON SEZ

Turn the page for a sneak peek!

Prologue

TRIAL RUNS FOR THE PERFECT MURDER

A LESS THAN
SUCCESSFUL ATTEMPT

Chicago, IL—Four weeks ago

THE COMPULSION WAS strong. It went against everything thirty-three year old Philip Kepler, office manager, husband, and father of two, believed in. In fact, it violated every fiber of his being. But the compulsion—the urge—was just too strong to ignore.

And then there was the voice. Philip had been hearing the voice for months—steady, repetitive, *demanding*—constantly urging him on. He'd been hearing it on the phone all that day. Even when he wasn't on the phone, he seemed to be hearing the voice echoing over and over again in his head.

He had no choice. He had to do as he was told.

Rain had been falling ever since Philip parked his family's Kia Sorento in front of a brownstone on 18th

Street. He double checked the building's address against the information in the text message he'd received. This was the place. His heavy breathing had fogged the windows over multiple times during his wait, which he'd clocked at forty minutes. Thoughts of cranking the vehicle and speeding off as fast as possible and racing home to his family were drowned out by the steady, demanding tone, of that voice.

His heart raced, and pounded furiously in his chest. His head throbbed. *What am I doing? Why can't I go home?* The questions lingered in his mind until they were answered by that voice: *You can't go home until the job is done. It's just that simple; you must complete the job first. It will be better for you and your family*, the voice echoing in his head went on, *complete the job Philip. Do as you're told.*

Philip's cellphone rang. He hesitated for a moment, and then answered.

"Have you been taking your medication, Philip?" It was the voice again, but this time it was "live" so to speak, not just a creepy phantom rattling around in his head. A quick chill flashed over him, yet he managed to answer, "Yes…yes, I have."

"Good. You know what you must do. It must be done," the voice said, repeating the words Philip had been hearing all day. There was a click, and then Philip heard a faint but steady dial-tone, then immediately, he was calm again—relaxed and ready to complete the job so that he could go home and be with his loving family.

He disconnected the call and then pawed at the fog on the interior windshield. His vision improved somewhat; enough anyway, to see the door of the brownstone slowly open. Philip stared hard at the petite, dark haired, African American woman that made her way onto the porch and opened her umbrella. He studied her face carefully. It was *her*.

Philip reached over into the glove box and pulled out the Smith & Wesson .38 Special. He pushed the cylinder release button, double-checked that the gun was loaded, and then he snapped the cylinder back into place. Philip Kepler hesitated for a split second, and then cocked the hammer back. He opened the driver side door just as the diminutive woman stepped off the porch of the brownstone and set on her way up the block.

Philip stalked behind her, the pouring rain running down into his eyes.

Finish the job, the calm yet demanding voice had returned. *Do it! Finish the job!*

And after this? *Finish the job!*

Will I be free after this? *Finish the job!*

Philip steeled his nerves once again and quickened his pace. His footsteps sloshed along the rain drenched sidewalk, and attracted the attention of the tiny woman who had just left the brownstone. She turned and offered a slight smile. "No umbrella?" she said. Philip ignored her, and continued approaching her.

It had to be done. It's just that simple, this had to be done!

Philip raised the revolver. The tiny woman's eyes dilated with terror. She froze in place, and just as she had begun to utter a scream, Philip pulled the trigger. The woman collapsed in a heap and Philip stood directly over her. He raised the revolver over her prone figure and

SHAWN SCUEFIELD

fired three more shots into her motionless body. The rain continued to pour and thud over them both. This went against everything Philip stood for, but it had to be done.

Philip pulled out his cellphone and dialed. After a moment, he spoke into the receiver, "It's done. I did just what you said. She's dead. Can I go home now?"

"Where are you?" the voice asked, still with that same smooth and steady quality that it had when the idea of putting four bullets into *little Miss Umbrella* was first broached months ago.

"I'm still here," Kepler said.

"I'm going to need you to be more specific, Mr. Kepler," the voice continued.

"I'm still standing over her body," Kepler choked out, his voice cracked as he stared down at the prone figure on the ground at his feet. Tears mixed with the rain and streamed down his face. "I…I…I don't know… what's wrong with me. I just want to go home."

"First things first, dear boy. Has anyone seen you?"

Philip Kepler looked around. With his mission front and center in his mind, he didn't notice the gaggle of onlookers that had gathered around, mouths agape with horror at the scene in front of them. Many of them already with cellphones in hand; some were recording the scene, while others were calling the police.

"There're people," Kepler garbled in that cracked voice of his. "There're people here."

"We have a bit of a problem then," the phone voice said. "Question for you, Mr. Kepler. Why did you shoot this woman?"

"Because *you* said I had to."

390

"That is most disappointing, Philip. Most disappointing. As a matter of fact, my dear boy, I really wish you hadn't said that."

"But it's true. You told me to do this. You made me do this!" Kepler's voice had begun to raise, the sight of the dead woman at his feet stirring his emotions.

"That's true, dear boy. However, as previously discussed, that simply was not the answer you were to give, if asked. You do know what this means, now, don't you?"

"P-plan...b? Plan...b?"

"Yes, Mr. Kepler. I'm afraid we're going to need you to move forward with plan b." The voice continued on, calm as ever. There was another click, and then Kepler heard that faint yet steady, dial tone through the receiver.

"Yes. I must go to Plan b," Kepler said, suddenly calm and relaxed again. A serene look came over his face. His tears seemed to stop instantly, only the rain continued to streak down his face. After the tone ended, Kepler went on, "Would you be sure to tell my family, that I love them?"

"That will be communicated, Mr. Kepler. Now please, execute plan b. Thank you."

The call ended.

Philip Kepler, thirty-three year old husband, and father of two, took the revolver and put it in his mouth and then pulled the trigger.

SUCCESS, AS INTENDED

Two days ago

MICHIGAN AVENUE IN downtown Chicago was busy as usual. Rush hour traffic was snarled on the Magnificent Mile and its surrounding streets and the number of bodies hustling along the sidewalks and into intersections only exacerbated the problem.

The congestion wasn't what had James William McClintock spinning in circles, however. He'd been up and down Michigan Avenue plenty of times, but this day, he somehow seemed lost. He felt like he was sleep walking. Everything looked familiar and unrecognizable at the same time, yet he continued on his way.

He had to get *there*. The voice on the phone had told him so. None of it made sense. What the voice was telling him, demanding actually, that he do. Yet he couldn't say no. It didn't make sense, while it seemed perfectly rational at the same time.

James looked up and caught a glimpse of the marquee. There it was—his destination. Moments later he walked into the lobby of the Grand Luxe Hotel. An air conditioned breeze rolled over him; a noticeable difference from the temperature outside. The weather had been rainy in city the last few weeks. Now that the rain had moved completely out, the heat was back. And so was the humidity. That was rare for this late in the fall, however, not unheard of in Chicago.

But the question that wormed its way through James McClintock's mind wasn't about the weather. No, the real question, the one that he had no answer to, was: Just what was he doing *walking* up and down Michigan Avenue? Normally, he'd be driven wherever he needed to go. His phone began buzzing in his pocket and he quickly forgot about why he was walking as opposed to being driven.

"Have you been taking your medication, James?" the voice on the other end of the call asked. It was a strangely familiar voice; seemingly from a half-remembered dream.

"Yes," James McClintock responded. His hands began to tremble. He felt beads of sweat form on his brow.

"The increased dosage?" the voice asked, again.

"Yes. Yes, the increased dosage."

"Excellent. And have you arrived?"

"Yes I have," James answered again. He wanted to hang up, *didn't he*? He found though, that he could not, and he continued to listen.

"You know what you have to do, now, don't you? It has to be done, James. It has to be done."

"Yes. Yes I know." He found that he simply couldn't say "no" to the voice.

"And why are you doing this?" the smooth talking voice asked.

"Simply because…it has to be done," James answered, his voice cracked a little and his throat suddenly felt dry.

"Very good, my boy. Very good. Carry on."

James heard a click followed by a faint, steady dial tone. A moment later, he ended the call and put his cellphone back into his pocket. He felt a calming peace suddenly—surprisingly even—wash over him. He entered the hotel, and stared around the lobby until he found the hospitality counter. He made his way over.

***

Behind the service counter, Brian Grazer, had just clocked in. He had been late nearly every day so far during the week and, as his boss had put it, he was on thin ice. He may have hated the job, but he needed it, and he felt good that this day, he'd made it on time. He'd been ten minutes early, actually. *Not that there would be any praise or recognition for that*, he thought.

Just the same, he was ready to get his shift started. He noticed a man standing near the entryway on his cellphone. The man looked lost, confused even. Brian waved the man over.

"Yes. How may I help you, sir?" Brian asked, with his professional smile—all teeth showing—in full effect.

The man said nothing. He lifted his Ralph Lauren Polo shirt and pulled a chrome plated Kimber 1911 from his waistband. Brian's eyes stared back at him, wild and wide with terror. James William McClintock opened fire.

CPSIA information can be obtained
at www.ICGtesting.com
Printed in the USA
LVHW010722010719
622841LV00001B/80